W9-AUU-736

FOREVER KNIGHT™
A STIRRING OF DUST

SUSAN SIZEMORE

BOULEVARD BOOKS, NEW YORK

For Scott, Christina, Arwen,
and Shannon Ham.

FOREVER KNIGHT: A STIRRING OF DUST

Based upon the television series created
by James D. Parriott and Barney Cohen.

Produced by Paragon Entertainment Corporation in
association with TriStar Television

A Boulevard Book / published by arrangement with
Sony Signatures Inc.

PRINTING HISTORY
Boulevard edition / April 1997

The Putnam Berkley World Wide Web site address is
http://www.berkley.com/berkley

ISBN: 1-57297-238-6

BOULEVARD
Boulevard Books are published by The Berkley Publishing Group,
200 Madison Avenue, New York, New York 10016.
BOULEVARD and its logo are trademarks
belonging to Berkley Publishing Corporation.

PRINTED IN THE UNITED STATES OF AMERICA

10 9 8 7 6 5 4 3 2 1

How does Nick Knight
track down a murderer?

Experience.

He's been a cop for years.
But he's been a vampire for centuries.

FOREVER
KNIGHT™

A STIRRING OF DUST

Nick knows one of his own kind is
responsible for several brutal murders.

But who is the hunter . . .
and the *hunted*?

All-new, original novels based on
the hit TV show created by
James D. Parriott and Barney Cohen

Produced by Paragon Entertainment Corporation
in association with TriStar Television

PROLOGUE

THE THIEF WALKED OUT OF THE SHADOWS TO THE REAR entrance of a shop that wasn't officially open. He had to knock for quite a while before the old man came to the door. He didn't think he'd been followed, but he felt like it. He'd felt like he'd been hunted, played with, since the moment he'd broken into the disc jockey's apartment.

That place had been weird, full of valuable things, things that had been almost too easy to steal. It had been like an invitation. Yeah, like an invitation to do evil. And then face the consequences.

The thief shook his head to clear it of these strange thoughts. He shivered, and when the old man opened the door just a little, enough to let him into the back room, he hustled inside.

"Full moon tonight," the antique dealer said. He closed the door, then raised a window blind.

"Hunter's moon," the thief answered. He didn't know why he'd said it.

"It's not like anyone can see us back here," the old man said. "Besides, I like the moon." The silver moonlight covered his desk. His attention was caught by an object already on the desk as the silvery light sparked for a moment on the polished steel of a British cavalry saber. When the moon was overpowered by the brighter electric light as he turned on the desk lamp, the sword lost its almost magical glow. The old man looked curiously at his nervous protégé. "What have you got for me?"

The young man laid a briefcase flat on the desk. The old man leaned over him eagerly as he opened the case. Inside were two very special items, for the antique dealer's very private customers. The young man had a good eye for what those special customers liked to collect.

The old man picked up the silver box and lifted the lid. "What's this?" he asked.

"I don't know. I haven't looked inside it."

"Looks like ashes." He chuckled. "The work's exquisite."

"Turkish," the young man said. "Sixteenth century, I think."

The old man sifted his fingers through the small pile of gray ashes in the bottom of the silver box. "Ashtray, you think?" He gave a short bark of laughter. "Funeral urn?"

"God, I hope not." The thief shuddered again. Maybe he'd been carrying around the ashes of a cremated dead man. Maybe he was being haunted.

He took the box from the old man and tossed the ashes away. They flew toward the window, toward the moonlight. They danced and glittered in a moonbeam, but neither man noticed as they turned back to the second item in the briefcase.

The old man picked up a marble statue. It was about eight inches high, of a nude man holding a trident. "Roman."

2

"Roman," the young man agreed. "First century. A household god, I think."

"A *numina*, yes." The dealer ran his fingers lovingly over the cool skin of marble. "I have just the buyer for this." It was time to discuss prices.

Behind them, the dust stopped swirling. It hung suspended on the air. It swayed back and forth, as if to music. It pulsed, as if to a heartbeat rhythm. It thinned and stretched and writhed. It changed color, from ash gray to silver to pearl. For a moment it was blue-veined molten lava. Then blood red. It turned into arms and legs, a torso, and finally a man. Or at least something shaped like a man. A naked, dark-haired form, with glowing yellow eyes. The creature stretched out its arms, looked up into the moonlight, and grew fangs.

It turned around, toward the heated scent of life. It saw two men, and moved forward silently to feed. Then it saw the weapon resting on the table. The monster snatched it up with a howl of joy. It sliced the air with the sharp blade, then turned toward its first victim. The sound of steel severing flesh was as satisfying as the taste of blood.

The old man died the true death, the saber slicing off the drained body's head, but the monster was too gorged to finish off the young one. The young one it tasted but didn't drain, didn't sever the spine. When it was done with its prey, the monster found the door, wrenched it off its hinges, and ran out to dance in the moonlight.

After a long while, the young man stirred. He saw nothing, felt nothing, was nothing. He walked out the door and into the street. He had two needs. All that was left to him was the terrible, driving compulsion to find his maker, and the burning hunger.

He followed them both into the night.

3

1

"ILL MET BY MOONLIGHT, OR SO THE SAYING GOES. THERE'S A full moon out tonight, my children. What does that mean? Is it ill or fair? What does the full moon really mean?"

The voice on the radio was at once seductive and mocking. Not only was there a full moon, but LaCroix was in the mood to howl, Nick Knight thought, as he moved across his living room to open the specially made window hangings. There was a time when Nick would have been nervous to hear that tone in his maker's voice.

He was still a little nervous, but not worried that LaCroix was going to go on one of his mad rampages. Not tonight. LaCroix was having too much fun taunting the citizens of Toronto as a call-in talk-show host. As the Nightcrawler he spewed equal amounts of vitriol and philosophy five nights a week. He enjoyed creating chaos as much as he did killing, and was gathering quite a fan following.

Even Nick listened more nights than not. Monitoring the monster, he'd told Natalie when she'd asked why he bothered. And maybe missing him a little, which was something Nick didn't like to admit to himself.

"Maybe one of us is mellowing in our old age," Nick said to the radio voice as the metal curtains rose noisily on their motorized tracks.

Though he didn't need to breathe, he waited with held breath as the full silver disk came into view above the skyline.

"Ah," he said when he could see it, and held his arms out wide. The ancients were right, there was magic in moonlight. He could feel it tingling along his skin and deep into his bones.

Nick could not stand in the sun, but he loved moonlight. All of his kind did. He would have been happy to stand naked and bathe in it, but Natalie was coming over to share a rare night off. He didn't want to shock the lady, though he doubted there was anything that could shock a coroner who'd made friends with a vampire.

"It makes you want to howl, doesn't it? To scream. To conjure demons. To writhe in ecstasy or agony under its cold, hard light. To make love. Love."

LaCroix had a way of saying the most tender human word that gave it the same meaning as pestilence. In LaCroix's hands, love *was* a plague. Nick had known LaCroix's kind of love for centuries. Someday he was going to escape it. For now, he crossed the room, found the remote, and turned off the stereo receiver.

As LaCroix's voice disappeared, Nick heard the sound of the elevator coming up from the ground floor of the warehouse he'd turned into his home. He closed his eyes, and he could feel Natalie Lambert. Her heartbeat and the scent of her blood were as familiar as her face. He could feel her anticipation, and a sense of serenity as well. He shook his head and smiled. Nick could never understand why she enjoyed spending time in the company of a vampire.

Tonight, he knew Nat was looking forward to watching a video of a film she hadn't had time to catch in the theaters. Nick had hopes that he could talk her into a walk in the moonlight instead.

"No way. At least not yet," Natalie answered Nick's suggestion. She held up the yellow plastic bag from the video rental store. "I had to go to three places before I found this." She pointed a finger at her friend. There was a teasing light in Nick's eyes, a certain boyish set to his tilted head. It was all very charming, but he wasn't going to get away with it. "We're going to watch *Slash and Burn*."

Nick made a face. "Oh, Nat, not another horror movie."

"You said it was fine when I asked."

He ran a hand through his dark blond hair, then gave her his best toothy smile—not the patented, yellow-eyed, fanged fiend look but the very human charm he turned on her when he wanted his way. "I changed my mind?"

She had already put her Chinese carryout food down on the counter. Now she was ready to kick off her shoes and put the tape in the VCR. She was looking forward to a hot dinner and a gory movie. Considering what she did for a living and that she had a genuine vampire for a best friend, she didn't know why she liked horror movies, but she did. Maybe because horror movies weren't real.

She glanced at her watch. "We can go for a walk at midnight." She smiled at him. "Now, doesn't that sound . . . ?"

"Like a reasonable compromise," Nick supplied for her.

She almost said "romantic," but that wasn't a word that they allowed to enter into their relationship, though they danced around it often enough. He was too pale to blush. She had a redhead's complexion, and turned her face away to hide the momentary embarrassment.

He took the tape from her and moved to put it in the VCR. She grabbed her meal and a pair of chopsticks, and joined him on the leather couch as the credits rolled across the large-screen TV. While she ate her dinner, they stayed at opposite ends of the couch. By the time the white box was abandoned on the coffee table, they had sidled closer. By the time the werewolf hero of the movie had been captured by the ecoterrorists, they were seated close together in the center of the couch. Nick's arm was around her shoulders and she was leaning easily into his friendly, familiar embrace.

It didn't bother her that his skin gave off very little warmth. And for once she didn't nag him because she knew that wasn't red wine he was sipping out of a champagne flute. Sometimes it was more important for them just to relax and be together than to remember that she was a doctor trying to cure a homicide detective of a nearly eight hundred-year-old case of what she persisted in referring to as a genetic disorder.

"You on call?" he asked as the werewolf made kibble out of a couple of its tormentors.

"'Fraid so. You?"

"There aren't that many of us who volunteer for the night shift. Captain Reese seems to think my time is his, no matter what the schedule says."

"Let's hope for a quiet night."

"Amen."

Natalie did not point out the word he'd just used. She made a mental note of it, and smiled to herself. On the

8

night she'd met Nicholas Knight, he'd told her quite fervently that he was damned. She'd seen how he'd reacted to crosses, had seen burn marks on his hands from actually holding one. That he could casually say a simple word like "amen" was a breakthrough. At least for his self-image as a creature of irredeemable evil.

Natalie turned her attention back to the screen, but her thoughts remained on the perception of evil. What makes a monster? she wondered, as the werewolf in the movie looked at a beautiful woman. This was the point where the werewolf realized how different it was from the rest of humanity.

"I love this part."

"It's maudlin," Nick replied. He glanced at her suspiciously. "I thought you hadn't seen this."

Natalie feigned innocence. "Did I say that?" He frowned. "All right, I rented it the last time I had a night off." She gestured toward the screen. "I wanted you to see it."

His eyes narrowed. "Why?" Nick took his arm from around her shoulder and sat up straight. It was his turn to gesture toward the screen. "Is this an object lesson of some sort? Is your poor, misunderstood werewolf symbolic for us real monsters?"

Natalie was in too good a mood to let him get serious now. She kept her tone joking as she asked, "There's no such thing as werewolves?"

He stood. "Don't be ridiculous. Of course not."

She hit the pause button on the remote, then jumped up to face him. On the frozen screen, the werewolf was silently baying at the moon.

"Whoa. Wait a minute. If vampires are real, there's no reason werewolves shouldn't exist. Have you ever met one?"

"No." He hesitated a moment before he pointed a finger at her. "Just because I've never met one doesn't mean they're real."

She pointed a finger back. "But you have no proof that they aren't."

"You sound like some tabloid television show. Do you believe in UFOs? How about Bigfoot? Ghosts?" He looked thoughtful for a moment. "No, ghosts are real, I've met a few."

"If ghosts are real, why not all sorts of—things?"

"You're trying to distract me from arguing, aren't you?"

Natalie did her best to look wide-eyed and innocent. "Me? I'm just trying to watch a movie."

She slipped her arm through his and drew him toward the couch. He laughed, and they sat down, her arm around his shoulders this time. Nick picked up the remote and started the tape again. The room reverberated with the werewolf's howling anguish. Natalie felt Nick shiver at the sound.

She made no comment, she just concentrated harder on the fictional troubles of the creature in the movie. Neither of them said anything through the rest of the tape. As the credits rolled at the end, Natalie let her curiosity get the better of her.

"Are there others, Nick?"

"Other what?"

There was a coldness in his voice that should have warned her. Natalie Lambert had long ago made the decision to face any truth about Nicholas Knight and his dark world squarely. It was the test of friendship, and the price of finding a cure.

She chose her words carefully. "Other supernatural beings. Are there any?"

He turned pain-stricken eyes on her. "Other cursed creatures, you mean?"

"You have a blood disease," she answered promptly. "Kindly get your mind out of the Middle Ages and remember what century you're in."

"A century where no one is required to take responsibility for their own damnation," he shot back.

"A century where people don't blame God or the Devil every time they catch a disease. Damnation doesn't show up under a microscope. The aberrations in your DNA do."

Nick gave a reluctant nod. He turned away from her for a moment. "I keep trying to be adaptable enough to believe that."

Natalie rubbed her hands up and down her arms. She hated when they got into this sort of discussion. She didn't back off, however. That was another of her rules for dealing with this vampire: never to let him withdraw emotionally from her.

"You didn't answer my question," she reminded him, "about other monsters." She hated the term, since he equated himself with it. She also knew he hated any attempt to be politically correct about his background.

Nick sat on the couch, hunched forward. He rested his hands between his knees, fingers laced tightly together. As pale as he was, Natalie noticed that his knuckles were whiter than the rest of his skin from the pressure.

"There are monsters," he said.

She could tell from the remote expression on his face that despite her efforts, he'd withdrawn.

"There are other monsters, Nat. And believe me, you don't want to know about them."

"Is the night not beautiful, Nicholas?"

Nicholas didn't answer as he turned to help Janette

11

from the heavily curtained carriage. He hated the carriage. It was large and luxurious, but it was like traveling in a sarcophagus. No, he thought with a twisted, ironic smile, the pharaohs' stone tombs were no doubt better equipped for the journeys of the dead than this coach. Though they probably carried about the same amount of luggage.

Janette could travel with the speed of the wind if she chose, but she did not like to travel without her wardrobe if she could help it. Since they were on their way to visit an old comrade of LaCroix's, she had packed for a courtly occasion. So they traveled by day in the coach Prince Radu had sent.

"Ah, the night," LaCroix said as Nicholas helped Janette step down from the coach. "I never get tired of it."

"That's a good thing, isn't it?" Nicholas replied. "All things considered."

"Is that a tone of bitterness I hear?"

"Yes, I think it was," Janette said. She moved to LaCroix's side in a rustle of silk. The elder vampire took her hand and bestowed one of his rare smiles on her. She preened under his approving look.

"Our Nicholas is beginning one of his fits of conscience," LaCroix said. As usual, his tone was full of mockery.

"So it seems," Janette answered. She looked Nicholas over with a gaze that was anything but approving. "I think it is only because he did not want to come. Are you sulking, Nicholas?"

He could not tell if dear Janette was teasing or truly annoyed. He tried to be placating. "I hesitated at accompanying you only because I find the conversations in the salons of Paris interesting. This new philosophy. . . ."

"Will wait for your return, Nicholas." LaCroix held out his hand, and the gesture seemed to encompass all of time, and the forest. "Can you not feel the wildness of this place? The freedom? Our kind needs to retreat from civilization upon occasion. To find our prey without any fear of mortal retribution."

"I doubt the local peasants see it that way," Nicholas countered.

"Their duty is to die, Nicholas, not to offer their opinions." LaCroix's expression held the stern pride of the Roman general he once had been.

Nicholas stood stiffly by the side of the rutted road. The forest at his back was full of life. Some of it was human. He was hungry, and though he fought the urge to hunt, the excitement of the coming chase pulsed through his blood. He hated to admit that LaCroix was sometimes right.

It was true that he had not wanted to come. He had wanted to settle for a while in Paris, to study the new science and philosophy the mortals were so excited about. He had never been to this land of rugged mountains, not even in his Crusader days when holy armies had pillaged their way through this part of Europe. He'd taken another route. If he hadn't, he might still be alive.

He smiled at the incongruity of that thought, letting his fangs show. He let his senses drink in the echoes of the life and death that surrounded him. LaCroix laughed at the sight of him like this. Janette smiled. They both showed fangs. Neither of them had any qualms about what they were. Nicholas allowed himself to forget his own as he turned and ran into the forest. Tonight he would hunt alone.

He moved silently through woods that were darker than the night above the ancient trees. Clouds and thick branches obscured the stars, but his vision required very little light. He could see life by the heat it gave off, catch the scent of emotions on the wind. Some were sentient, some were not.

He vowed that tonight he would feast on whatever creature first crossed his path, and his conscience could go to hell. He'd let fate decide whether it was a deer, a boar, some adulterer coming home late from a forest tryst, or perhaps a midwife rushing to attend a birth. Good, evil, indifferent—tonight he would pretend that all mortal blood was the same.

He ran for miles and miles. He dodged giant trees and tumbled boulders. He leapt over wide, rushing streams and raced a waterfall down the side of a cliff. When he came within a hundred yards of a village, he stopped dead to sense the life within the locked and shuttered houses. Nicholas flew above the treetops. He hung suspended on the air by an act of will, and floated forward on the breeze.

But he did not go far before he hit an invisible wall. There was garlic hung over every mantel and door frame of every house. The reek of it burned his nostrils even from high over the squat buildings. It made him cough. He flew back to the ground, where he snatched up handfuls of earth. He held the soft, wet mass to his face and took deep, ragged breaths. It filled his lungs with the scent of pine needles, of moss and earthworms and the sweet rot of the earth renewing itself. Anything was better than the assault of garlic on his senses.

When the reaction from the garlic had faded, Nicholas moved away from the village as quickly as he could. Once safe in the depths of the forest, he couldn't help but lean back against a tree and laugh.

He looked up at the arc of stars visible through the

14

branches. LaCroix was wrong for once. The local peasants didn't think it was their duty to die for them. They knew who the enemy was, and how to protect themselves from it.

Nicholas was growing tired. He'd used up a great deal of energy, first playing games with the night, then in flight. Blood hunger gnawed out from his heart. Soon the need would control him. He had no time to linger in solitude any longer, or to think about the vampire-protected houses. Nicholas had to make his kill and get back to the coach while darkness lasted.

When he stepped away from the tree, a stench hit him that was far worse than the clean burn the garlic had been in his lungs. The smell crept out of the forest to his right, like invisible ground fog. He realized that the stench followed a worn path that led back toward the village.

He was used to the smell of death, but this foulness reminded him of the charnel pits in the days of the Black Death. This was a concentrated rot tainted with evil. Tainted with obscene magic.

There was a vein of energy mixed with the stench. Energy that reminded Nicholas of his own kind, but other. Worse, somehow. This was the trail of some hideous entity that moved through the forest. It was a dead thing walking. It frightened him, and he'd been dead for hundreds of years.

His fear turned into terror when he stepped onto the path, looked to his right, and saw the glowing eyes of the monster that watched him.

Nick blinked away the memory, but cold dread remained in the pit of his stomach.

He needed a drink.

He would have smiled reassuringly at Natalie, but he

felt his fangs pressing into his lower lip. She had no idea how inviting her throat was right now as he drew back from that long ago night of shock and unsatisfied hunger. He had no intention of letting her know. He avoided her worried gaze as he got up and went to the refrigerator. He drank the chilled cow's blood straight out of the bottle.

"See, you are becoming human," she said as he finished taking a long gulp. She'd followed him across the room.

He wiped the back of his hand across his mouth, then glanced at her in confusion. The substitute for human blood had calmed him enough to keep him from perceiving his best friend as prey, but he was still shaken.

"Human?" he asked. "How am I in any way human?"

She crossed her arms. "Human males always drink straight out of the milk carton. That's what you reminded me of just now."

"It's a guy thing," he told her, trying to match her light tone. "Vampire, mortal, doesn't matter. All men are pigs." He put the bottle back in the fridge, and closed the door with more force than he intended. He leaned his head against the cool enamel surface.

Natalie didn't know what was disturbing Nick, but she had a feeling she wasn't going tease him out of it. She looked at her watch. "How about that walk? It's nearly midnight."

Nick rubbed the back of his neck. "I've lost the mood for moonlight."

She had the feeling he'd been speaking more to himself than to her. In fact, she thought it might be best if she left him to whatever memory he'd obviously conjured up from his past. He usually told her just what it was he recalled, but in his own good time.

She faked a yawn. "I think it's time I went to bed."

16

He gave a perfunctory nod. "See you tomorrow."

Natalie wasn't surprised when he didn't walk her to the door. In fact, he was halfway up the stairs to his bedroom by the time she'd gathered up her things and stepped onto the elevator.

"Get some rest," she called, and got only a brief wave in reply.

She leaned her head back against the elevator wall as it slowly descended and closed her eyes for a moment. "Oh, Nick. You need eight hundred years worth of rest."

For some perverse reason she tuned the radio to the Nightcrawler when she got in the car. His voice filled the car as she drove along the empty streets.

"The moon's my constant mistress," LaCroix recited.

"I know that poem," a young woman's voice responded. *"Tom O'Bedlam's Song. It's lovely."*

LaCroix had obviously finished his preliminary rantings and was on to the call-in portion of the show. Why would anyone want to talk to him? Natalie wondered. Even when he was disguised as a mortal, contact with LaCroix seemed like an invitation to suicide. What a pity he hadn't stayed dead after Nick staked and burned him a couple of years ago.

"Can't keep a bad man down, eh, LaCroix?"

Though she could joke at the radio presence, she hoped she never had another actual encounter with the old vampire. Just dealing with Janette occasionally had been quite enough for her very steady but not made-of-titanium nerves, thank you.

"That poem was written by a madman, Tammy. Bedlam, my dear, was not a luxury resort. Or perhaps you would think it was. Are you mad? Of course you are."

"Why?"

17

"Because you've phoned in at least three times this week."

"I enjoy talking to you."

"Tammy, do you think of me as, perhaps, your— friend?"

Natalie switched off the radio before Tammy's answer.

"Nobody is that monster's friend, honey," she said as she stopped at a red light. There was no traffic. There was no one around this area of small, closed shops. Natalie was tempted to ease through the intersection and continue on her way home. Hardly a proper way for a coroner for the Province to behave, however.

She was glad she didn't give in to temptation when a naked man ran across the street in front of her just as the light changed. He moved fast, gave a swift glance her way, and disappeared into the shadows before she could get a good look at him. Her headlights caught a glimpse of pale skin, long dark hair, lots of hair. Was that a sword in his hand? His face—

Glowing eyes? Fangs?

She wasn't sure. It happened too quickly. Maybe he hadn't even been naked. Just a trick of the light. She was tired, susceptible. She'd just spent the evening watching a werewolf movie with a vampire. Her mind was on monsters after listening to LaCroix.

It must have been her imagination.

Natalie drove cautiously toward home.

2

TRACY VETTER TUCKED A STRAND OF HER CHIN-LENGTH BLONDE hair behind her ear and glanced calmly down at the body. The head was on the other side of the room, having its picture taken by a forensic technician. The coroner hadn't arrived yet, so Tracy had only the visual evidence of a headless corpse to guess the cause of death. It was a gruesome, bloody sight, but she made herself take a good, long look.

She only looked calm; inside, her emotions were roiling. She didn't let anything show, though. She was young, relatively new to the homicide detail, female, and, worst of all, an assistant police commissioner's daughter. Her squad was supportive, maybe even overprotective; everyone kept telling her she was a good cop. That didn't mean they didn't think she had plenty to prove. Tracy agreed with them. She liked to think that she'd gotten the job on merit, but she didn't rule out that a certain amount of nepotism had been involved in her rapid rise. So she worked hard, not just to prove herself but because she loved her job.

Along with the crime scene crew there were quite a

few uniformed officers in the shop, but she was the first homicide detective on the scene. This left her nominally in charge of the investigation while waiting for her partner to arrive. The fact that there were several civilians peering past the official yellow tape strung across the shop entrance gave her an excuse to walk away from the body. She hadn't paid much attention to them on her way in. Now she turned to the officer who'd been the first on the scene.

"Who are those people, Lorri? Gawkers or witnesses?"

"Neighbors."

Tracy nodded. This area was the sort of Eastern European enclave where shopkeepers lived over their stores and everyone knew everyone else's business. All very colorful and quaint, and hopefully useful for a homicide investigation. "Anyone see anything?"

Lorri chuckled. "We're not that lucky on this one."

"Too bad."

"That doesn't mean they don't all have opinions."

"I'll see if anybody at least heard anything."

Her partner arrived just as Tracy started toward the door. She watched Nick slip under the tape barrier, his pale hair and skin emphasized by the clothes he wore. He was dressed all in black, including a widely cut, long black jacket. She supposed he was a handsome man, for someone in his thirties. His skin was too colorless from a sun allergy that forced him to work nights exclusively; he was too mysterious about his private life. Not her type, though she liked and trusted him as a partner.

Not her type. Too old. Mysterious. She couldn't help but smile at herself at her assessment of Nick Knight as a male rather than as a coworker. As if the person she was interested in wasn't a great deal older and more mysterious than Nick Knight could ever be. Pale, too. And as for Javier Vachon being her type, actually it was probably the other way around—but there were some things about him she didn't want to think about too closely.

So Tracy got her mind back on business, and glanced once again at Nick. They nodded to each other, then he turned his attention to the crime scene, leaving her to get statements from the bystanders.

Nick didn't speak to any of the busy technicians when he came in. He left Tracy to deal with the civilians for now. He looked around, noted details, absorbed the atmosphere. He glanced at the body, noted the spatter pattern of blood where the corpse had landed, but his attention was drawn to a number of objects on a desk near the large window. He wondered if the scent of blood was as strong to the others as it was to him as he crossed to the desk. Did it disgust them or bring their senses to life? Did they even notice? Or was it part of the background noise of what they did, a scent that would be conspicuous only if it were absent? Should he point out that there wasn't enough blood, and that more than one person had died here tonight?

He almost turned to speak to one of the lab people. If the moon hadn't been so brilliant tonight, so potent, he wouldn't have been so tempted to start an impossible conversation. He was feeling more alive than he had in a long time, more reckless. It made him curious to talk about the wrong subjects with the wrong people.

Instead he kept his mind on the job and looked down at the desk. It was the glitter of silver and the sheen of marble that had caught his attention from the doorway. The statue he ignored after a cursory glance. He reached out for the silver box.

"That hasn't been dusted yet," the fingerprint technician warned before Nick's fingers came in contact with the box.

"Then do it, Paul." He gave the young man an annoyed look, then took a careful step back to avoid temptation, and to get out of the tech's way. He turned and motioned Tracy over. "What have we got?"

"Antique dealer named Adre Matescu. No priors, but suspected of dealing in stolen art treasures."

Nick gestured at the objects on the desk. "Like those?"

Tracy gave the statue and box a cursory glance. "Probably. Want me to check those out?"

A surprising wave of possessiveness came over Nick. "No. I'll take care of that." He pointed at the body, then the head. "How did that get detached from that?" Tracy didn't look at either. He noticed that Natalie had arrived and was kneeling beside the corpse. "Never mind, I'll let the coroner fill me in on the gory details. What do the neighbors have to say?"

"That Constantine Drezerdic is responsible for the murder."

"Who?"

She gave him a wry look. "That's something I suppose I'm going to have to find out. The neighbors claim he's a crazed killer—when he isn't a mild-mannered store clerk. Everybody wants to talk about him, and how he must be responsible, but I got a lot of mixed signals. Apparently he found his wife with a lover, accidentally killed her in an argument, then cut off her head as some kind of trophy. Neighbors don't think he was wrong to kill his adulterous wife, but the decapitation thing disgusts them. He just got out of prison."

"How does that connect him to our victim?"

"Don't know if it does. No one heard or saw anything. They just don't think it's a coincidence that a man who

22

beheaded someone lives in the same area as someone who got beheaded."

"So they've handed you a lead but not a real suspect."

She nodded. "At least that's something."

"Find out about this Drezerdic. Fancy meeting you here," he said to Natalie as she came up to him. He didn't need vampire senses to detect that she was tired and irritated, but also more troubled than usual by this crime scene. The question was, Why?

"Beepers," Natalie said, "are the spawn of the devil. If I hadn't answered mine, I could be in bed right now."

"And miss the pleasure of my company?"

"I've already had that pleasure this evening." She nodded toward the corpse. "Anything I should know before I get to work?"

Not wanting to be overheard, Nick took Natalie by the elbow and moved her to a quieter part of the room, by the desk. He looked at the box again. There was something that attracted him to it, something . . . familiar.

The castle hall was something out of the thirteenth century, lit by a giant fireplace and dozens of branches of candles. The floor was rush-covered, and Nicholas could sense the scurry and squeak of mice near his feet. Two of the walls were hung with tapestries in dark colors that depicted even darker deeds. The furniture was sparse, made of heavy, ornately carved dark wood. The large room held one long dining table, a few high-backed chairs, and a cabinet where the light gleamed off a large collection of silver plate and utensils. The mantel and walls beside the fireplace were ornamented with ancient weaponry. There were enough swords and spears to supply a small army—one that could easily be blown away with a few well-placed rounds of cannon fire.

As he looked around, Nicholas murmured, "This is ridiculous."

"What is?" LaCroix asked. As he followed Nicholas's gaze around the large room, he murmured, "Ah, the decor offends you, Nicholas." The elder vampire put a hand on his arm. "Radu's the sort who finds a style he likes, then stays with it."

"It's primitive."

"Does it matter? Luxury is pleasant, but hardly required for our kind."

"I prefer living in luxury myself," Janette contributed.

"As do I," LaCroix conceded.

"I prefer progress," Nicholas said.

"For Radu this is progress. When I first met him, he lived in a skin tent; a young vampire who'd barely made the transition from drinking mare's milk to mare's blood. We must give him time."

"That time appears to be 1200," Nicholas said.

Janette laughed, drawing Nicholas's attention away from LaCroix. Candlelight and blood from fresh feeding gave Janette's skin a warm glow; her dark eyes held both the glint of merriment and the predator's sharp look. She was lovely, dressed in midnight blue and stiff, pure white lace, her shining dark hair elaborately dressed in the latest curled style. She looked as out of place in this medieval setting as Nicholas felt.

He didn't know why it should be so, as he had first seen her in a setting more ancient than this one, in a time and place where he belonged. It had been in a great stone hall similar to Radu's, but devoid even of such amenities as a fireplace, or hangings to cover the cold stone walls, when he had first felt her gaze on him. He had been Nicholas de Brabant, a Crusader who had stopped at an Outremer fortress to recover from a wound. She had been an unknown beauty who came to his pallet just before he settled down for the night. He had wanted her instantly. She was a temptress he'd followed to his doom. To LaCroix. Sometimes he regretted the results of that meeting, but Janette remained forever beautiful to him.

Since that day he had seen Janette in velvet and silk, sometimes in rags, but always in a setting suitable for the times. The effect of seeing her in her very fashionable clothing in a place that the changing world had passed by disturbed Nicholas. It bothered him almost as much as the hideous creature he'd encountered outside the village the night before. He didn't know why, or how, the two could possibly be connected, but all his senses were alert to the strangeness of the place.

"This Radu sounds like quite the barbarian," Janette said to LaCroix as Nicholas continued to inspect the hall. His attention was drawn to the collection of silver on the side table. Besides the usual round and oval platters and plates, Radu had amassed a wide variety of ornate jewelry boxes, reliquaries, and delicate containers from many eras and places. While Nicholas examined a fine piece of Florentine silverwork, the conversation continued behind him.

"Oh, he was quite the barbarian," LaCroix answered Janette. "Completely ruthless. And still is, I should imagine."

"I trust he has moved on from mare's blood to more suitable prey."

"Centuries ago, my lovely one." The voice was a deep, rough rumble. Radu, come to greet his guests, Nicholas supposed, making the dramatic entrance so typical of their kind. Still holding the Florentine jewelry box, Nicholas turned to face the newcomer.

"And tell me why, LaCroix," Radu said as he stepped

into the light, "is that young man fingering my silver? Have you brought a thief into my domain?"

"You tell me what's bothering you, and then I'll tell you what's bothering me," Natalie said, drawing Nick's attention from the objects on the desk, and away from the memory.

They had as much privacy as they were likely to get in the crowded room. So Nick said quietly, "Not enough blood. And, I think——." He closed his eyes, and let his other senses roam. After a moment he nodded in confirmation. "Two people died here."

He was glad Natalie didn't ask him how he knew. She accepted that he had some psychic knowledge of events. At one time he would have agreed, but in this age of science he knew the truth was that he could taste molecules of blood that still lingered in the air. In this room the blood of two mortals mixed and mingled, with a residue of something else, something other.

Natalie asked, "Where's the second body?"

He shrugged.

She looked around carefully before she said, "You think one of your kind is involved?"

"Why would you ask that? This is a decapitation," he reminded her.

"I ask because you're looking—furtive is a good way of describing that look on your face."

He shrugged, and tried to look innocent. "Maybe it's just indigestion?"

"Nick!"

"I'm not sure if it's one of my kind." The sensation he felt might be the lingering energy given off from the fear the two victims had experienced. It could be the influence of the full moon impairing his judgment. Something didn't feel right; it did feel familiar. He wasn't sure there was a vampire involved, either. "It doesn't take a lot of strength to cut off someone's head with a sharp sword," he said. "A mortal could easily have done that. But there is a lot of blood missing."

It was Nat's turn to shrug. "I haven't done the autopsy yet. Decapitation might not be the cause of death."

"You've looked at the corpse, haven't you, Dr. Lambert?"

"Don't get sarcastic with me, Detective. Or tell me how to do my job."

Nick refrained from pointing out that he had far more experience with death than she did. Why state the obvious? Besides, he wasn't trained in forensics. "Maybe his head just spontaneously flew off."

"Maybe I'm being a little touchy," she admitted. "I saw something near here on my way home."

"Something to do with the case?"

"Maybe. Or I imagined it. I probably imagined it." She looked at the body. "Then again, I thought I saw a sword."

He put his hand on her arm. With the touch, he sensed her confused frustration. "You did say you'd tell me what's bothering you."

She nodded. "I heard Tracy say that you have a human suspect."

"That's right. Tracy's going to check him out."

Natalie bit her lip and looked carefully around.

"No one can hear us. What did you see?" he urged.

She took a deep breath. "Okay. I think I nearly ran down a big, naked, sword-wielding vampire not two blocks from here about a half hour ago."

He moved very close to her, and whispered, "You're sure?"

"No, I'm not sure. I told you it might be my imagina-

27

tion." She stepped back. "I did see somebody running, but I was sleepy and my mind was on spooky stuff. It might not be connected at all."

He gave a faint laugh. "Not connected? How can you . . . ?"

"Because humans are far more likely to commit grisly murders than your kind," she cut him off. "That's why I'm going to conduct an autopsy and you're going to check out normal leads before either of us gets carried away with supernatural theories."

She was reminding him that thinking like a human might help him in his quest to become human. Natalie had all sorts of notions that his affliction was caused as much by behavior as it was by a blood disorder.

"Police procedure first," he agreed.

But as she moved away to go about her work, he turned and slipped the silver box into one of the deep pockets of his black coat. Fingering the silver, indeed, he thought, and went to make a statement to a television reporter who had somehow gotten into the room.

3

Screed was rat hunting when the two-legged *thing* came stumbling toward him. It was as tall as he was, man-shaped like he was, but dead. Far more dead than he was.

Screed understood fear, but mostly from the superior side of the equation, having caused a bit more than he'd experienced. There wasn't much the *carouche* found disgusting. He'd seen it all, done it all, been it all.

Or so he'd thought.

He hadn't seen anything like this before. He didn't want to see it now, but he couldn't do anything but stare for a few moments. The skin on its neck was torn away, its clothes brown with dried blood. The eyes that were fixed on him held no life, but they did convey a piteous, confused need. It had a fresh meat smell about it. He was thankful for that, at least. He didn't think it was going to stay fresh for long. He had no trouble imagining this creature a few days from now, stumbling about with rotting bits falling off it.

He didn't like the thought of rotting corpses walking. Corpses were supposed to stay where they were put.

Things should be alive, dead, or undead, not moving somethings that looked to be even lower on the food chain than a *carouche* like himself.

This thing wasn't natural. He'd never seen anything like it, never heard about anything like it. It sent a shudder through Screed's skinny frame.

"You're breakin' the laws of nature, mate," he murmured as the thing took a step further into the alley, its gaze fixed longingly on him.

Screed put a dumpster between himself and the thing. He waved it away. "Go on 'ome, cobber. Sun'll be up soon," he added, unable to prevent himself from giving advice even to a creature who didn't deserve it, and probably had no comprehension.

"Going to get a dreadful sunburn. I 'ope," he added, taking to the air as the thing kept coming toward him. He was grateful when it didn't follow him. He hovered above the alley for a few moments, just to make sure the thing couldn't fly. It lifted its head and watched him, but it stayed next to the Dumpster.

Screed nodded. "Well, there's a blessing."

He flew away, not toward his own place but toward an abandoned church where a mate made his home. This friend fancied the irony of a vampire dwelling on sacred ground. Javier Vachon had never taken to the notion that he was a damned creature of Satan. Screed liked him for that. A very New World sort of vampire was Javier, not like those old-line European sorts who sniffed around Princess Janette when she still ruled the roost over at the Raven. Even welcomed a *carouche* into his crew, did Javier. For that reason, and because the rats in the church's deep basement were particularly tasty, Screed sped off to bring Vachon the news of what he'd just seen.

• • •

In one thousand nine hundred and eighteen years of living in the dark, Lucien LaCroix had never once desired to see the sun rise. He wasn't waiting for it now as he stood on the empty sidewalk outside the Raven, seemingly gazing toward the east. The moon was long down, and daylight was fast approaching. He had less than an hour of safety left, so it was understandable that he was getting a bit impatient. The nightclub was closed, all the mortals and immortals who frequented the place had gone about their business. He was the only one left, he and the girl who stood in the shadows behind him. She didn't think he knew she was there, or she pretended not to want him to know.

They'd been playing this game for some time now, both inside the crowded darkness of the Raven and now here in the empty darkness of the late night street. Where he went, she followed, a discreet, almost covert presence. He wasn't quite sure what to do, being more used to being the stalker than being the stalked. He smiled, knowing full well that on his face a smile was not a charming thing. Perhaps if he turned it on the girl, she would go away, flee screaming into the night, and let him get on about his business.

The business he had in mind for the rest of the evening had originally been to end his cat-and-mouse game with the young man who had stolen his *numina*. It had been his intention to make a meal of the foolish boy, then go to bed. It was too late for that now, so he would have to seek his entertainment elsewhere. Having been seared by the hungry looks from this young woman since he came from the back of the club after finishing his radio broadcast, LaCroix was intrigued. She was a fragile-looking thing, gamin-featured, with a bruised soul gazing out of her big, dark eyes. She watched him the way another young woman had once watched him one thousand nine hundred and eighteen years ago.

"'*Her eyes have feasted on the dead,*'" he quoted as she finally moved closer.

The girl was being furtive, but he could tell by the steady thrum of her heartbeat that she wasn't nervous. She wasn't afraid, she wasn't even sexually excited. He didn't think she wished him harm as she came closer, which was a pity. It would be far easier to deal with a simple assailant than to have his curiosity piqued. He felt the warmth of her fingertips as she stretched a hand out to touch his shoulder.

"'*Her mouth is sinister and red,*'" he said.

And was standing close behind the girl before her hand reached him.

He leaned down to whisper more of the poem in the girl's ear as his arms came around her. "'*As blood in moonlight is.*'"

Rather than screaming, or fainting, or making any other sort of sane response, the young woman relaxed against him. "You can't seem to get your mind off moonlight tonight, Nightcrawler," was her calm reply.

Ah, yes, a familiar voice. He should have guessed sooner. "Tammy."

"You sound disappointed."

Why wasn't she surprised that their positions had been so suddenly reversed? Why was she so comfortable in his less than warm embrace? He stepped back. She turned to face him, looking eager.

LaCroix shook his head. "Go home."

"How?"

"Don't you have a home?"

The word sent her blood racing with anger; it was a

delicious roar in his ears. "I have a place to stay," she answered. "It's not the same as a home."

"But it's so trite to admit to the loneliness, isn't it, my dear?"

"I'm not afraid to admit it to you. Not to an anonymous voice on the phone, but to you, face to face."

He cocked his head to one side as he regarded her. The bitterness of her tone, mixed with the trust in her words, was charming. His answer was caustic. "You're a poor motherless lamb with only me to turn to. Is that it?"

He expected her to wince, but she laughed instead. "Something like that. Only lambs," she added, "get slaughtered."

"Didn't I say something like that last night?"

"You say something like that every night."

"I thought you were a fan, not a critic."

"I'm whatever you want me to be."

LaCroix briefly touched a finger to the side of his nose. "I see. What a generous offer. What if I want you to be my dinner?"

She held her arms away from her sides, showing off the slender body clad only in a short, too-tight, black dress. "Too skinny," she said. "No meat on me."

The sky was lightening. What few stars were visible above the lights of the city were fading away. LaCroix found himself slowly walking around the girl, as though examining a slave offered for sale. When they were face-to-face again, he glanced once more at the traitorous sky before turning his back on the girl.

"Time to go."

She followed him without question, something no one had done for a long time.

Her shift was officially over by the time Tracy knocked on the apartment door. Before coming here she'd taken the time to do a little homework on the man she was about to talk to. While she didn't like what she'd read, it gave her some idea of what to expect. The time she'd spent reading the file gave the part of the world that didn't work the graveyard shift time to get out of bed. The man she'd come to see looked wary when he answered the door, but he also looked awake. Actually, he looked like he hadn't slept—not a point in his favor.

"Constantine Drezerdic?" she asked as she showed him her badge.

Dark eyes narrowed as he nodded. "Is this about my daughter? Have you found her?"

He was short, with hands that seemed too big for his wiry frame. There was a fanatical concentration in the way he gazed at her that kept Tracy on her guard.

"I filed a missing person report with the police," he went on before she could answer. "Was told the system didn't work that way, that Tamara wasn't missing, that her whereabouts are none of my concern. She's mine. Of course they're my concern."

Though her curiosity was piqued by Drezerdic's single-mindedness, Tracy knew from studying his file that his daughter was an adult. The woman he searched for hadn't seen her father since she was seven, and had witnessed his decapitation of her mother.

"May I come in?" Tracy asked, and took a step forward, forcing him to move hastily backward. Once she was inside the apartment, she closed the door behind her. She took in the spotlessly neat efficiency unit with a glance. A pile of papers, manila folders, a notepad, and a telephone on the dining table were the only evidence of the place actually being lived in. No swords were sitting conspicuously in view. "May I ask you a few questions?"

"I report to my parole officer once a week," he

answered. "I'm never late. I never miss work. I'm doing everything I'm told. All I want is my daughter back." He leaned close to Tracy. His voice was a husky, earnest whisper. "I'll do anything you want to get Tamara back."

Tracy forced herself to meet his fanatically bright gaze. "I'm not here to talk about your daughter, Mr. Drezerdic, but your cooperation will be appreciated."

He smiled eagerly, showing too many stained teeth. "I spent fifteen years in prison being cooperative. I've had practice at doing what needs to be done. All so I could get out and find my child."

A chill chased up Tracy's spine at the way he said "my." She knew that it was possessiveness turned murderous that had gotten him fifteen years in prison. In her opinion, fifteen years wasn't nearly enough time for what he'd done. She didn't offer her opinion, however, but gave a brisk, professional nod. "Fine. Where were you last night, Mr. Drezerdic?"

"Looking for Tamara, of course." He gestured toward the table. "I was on the phone most of the evening."

Early morning sunlight coming in the apartment's only window slanted across the table. "Do you remember the amount of time you spent on the phone?" She'd have to check phone records against the autopsy report, but she suspected the man had an alibi for the time of the murder. There was no eyewitness to put him at the antique shop. She'd have to wait for the forensics people to finish the preliminary physical evidence report before she'd know if Drezerdic's prints were at the crime scene. She didn't have a warrant to search the premises. All she could do was talk, and listen, for now.

"I didn't pay attention to time," he told her. "You don't notice something like that when you're looking for your child. Time is nothing, finding her is everything. She belongs to me."

"Do you know Adre Matescu?"

"He's the antique dealer. His shop is up the street. Too many young people come in and out the back door there. The wrong sorts of young people."

"You've seen these young people?"

He nodded. "Oh, yes. Everyone knows about the young men who come to Matescu's in their long hair and leather coats, their shaved heads and pierced noses. Some of them are my Tamara's age. Mrs. Sijan suggested I ask them if they know my girl. She knew my girl when I was in prison, but lost track of her. She thinks Tamara might have ended up in that sort of crowd. That's why my child needs me, to keep her safe from young men like that."

Despite their insistence on checking out Drezerdic, the neighbors had also mentioned the young men to Tracy. She'd been told the murdered antique dealer had been under investigation by the burglary unit. She had quite a few people besides the creepy Mr. Drezerdic to talk to in connection with the death. The fact that Drezerdic admitted that he'd talked to people associated with the victim wasn't anything like a motive, but it was something.

"Did you have any contact with Mr. Matescu?"

He shook his head. "I stopped a young man coming out of the shop once, but he didn't know anything about Tamara. He did tell me the names of clubs where pretty young girls go. Then Matescu came outside and told me to go away."

"And what did you do?"

"I went away. I'm on parole. I don't want trouble." He

looked pointedly at his watch. "I have to go to work. I don't want to be late."

"You've never been in his shop?"

"No."

"Why would your neighbors think you had something to do with his death?"

Drezerdic's eyes grew round. "You didn't tell me he was dead." His surprise seemed genuine. It was followed immediately by a fierce, restrained anger. "I'm not a murderer. Yes, I took my wife's life. She was an adulteress, it was my right. They told me it was wrong and they punished me for it. I would never take a stranger's life. Why would I?" He eased past her and opened the apartment door. "I want to go to my job now."

Tracy decided to let it go. Being near him set off alarm bells in her mind, but mental alarms weren't just cause for taking him in for questioning. Not yet. She found him creepier than Vachon's friend Screed, but that wasn't a good enough excuse to hold him. It was time for him to get to work, time for her to go home from work after she set an investigation of his whereabouts last night in motion.

"I'll be in touch," she said, and let him close the door in her face. "And I want a shower to get your slime off me," she murmured as she headed toward her car. She hoped she didn't have nightmares about fanatical fathers or headless corpses once she finally got a chance to get some sleep.

His dislike for the older vampire was instant. Even before LaCroix laughed at his expense, Nicholas felt cold anger settle around his heart.

"I'm no thief," he said to Radu.

37

"Except of hearts," Janette added, with a low, seductive laugh.

Her comment caught Radu's attention. The smile she turned on him held it. The light that appeared in the older vampire's eyes as he returned Janette's smile was no sign of otherworldly power, but an indication of primal, earthy, masculine interest. That she looked Radu over with the same assessment was almost enough to bring a jealous growl to Nicholas's throat. It was a reaction he forced himself to curb.

With a casual-seeming flick of his wrist, Nicholas tossed the tiny Florentine box back onto the treasure-laden table. It crashed against a larger container, one stamped with a twined sun and moon pattern on the lid. Nicholas was not upset to see that the soft metal of the second box took a deep scratch from the force of the encounter.

He moved to stand beside LaCroix at his maker's silent signal. When Radu would have taken her hand, Janette came to LaCroix as well. She cast LaCroix an annoyed glance as he said, "It is good to see you, my friend."

"It is good to see you, General," Radu replied. "You and your obedient children."

LaCroix nodded, always happy to acknowledge his control over them. Nicholas deliberately ignored any provocation from either male. Janette looked between them, then stepped away. She went to the hall's massive dining table and took a seat rather than involve herself in any confrontation. Nicholas could feel her cool gaze from the depths of the torchlit room, but he wouldn't let himself look at her. He studied Radu instead, and saw no outward reason why Janette would be attracted to the old-fashioned vampire.

Radu was dressed to suit his surroundings, in a long surcoat of dull gold brocade, the wide sleeves lined in dark fur. A heavy silver collar, embellished with uncut gemstones, circled his throat. A harness bristling with knives in studded leather sheaths was fastened across his broad chest. Black hair hung down his back in a waist long braid. A curved Turkish sword rested against his thigh.

Radu curled his left hand around the ornate hilt when he saw Nicholas's gaze on the weapon. "You stink of disdain," he said to Nicholas. "You wonder why one of our kind carries so many blades when these—" he curled back his upper lip to show massive fangs—"will suffice. The answer is easy, little one." Radu touched a knife. "I like them."

"Ever the barbarian, aren't you?" LaCroix asked.

"Always."

LaCroix clapped Radu on the shoulder. "Good. I've missed that."

Radu's laughter boomed and echoed through the cavernous hall. "I've missed hunting with you. It's a pity the Austrians drove out the Turks," he added. "They made excellent quarry. And their women—delicious. Still, there's plenty of elusive game in the forest."

"Elusive, yes," Nicholas said. "I've already noticed the villagers' fondness for garlic. No doubt they take exception to your treating them like deer in a royal game park."

Radu gave an offended sneer. "I do not hunt peasants. Their blood tastes of dirt."

"If you don't attack the villages, why do they protect themselves from our kind?"

Radu shrugged. "There is a plague. It's easy to blame our kind for any unexplained deaths."

"A plague doesn't explain what I saw last night."

"And what was it you saw?" Nicholas didn't like the amused glint in Radu's eyes. "Was it something like this?"

He gestured, and footsteps shuffled toward them through the rushes. Its stench preceded it. Nicholas wondered why he hadn't at least smelled the creature sooner as it appeared out of the shadows. It was a bundle of rotting flesh dressed in rags. Blood was caked on its lips and cheeks. Its gaze was fixed worshipfully on Radu.

"Pretty, isn't it?" Radu asked them. "I keep it as a pet."

Nick woke up at the sound of the alarm, thoroughly annoyed with dreaming of Radu, and that his past kept coming back to haunt him. The clock told him the time, his senses told him that it wasn't long until sunset. He ran his hands through his hair and shook his head to clear it. His attention was caught by the glint of silver on the bedside table. Glancing over, he saw the box he'd taken from the crime scene. It was cool to his touch when he picked it up. Cool and smooth, except for the raised sun and moon pattern on the lid, and the long scratch that marred one side. He knew where the scratch came from. He remembered now where he'd seen the box before.

The question is, he thought, *what's it doing here? What does it have to do with last night's murder?*

He supposed he was going to have to go to the Raven to find out.

4

"*WHAT MAKES A FAMILY? A HOME? WHAT DO THOSE THINGS MAKE of us? What molds us into the things we become? What bends us into the shapes that horrify us when we look in the mirror?*" LaCroix asked, speaking into the mike, warming to the prospect of another evening spent taunting the sensibilities of this fair metropolis.

It was odd, how he'd come to enjoy the prospect of ripping rhetorical fangs into the complacent veneers of those mortals who chose to listen. It almost gave him the same thrill as hunting. On his best nights, dissecting the city with words was better than hunting. Because it was the prey's choice. They could simply switch to another station anytime they wanted. Or they could let him in, listen to his anything but soothing voice, spend a sleepless night with him. It was their choice to let him lacerate their souls and suffer having all their doubts, their fears, their questions spill out. He'd found a way to let a thousand souls bleed to death in a night without ever having to take a drink. It was almost as good as blood.

41

Technology is a wonderful thing, he thought before he went on.

"What makes us monsters to others? To ourselves?" he asked. He spoke slowly, relishing the sound of his own voice. *"Biology? Environment? Society? Our own perverse wills? All of the above? This is a multiple choice exercise, my children. Think hard before you answer. Choose as if your life depended on it."*

Tonight's monologue was his musings after a long conversation with Tammy. The girl had a lot to say about family values, none of it pleasant, while at the same time she seemed to crave acceptance, guidance. She was a mixed-up, modern kid—much as Nicholas had been in his time, and Janette in hers. And Divia in hers, for he found that Tammy reminded him more of his somewhat perversely devoted biological daughter than of the children he'd made since being brought across. Or was he the one who'd been perverse in that relationship?

"Things change," he said. *"They stay the same. Nero came from a dysfunctional family. Vlad the Impaler never quite recovered from his childhood traumas. How glorious to be able to take all that childish anger out on the rest of the world. Pity most of you can't play monster the way you'd like to, on the grand scale. Tell me, what did your father do to you? Or is it your children who commit crimes against you? What do you dream about doing in payback? Revenge, someone once told me, is the best revenge. Let your demons out to walk the night. The Nightcrawler's always happy to listen."*

LaCroix glanced up from the microphone as Tammy leaned over the table. What little she was wearing gave him an excellent view of the veins pulsing blue beneath the soft skin of her throat and chest. He clicked off the microphone. "If you're trying to show off your breasts," he told her, "you're not being very successful."

"That's because I haven't got anything to show off. You're still looking, though."

"What I'm looking at, I find very attractive."

Her smile was bright with pleasure that was more childlike than seductive. "Talking too much must make you thirsty." She held out a full wineglass. "Miklos said you drink this."

LaCroix was, unreasonably, charmed.

"When nothing better is available."

He took the wine mixture and downed it to ease both his throat and a growing fascination with hers. He was enjoying the cat-and-mouse game they were playing and wanted it to go on longer. Possibly because he wasn't sure which was the feline and which was the rodent. He wasn't sure what the girl really wanted. Or what he wanted from her, for that matter. He found her combination of neediness and defiance interesting. She reacted to him with fearless, biting humor, but at the same time her gaze spoke of her need for his approval.

He wasn't sure what to make of her yet, so he'd let her sleep on his couch, keeping his bedroom door locked in case she tried to join him. If the door had so much as rattled during the day, he would have taken her. Instead, while he stayed awake, waiting, she'd slept as soundly as a trusting child. When darkness came, he brought her dinner, talked to her, let her come with him to the Raven. Now she'd followed him from the club back to the broadcast booth even though he'd told her he wanted to be alone.

"I'm not used to being disobeyed," he said to her.

"Then perhaps it's a habit you should cultivate," Nicholas said from behind her.

43

"Correction," LaCroix answered his favorite child. "Being disobeyed is something I occasionally tolerate."

Tammy whirled to look at the newcomer, then glanced back at LaCroix. She must have heard the affection in his voice, for her expression was a combination of jealousy and wariness. It deepened when LaCroix gestured toward the door, making the command for her to go a mental one as well. She obeyed, compliant but also angry.

Nick was surprised by the girl's presence. He was even more surprised by the venomous glance she gave him as she sidled past to leave the broadcast booth. "Isn't she a little young for you?" he asked, raising a quizzical eyebrow at LaCroix.

"Aren't they all?" LaCroix responded, just as his engineer signaled an incoming call.

Nick waited while the Nightcrawler fielded the comments of what Nick's late partner, Schanke, would have dubbed a certifiable loony-toon. From the conversation, Nick assumed that tonight's theme was a riff on the subject of family. He was glad he hadn't tuned in to CERK while driving to the Raven. It was a subject he didn't want to hear LaCroix discourse upon. Especially the subject of vampire family values. They'd been over it too many times. Some of those times had involved violence, rebellion, escapes, captures, betrayals, stakes, flames, rebirths, threats. . . .

"*Sex, lies, and videotapes,*" LaCroix said to his caller, interrupting Nick's chain of thought.

"Those, too," Nick murmured to himself, getting an ironical look from his maker in response.

He almost smiled at LaCroix, caught himself, then gave in and actually smiled. Partly because he and LaCroix were living in a state of truce these days, with his maker almost treating him like an adult. Almost.

Partly because there was no use being petulant, which he supposed was almost acting like an adult.

LaCroix's look turned hard as he switched off the mike. "I'm seeing far too much of you lately, Nicholas. I thought you wanted a life of your own." He stood. Tall, straight, vaguely threatening.

Nothing unusual in that.

Nick smiled again. "You're about to accuse me of wanting to use you for my own purposes."

"Aren't you?"

"Yes."

LaCroix frowned at his honesty. "Have a drink. We'll talk when I'm done here."

Nick took in the broadcast booth. "Your sense of responsibility to your fans—and I'm sure the young lady who just left is a fervent one—is admirable."

LaCroix's frown deepened to a dangerous glower. "We can discuss her, or why you came to see me," he answered. "The choice is yours."

Nick weighed curiosity, tinged with worry for the girl, against one headless corpse and a strong feeling that something horrible was loose in the city. "We'll talk about my problem," he conceded. "I'll go get that drink."

By the time Nick came back to the broadcast booth, fortified with one of the bovine brewskis the club's very special bartender had concocted especially for him, LaCroix was finished for the evening. The engineer was gone. Nick had felt the girl's jealous gaze on him when he'd left the bar, but a commanding look had kept her from following him.

He was alone with his maker, with more on his mind than when he'd arrived at the Raven. He was worried about the girl. He'd watched her dance with a mortal boy her own age, but her attention had never really left the door to the back of the club. He'd watched her carry on a brief conversation with Urs. Something the mortal girl said made the moody vampire girl smile. He'd also gotten the feeling the mortal girl was questioning Urs, especially after Urs made a swift, angry exit from the club.

He wasn't going to ask, he told himself as he took a seat opposite LaCroix. Not just because LaCroix had given him the choice of topics, but also because, as much as he tried to live in the mortal world, there were immortal rules he still lived by. He could police the mortal world but not his own. If the girl was LaCroix's chosen prey, then so be it. If the girl was playing games with vampires and got burned, there was nothing he could do. He didn't want to destroy vampires, he just wanted to stop being one. That the effort involved some hypocrisy was just another bit of guilt he had to deal with.

When he fished the silver box out of his coat pocket and set it on the counter between them, LaCroix said, "Ah."

It was a very significant sound. "You've seen it before?" Nick asked.

LaCroix steepled his fingers. "You know I have."

"My questions are, What's it doing in Toronto? What was it doing at a crime scene? And most importantly, what was in it?"

LaCroix gazed at Nick over the pyramid of his fingers. His eyes glowed ever so slightly in the dim room. His soft voice held an infinite amount of threat. "Are you asking these questions in an official capacity, Detective Knight? Am I a murder suspect?"

LaCroix did not cut off his victims' heads, nor was he the indiscriminate killer he had once been. Times changed, LaCroix changed with them. All of their kind did if they wanted to survive. Those who could not adapt were dangerous to their own kind, and measures were taken to eliminate them.

Nick ignored the angry tension that radiated from his maker. "You're not a suspect," he answered. "I only want answers to my questions."

"You assume I can give them to you." LaCroix sat forward. "You assume a great deal, Nicholas. You always do." He picked up the box, stroked long, pale, strong fingers across the embossed lid. Lovingly, Nicholas thought. "This is mine," he said. He lifted the lid, then slowly closed it. The sigh would have been inaudible to anyone but another vampire. After a significant hesitation, he added, "A gift from our old friend."

Nick didn't contest the lie. "How did it end up in a dead antique dealer's office?"

LaCroix smiled. It was a predatory sight people usually experienced just before they died. Nick had endured it for over seven hundred years. He'd learned not to flinch. Nick noted that there was actually a hint of embarrassment in this version of the expression. The laugh that accompanied the smile was brief and bitter. "I imagine the antique dealer was the burglar's fence."

"It was stolen from you?"

LaCroix nodded.

Nick couldn't keep the shock out of his voice. "You let someone invade your home?"

LaCroix gestured around the room. "I was at work."

Nick wasn't going to laugh. He wasn't going to let a hint of glee at someone taking advantage of LaCroix show. Besides, this was serious business. Nick remembered his own furious reaction the few times outsiders had invaded his warehouse home. "I don't suppose you reported the break-in to the police?"

"Don't be ridiculous."

"What did you do?"

LaCroix replaced the box on the counter. "I tracked the thief myself. I have every intention of punishing him for his crimes."

"Have? Not had? You haven't caught him yet?"

"I know who he is. Until yesterday I knew where he was. Then I became distracted." LaCroix leaned forward, gaze intent. "I assure you, Nicholas, I will dispose of him in my own way, and in my own time."

"I'm not arguing your rights in the matter."

"What, no lecture on the workings of the mortal justice system, Detective?"

Nick shrugged. "A man's home is his sarcophagus— castle. We have a right to defend our privacy."

"You mean we have a necessity to defend our privacy."

"There are a few things we agree on, LaCroix."

"Better a soft bed than coffins and holes in the ground."

"Safer as well as more comfortable, as we both know."

"I recall the incident, Nicholas. Most distasteful."

The late night wind howled with the fierceness of a pack of wolves, tearing indigo rags of clouds across the stars. A storm had come and gone. They had hunted through it, defying the lightning, bellowing with the thunder and the muskets of the soldiers who'd been their prey. It had been a small patrol out chasing bandits, well-armed for the task of capturing mortals, ill-equipped for what came after them. It had been exhilarating, the hot blood of the soldiers delicious with the tang of fear and fury. Nicholas could not fault Radu for his choice of entertainment.

He did fault their host for plunging deeper into the forest after one last fleeing mortal as the time grew late.

He faulted Janette for laughing wildly and joining the barbarian in the chase.

Nicholas turned to LaCroix as they skirted the edge of the village. "Dawn's too near for us to reach the castle."

LaCroix nodded. "Inconvenient. We'll have to find what shelter we can."

"What about Janette?"

LaCroix sneered. "Radu will, no doubt, provide for her."

Nicholas tried not to think of the pair of them sharing some dark, private place through the long daylight hours, especially with the wildness of the night still burning in their veins. He well knew how he and Janette would work off that charged energy. He well knew how she and Radu had been looking at each other. He well knew there was nothing he could do about it.

LaCroix put a hand on his shoulder. "It's eating away at you, isn't it? You see her looking at him, and you begin to understand, if only a little, how I feel about you both."

What he felt had nothing to do with possessiveness, with ownership. He didn't answer his maker—his master. Instead, he pointed to where their path crossed with another track up ahead. "I think there's shelter this way."

What they found at the crossroad was a mound of fresh earth and a small stone building, the entrance barred by a heavily rusted iron door. "Unconsecrated ground," Nicholas said. "Where they bury criminals, heretics, and suicides." He ran his hands over the rusty door. It was difficult, but he managed to pry his fingers into the metal. "Someone paid dearly to see a relative unworthy of proper burial placed here." Whatever else was inside, there would be no crosses in the tomb to prevent them from entering.

"What do I care what or why old bones are resting here? What I don't like is having to join them."

"It's this or bury ourselves as best we can in the forest," Nicholas answered as he pried the door open.

His fingers left clear marks in the edge of the door, his palms came away covered in rust. For a second he glanced at his hands. Though the smell of iron permeated his nostrils, it looked as if his hands were covered in dried blood. He wiped them on his cloak.

I hate this life, he thought.

"This will do," LaCroix grudgingly conceded, and preceded Nicholas through the opening.

Nicholas shook off the mood, and followed. From the inside, he pushed on the resisting door until less than an inch of space remained open. Nicholas couldn't bear the thought of closing the door all the way, or being completely entombed. It wouldn't hurt to have a little light, especially if the day proved to be as dark as the clouds of another approaching storm promised.

"We'll have to spend only a few hours with the dead," he said, as LaCroix swept a skeleton off its resting place and took a seat.

"Nonsense, Nicholas. We'll always have each other."

Nicholas was not in the mood for LaCroix's attempts at humor. He stayed near the door, away from the line of light but close enough to look outside as the dawn came and the day began to pass. His mind was on Janette. On Radu. On the tryst he envisaged in some deep forest cave. When those thoughts set him burning with jealousy, he forced his mind back, back to Rome, to the ninety years LaCroix had left them alone to live together in one long, intense, passionate moment. It had been the happiest time he'd known since being brought across.

He'd been furious when Janette broke the spell, when

she'd gone away. LaCroix found him soon after. Janette returned with him. She never mentioned their time together, so Nicholas carefully kept quiet as well. And life went on and on and on.

"You don't want to lose her again."

No, he didn't. He didn't intend to talk about it, either. He said, "Someone's coming."

"Did you notice how Radu reacted to the musketeers? How he tore the weapons from their hands and beat them with them? How he dismembered and beheaded the corpses of most of those who'd dared to fire at him? I don't think he likes guns, Nicholas. He hasn't any at the castle, I noticed. How strange."

As Nicholas listened to the sound of approaching feet, he turned to look at LaCroix. "I thought you liked Radu's old-fashioned ways."

LaCroix gestured around the crypt. "I don't like very much about Radu just now. Very inhospitable."

"You enjoyed hunting the musketeers."

"Of course. But I don't see their guns as personal enemies. And that thing that follows him. . . . The creature bothers me," LaCroix admitted.

LaCroix looked at his hands while Nicholas counted the heartbeats of five people coming closer. A slow, steady rain pelted down outside, punctuating the passing seconds. He heard quiet voices, full of anger, dread, and anticipation. When they came into his field of view, a jolt of alarm went through Nicholas. He risked burning his face as he moved forward to get a better look. Then he nearly choked at the miasma of garlic that wafted from the group as they gathered on the other side of the crossroad. The men were carrying shovels, pry bars, hammers, and large wooden stakes. Nicholas took an involuntary step back, catching his foot on a leg bone and nearly falling.

He looked around wildly. The bone-filled confines of the crypt glowed red as his vision changed to peer into the darkness. Nothing he saw would be any help to them. There was no way out but the rusted door, and that led only to burning light and wooden stakes. They were trapped.

Nicholas, forcing himself to be calm, peered outside once more. Someone had struck a light to a pitch-soaked torch. It sputtered and hissed in the steady rain, but the flame held. Garlic, stakes, and fire. These men knew what they were about.

The blood that had coursed hotly through a soldier's veins a few hours ago went cold in Nicholas now. He was barely aware of whispering, "I don't want it to end like this."

"What is it?"

He waved LaCroix to stay silent, to keep still, but the other vampire was beside him instantly. LaCroix took a quick glance outside. He hissed, an animal sound of anger and fear. The noise rang like a shout in Nicholas's ears. It set his heart racing, but none of the peasants seemed to have heard. Their attention wasn't on the crypt, but on the fresh mound of earth on the other side of the crossroad. Their angry, nervous attention was completely focused on the grave. Nicholas almost sighed with relief. Curiosity kept him and LaCroix from hiding in the safer darkness away from the door.

When he saw them begin to dig, he wondered if there was another vampire in the grave, if there was something he could do to distract the villagers from their murderous intent. When LaCroix put his hand on his arm, Nicholas knew that it was a warning to stay out of the affair. There was nothing they could do, it was none of their concern.

But Nicholas was concerned. He didn't know whether he pitied the vampire or the people who were trying to rid themselves of a monster who preyed on them. Then he found himself almost hoping that this grave was a bolt-hole hiding place of Radu's, that the Serbian vampire was about to meet his end. Though he had no just cause to hate Radu, he did.

It didn't take long for the peasants to clear the dirt away. The thing they sought was barely covered with a thin crust of earth. It was more a burrow than a grave, a covered-over hole to hide from the sun. The stench that rose from the ground as they hauled their victim out overpowered the reek of garlic. Though the light was dim, it was enough to burn the unearthed thing. Already putrefying flesh quickly took on the stink of frying rotting meat. The men holding the ragged creature flinched and coughed as they hauled it toward the very center of the crossroad, but they didn't hesitate to be about their business.

As the crowd came closer, LaCroix whispered in Nicholas's ear. "What is it? Radu's pet?"

Nicholas shook his head. His stomach clenched with fear, but not at what the villagers were doing. "Another one."

"Another?" LaCroix sounded appalled.

"I think this is the one I saw the first time. I thought Radu's pet was the same creature, but it's different. I see that now."

"How can you tell the difference?"

"By the stench," Nicholas answered. "This one is further gone than Radu's." The truth was, he'd gotten a glimpse of this thing's eyes before it was thrown to the ground. The eyes had been different. He wished he hadn't seen the eyes. They showed no intelligence, but they had been filled with pain and terror.

It's going to die, he told himself. *Truly die. That is the help it needs.*

"Where do those things come from?" LaCroix asked.

"From hell, I think," Nicholas replied.

"There is no such place," LaCroix answered, adamant as ever that there was no God. The creature smoked as it was doused with holy water. "It's some trick of the mind," he added even though the words were nearly drowned by the thing's screams.

"That thing has no mind," Nicholas answered.

It took six men to hold the creature on its back in the center of the crossroad. Two other men stood on either side of it. One, thick-muscled and with the look of a blacksmith about him, held the hammer. The other one placed the stake over the thing's heart.

The blacksmith raised the hammer high over his head, then brought it down with all the force of his being.

"That's what comes of not having a place to call home."

Though he was still half-caught in the memory, Nick managed a faint smile at LaCroix's ironic comment. "It was fortunate for us that they were satisfied with their work that day and didn't bother looking in the crypt."

LaCroix nodded, his face shadowed and imperious behind steepled fingers. He leaned forward when Nick scooped up the box and slipped it back into his coat pocket. He held out a hand. "That is mine, Nicholas. You know how possessive I am of my property."

Nick stood. "I'm keeping it for now. Evidence."

LaCroix stood as well. "Evidence of what? My involvement? I had nothing to do with the death."

"One of our kind did."

One of our kind who knows how to use a sword, he added to himself. Which would be just about every vampire brought across before the middle of the nineteenth century.

LaCroix inclined his head. "Granted. Though I'm not sure whether to be flattered or insulted at not being a suspect." With the faintest glimmer of a smile, he added, "Perhaps Radu came back for his box."

"We both know that's not very likely." Though Radu was *very* fond of swords.

"It was just a thought."

"Do you know who it was?" Nick asked. "Was someone tracking your thief with you?"

"I was hunting alone."

"Perhaps it was some young one who stumbled on your game and decided to play as well?" Nick strongly suspected that the explanation for the fence's murder would not be that easy, that LaCroix was more involved than he claimed.

LaCroix's eyes went a cold yellow at the suggestion that another vampire had interfered with his fun. "Perhaps someone was trying to do me a favor. If so, they'll pay for it."

"Or perhaps it was a coincidence," Nick suggested. "Whichever one of our kind is responsible, I have to track him down."

"Or her. Don't be sexist, Nicholas."

"Or her. In the meantime," Nick added as he stepped toward the door, "I have to convince the Homicide squad that it's nothing more than an ordinary, run-of-the-mill, brutal, mortal murder."

He moved quickly out of the room, and out of the club, before LaCroix could demand the silver box back once more.

After Nicholas was gone, LaCroix threw back his head and laughed. "You never listen, Nicholas. Ah, well," he added with a chuckle as Tammy sidled back into the studio, "the fate of this fair city is hardly my problem."

5

"THERE'S A PROBLEM."

"More'n one, mate."

While Screed and Urs jockeyed for position in front of him on the sidewalk, Javier Vachon tried to inch past them into the club. All he wanted was a drink.

Urs batted at Screed. "Go away, rat catcher, this is important." She turned to Vachon. "I'm just glad you answered your pager when I called," she said. "You're terrible about remembering it."

"Uh, yeah."

Actually, Vachon wasn't quite sure where his pager was. Possibly in Tracy Vetter's refrigerator. He remembered its beeping at him the last time he'd been rummaging around her kitchen, looking for something for his rather specialized tastes, but that had been several days ago.

Screed stepped in front of Urs. He wagged a bony finger under Vachon's nose. "Trouble in big bright capital letters, cobber. Tried to tell you sooner, but you weren't at the church last night. Oh, no, 'ad to 'ang about

57

this place waitin' for you and gettin' dirty looks from the better sort of clientele in 'opes you'd show."

Vachon really wanted that drink. The band inside the Raven was playing loudly, something with a deep heavy bass line that rattled the walls and vibrated out onto the street. Vachon could feel it in the soles of his feet, in his chest, throbbing in the faintly aching fangs tucked in his upper jaw. He could hear the crowd laughing inside, and the mixed rhythm of a hundred heartbeats underlying the music. He wanted to be part of the crowd, to dance, to immerse himself in the hedonistic atmosphere of the only bar in town that served vampires. Mostly, he wanted one of Miklos's very special mixtures to ease the growing hunger he didn't want to slake the old-fashioned way.

But Urs and Screed wouldn't let him past. He'd known Urs—Ursula Comstock—for over a century; Screed, longer. She was blonde and beautiful, and just beginning to work her way out of a hundred-year-long suicidal depression. If he'd known in the 1870s that what she needed was a feminist therapist rather than a shot at immortality, she wouldn't be blocking his way into the club right now. But that had been the Victorian era, and Freud had still been a kid. Who knew?

Now there was a thought. He'd been considering what to do with his life lately. Maybe he should find an all-night medical school, specialize in psychiatry, then set himself up as a vampire shrink. He wondered if Tracy Vetter would like to go out with a doctor. Would she introduce him to her parents? Would they complain that, sure, he's a doctor, but look at the long hair?

"I'm hallucinating," he muttered as he ran one hand through his long hair. "I must need that drink more than I thought." When he took a step sideways, the obstructing pair did so as well, like a vaudeville comedy act.

People going in and out of the Raven were giving them strange looks. "Will you two get out of my way?"

"No way, not until we talk," Screed insisted.

"Not until we talk," Urs echoed the skinny *carouche*.

The pair weren't normally rivals, but now they were vying for his attention like he was some sort of authority figure. Things hadn't been the same since Vachon declared that they were no longer a crew. The minute he'd cut them loose, they'd suddenly become needy. They'd given him more space when he was their leader. He was tired of the constant companionship of his fellow immortals. He wanted some time alone. He had some thinking to do. It didn't look like he was going to get any privacy tonight.

"How about we get a table inside and talk there?"

Screed laughed. "Oh, right, mate, like 'is Straight-out-of-a-Hammer-Horror lordship is going to let the likes of me into 'is place."

"Point taken," Vachon agreed. "The Raven doesn't serve vin de rodent."

Urs made a gagging noise, then glanced furtively toward the club entrance. "I don't want him to know what we've been talking about."

"No time for girl stuff," Screed declared.

He took Vachon in a grip that was too strong for his near-skeletal frame and hustled him into the shadows by the wall of the building. The noise from the band was even louder over here, but they were out of the traffic pattern of people going in and out of the Raven.

Screed gave Urs an annoyed look when she followed. She made a face but said, "All right. You go first."

Vachon leaned against the wall and crossed his arms. "Hurry it up," he advised. "My fangs hurt."

Now that he had Vachon's full attention, Screed looked

like he didn't know how to start. He made a wild gesture. "It's a thing," he said. "A fiendish thingy. Smelly dead man walking thingy." He pointed. "Out in the city."

"I see," Vachon said with a slight nod. He exchanged a puzzled glance with Urs. "All right, no, I don't. What are you talking about?"

"I think he's gotten into rat poison again," Urs offered.

"Oh, don't I wish," Screed said. He looked around wildly, as though expecting something nasty to jump at him out of the dark. "Don't I wish."

Vachon put a hand on Screed's shoulder and looked deep into the *carouche*'s eyes. "Calm down. Talk to me."

"You believe in monsters, mate?"

"Of course not," Urs spoke up. When both Vachon and Screed gave her sardonic looks, she shrugged. "Other than us, I mean."

"And just about every weirdo mortal out on the street," Vachon added.

"This thing was like us," Screed said. "That's what made it so disgusting. It felt kind of like a vampire, but with the power turned way down low. Wasn't running on empty, not even fumes, you know? Gave off ugly, ugly vibes. Like it was projecting its complete deadness, but was lookin' for something at the same time. Brain-damaged, it was. Brain-dead, flatline special that one was."

A chill went through Vachon at Screed's words. One thing Screed did not do was scare easily. "Let me see if I have this correct—you saw a dead vampire?"

Screed's eyes lit. He smiled. "Got it in one! That's what it was!"

Urs put her hands on her hips and turned a sneer on Screed. "A dead vampire? Get real. You sure it wasn't another *carouche*? A really hungry one, maybe?"

"'Ey, Blondie, I know a *carouche* from a walkin' corpse."

"What about that crazy, dog-eating thing that lives in the park?"

Screed shook his head. "Worse'n that. Way worse."

Urs looked worriedly at Vachon. "An animated corpse? That's not possible. Is it, Javier?"

He shrugged. "I've never heard of anything like it. Outside of horror movies, Stephen King, and folktales, anyway."

"You've always gone to too many movies," Urs told him.

"Keeps me up days, reading Stephen King," Screed added, with an exaggerated shudder.

Vachon ran his hands through his hair. "We've gotten away from the original point, here—which, as I recall, was me trying to get a drink. Where did you see this alleged thing?" he asked Screed. "When?"

Screed scratched his head, stared at the wall behind Vachon's head for a moment, then said, "Harbour Street, near the ferry docks. This morning, just before dawn. Hope it fried when the sun came up. Save us all a spot of bother, that would."

Vachon sighed. So that was what this tale of a monster was about. "You're assuming this is our problem?"

Screed relaxed, and looked hopeful. "It's not?" Then his scrawny form tensed up again. "Can't call an exterminator about it. Can't call the cops."

"We can ignore it," Vachon told him.

"Your usual answer," Urs said disgustedly.

Screed looked at Urs. "But 'e usually comes around. That's why you want to talk to 'im, innit? 'Javier, you gotta help me, sweetheart,'" he mimicked in a high-pitched falsetto.

"This isn't for me," Urs said, then gave Vachon a pleading look. "There's this girl. A mortal girl."

Vachon didn't want to hear about a mortal girl's problems any more than he did about mindless monsters. "I have one mortal too many of my own to worry about, you know," he pointed out to his longtime friends. "You're turning into a social worker," he added to Urs, not quite sure whether he approved.

She frowned angrily. "You never take anything seriously."

He gently touched her cheek. "You never used to tell me what you really felt."

Except for a few minutes after he'd first brought her across, Urs had hidden her feelings and done everything she could to please him for years and years. After a few decades of dealing with her facade, he'd all but forgotten her initial death wish. That had changed recently, and she was starting to deal with her problems, to stand up for herself. And for others. And expecting him to help her.

The way Screed expected him to do something about this thing the *carouche* might have seen.

It was enough to make him wish he'd never told them that the vampire/goddess/whatever who had made him had ordered him to do good deeds before immolating herself. He hadn't exactly been an obedient son for the last four hundred years. He was a conquistador, not a crusader, right? Every now and then he'd found himself fighting for the underdog and saving the occasional maiden in distress, but it wasn't as if he'd made a deliberate choice to be a superhero.

The way the other two were looking at him, it seemed they thought that he had.

Vachon sighed. "All right, Screed. I'll check out the

area around the docks." *But not tonight*, he added to himself.

Screed nodded. "Fair dinkum. I'm gone." And he was, a moment later, speeding away over their heads.

Vachon looked after Screed as he streaked away. "What's his—?"

"Too many vampires in the neighborhood for his taste," Urs explained. She caressed his cheek. "Most of them aren't as tolerant as we are. Whatever it was Screed saw must have really frightened him, or he wouldn't have dared come near the Raven."

"Screed likes to keep to himself."

"He likes to keep alive. You know how most of us treat *carouches*. They're useful for disposing of our carrion, but not good enough to talk to."

Vachon shrugged. "Sometimes I forget."

"That's because you accept everybody."

"Life's too short not to. Even for us." He'd never had much use for class distinctions, not even when he was mortal and the bastard, half-Marrano son of Don Carlos de Sebastian Feria, Duke of Azuga. "There's not that much difference between what we are and what Screed is. We all had vampire parents."

Of course, Vachon had to admit, he'd been lucky in both his mortal and immortal parents. Don Carlos had given him an officer's commission and sent him off to make his fortune in the New World. The lady who had brought him across had had only the best of intentions, even if she had not bothered to ask him his opinion of the future she wanted him to pursue. She had at least had the power to make him a full vampire.

Screed's maker had been too weak to make a child, but that hadn't stopped him from making the effort. The result was someone who wasn't quite a vampire but wasn't mortal, either. *Carouches* were rare, but obvious, evidence to the vampire community that they weren't as all-powerful as most of them liked to believe.

Vachon scratched the dark stubble on his cheek. "Now there's a frightening thought."

"What?"

"Maybe this thing Screed saw was brought across by someone who can't even manage to create a *carouche*."

Urs looked both horrified and disgusted. "Yuck. I don't even want to think about that. Let's change the subject."

He put his hands on her waist and pulled her against him. She was wearing a lacy black bustier and a short leather skirt. The boned garment was both soft and stiff to the touch. She smelled of lavender, sweet and old-fashioned, rousing more than memories.

"Why don't we talk over dinner, Urs?" He kissed her shoulder, and let her feel the points of his fangs against her bare skin.

Urs laughed. She didn't do that often. She also slipped away from his grasp. "No, Javier. Not tonight. You'll make your mortal girlfriend jealous."

"She's not my—. Are you teasing me?"

"Maybe a little." She looked toward the door of the club. "But we don't have time for games. You need to talk to Tammy tonight, before she gets in any deeper. Or talk to him."

Vachon didn't like the way Urs said "him." "Who's Tammy?"

"A girl who's trying to seduce LaCroix."

"Oh, *that* him." Although his tone was calmly sarcastic, the mention of the city's oldest vampire did nothing for Vachon's peace of mind.

In the last few months LaCroix had taken over the Raven from Janette, but so far he hadn't tried to exercise any influence over the younger members of the community. He welcomed them into his establishment, asking nothing more than the price of their drinks from them. LaCroix was too intent on his involvement with Nick Knight to bother with pulling rank on the rest of them. This was just fine with Vachon. He liked the new situation, even though he missed Janette's regal presence. She had never been a dictator, but protector and adviser to those who sought her out. This sounded like the sort of problem Urs would have taken to Janette, but expected him to deal with in her absence.

"I don't get it," he said, curious, though he would rather not get involved. "Someone's trying to seduce LaCroix? Why?" Urs rolled her eyes in reply. "Well, excuse me if I don't see the attraction. Does this girl know he's one of our kind?"

"I think she suspects. She's a real Gothic, pib type— black clothes, pale makeup, languid attitude. You know, the way mortals think we're supposed to act. But underneath the attitude. . . ." Urs rubbed her bare arms as though she felt a chill. The old, haunted look came into her eyes. "She reminds me of me."

Vachon reached out to cup her face in his hands. "Then don't look into that mirror. She has to make her own mistakes. You have to get on with learning to like yourself."

"Something has to be done. I won't have her death on my conscience."

"If anything happens to this girl, it'll be LaCroix's fault, not yours. We can't interfere with him. We're all killers, Urs."

She walked away from him and turned her back. "I've never killed for pleasure."

"I know." Vachon had. He hadn't liked it for long.

"That monster is playing with her. I don't like watch-

65

ing, even though I know I can't stop him. I've tried warning her, but she won't listen to me. She's the sort who won't listen to another woman. She's looking for a man to tell her what to do. She's looking for a father."

"Which is why you want me to talk to her?"

Urs turned to face him. "Yes."

"I'm not the fatherly type, Urs."

"Then talk to LaCroix."

"Nor am I insane."

She put her hands on her hips. "Just do something, Javier."

"Yeah, right, I'm supposed to walk up to this girl and say, 'Excuse me, Miss, but the meanest bloodsucker on the planet is planning on having you for a snack. Would you prefer to be served on a bed of lettuce? Or would you rather run for your life?'" He waved a hand at Urs. "Do you think anything I say will matter?"

Urs looked like she was going to cry. "You could try."

He sighed. "All right. I'll try." Vachon was fairly certain that LaCroix would do what he wanted, but wasn't going to try to argue with Urs anymore. "Is the girl inside?"

Urs nodded. "Yes. But the last I saw of her she was heading back toward the radio studio. For the second time tonight."

That did not sound promising. He stepped forward and slipped his arm through Urs's. "Point her out to me—if she comes out again." He touched her cheek. "Can we go inside now?"

She nodded.

As they moved away from the wall, Nick Knight came out of the club. The door slammed behind him, and he turned their way. If Knight saw them, he gave no indication as he moved toward the shadows. Vachon might have said something to the older vampire, but Knight was radiating too much annoyance and concern for a casual greeting to seem appropriate. For a moment Vachon did consider asking if there was something wrong with Tracy. He didn't get the chance as Knight made a quick check to see that no mortals were watching, then took to the air.

"People come and go so," he began.

Urs put a finger over his lips. "Enough, Javier."

Urs never had been much of a film fan. "Okay," he agreed. "But if this place gets any busier, it's going to need an air traffic controller." Vachon got an actual laugh from Urs as they reached the canopy over the Raven's door.

6

THE FIRST ONE HE'D KILLED TONIGHT CARRIED NO COINS, NO weapon. After he fed, then sliced off its head with the sword, he took its clothing to cover himself. The peasant's clothes were filthy, the fastenings strange. They smelled of rancid wine and urine. They would have to do until he could find more suitable garb. He was used to fine silk and rich fur against his skin, to the gleam of silver and gold and sparkling jewels on his hands and about his throat. He was used to the blood of beautiful women and battle-tested warriors. He was a prince, a soldier, very nearly a god. He would have the best the mortal world had to offer, or the world would suffer for it. He laughed as he stood over the headless body, longing to make the world suffer even if it provided lavishly for his desires.

The thing he desired most right now was to put everyone in this new, frightening world to death. After that, he wanted silver.

Last night had been hard on him, but the day had been worse. The place he'd found to sleep had been a hot metal box full of offal—he should have slept surrounded by purest silver. He missed the silver's cool protection. He longed for that peace, for the formless dreams, almost as much as he longed for the night and blood.

The box had grown hotter and hotter as the day slowly passed. Without the sweet protection of the silver, his dreams and thoughts had been painful, incoherent, and troubling. He'd been assaulted with confused memories of the inexplicable things he'd seen the night before. He'd been wracked by hunger so strong it nearly drove him out of hiding to feed. Never-ceasing noise that was louder than the clashing of armies surrounded him almost as solidly as the metal walls of his hiding place. Worst of all was the fear of all of it.

Righteous anger slowly grew in him as the long, hot day passed. He nursed the fury to combat the terror, to help him fight off the ravenous hunger minute by minute. He spun out vivid scenes of how he would punish those who made him afraid.

Then darkness came.

The peasant he'd stripped had been standing nearby when Radu emerged from the day's prison. For all his dreams of torture, his hunger got the better of him. Once he was fed and finally clothed, the sword at his side as secure as it could be, thrust through a flimsy belt instead of into a scabbard, he left the drained corpse in search of someone who would give him answers along with blood.

Radu made himself go out of the alley into the street where everything was strange. Everything was wrong. The worst part was the lights. They came at him out of the darkness, strange torches, round like eyes, the fire so white and intense he couldn't bear to look at it directly. The twin torches were everywhere, attached to roaring metal chariots. Or perhaps the white lights were the eyes of armored beasts that had taken over the world. He wasn't sure what he was seeing. He wasn't sure where he was.

All he knew was the ancient hunger, and the remembered skills of his hunting kind. He kept his gaze on the ground, kept one hand on the solid bulk of walls to steady himself when he could, kept his concentration on finding the one perfect heart that beat for him among the herd that surrounded him.

Eventually he followed a young man down a street that was dark enough for Radu's liking but still busy. He hung back, moving in the shadows of brick and stone buildings that were each as tall as castles. The ground beneath his bare feet was paved in some smooth white stone, littered in places with discarded bottles of glass fine enough to be on an emperor's table.

The passing hours had taught him that this was no village he'd found himself in, but a city larger, finer than even Byzantium before the Turks. A strange place that stank of acrid smoke, but where the gutters were free of human waste. One full of far too much noise, too many people, not enough darkness. No one stayed decently and safely behind locked doors after dark. That made them easy victims for the taking. He was glad enough of that, for the hunger burned unslaked by only one feeding.

But it disturbed him as well. These mortals walked wide, torchlit streets in great, noisy crowds, heads high, like thousands of princes. The women had no modesty. They walked about less than half dressed, their heads bare, gazes bold, voices loud—worse than camp followers at the tail of an army. The men seemed to have no warrior skills, no weapons.

At least the one he'd picked out carried himself with a bold swagger. The young mortal was dressed in a leather vest with no tunic beneath. His bare arms were marked with colorful designs. The young man held his head up, looked at the others on the street with bold contempt. He knew he did not belong with the common herd. Radu smiled. If he could not taste bravery, he would settle for pride. It would be sweet to strip that pride away.

Radu watched as the young man stopped and made a furtive transaction with a street merchant, then turned up a dark alley mouth. The moment was perfect, and Radu struck. He dragged his victim to the far end of the alley within the space of two heartbeats, to a narrow spot between buildings where the darkness was nearly complete. With Radu's hand clamped around the mortal's throat, he had no chance to scream.

"We will talk for a while," Radu told him. "And then you will die."

The defiant look in the mortal's eyes told Radu that he would die hating him, and that was good.

Radu took a few sips from the vein in the man's wrist before he looked into his eyes and spoke again. "What is the name of this place?"

The mortal answered—he had no choice—but Radu did not hear. As the man spoke, Radu's attention was drawn upward toward a flash of movement in the night sky. It traveled with the speed of a falling star, but he *felt* the hunter overhead. One instant the dangerous life force was there, faintly familiar, disturbing, its attention on some distant goal. Radu had a glimpse of a dark streak against the dark sky. He had an instant's contact with an invisible blaze of concentrated emotion. Then the dark form was gone, speeding away as silent as any hunting owl.

"Strigoi," Radu said. "One of my kind."

No stranger, either. Oh, yes, he knew that cub, and all his fiercely sentimental emotions.

"I need you."

Janette's soft fingers caressed his cheek, a velvet touch that was gone too quickly.

"I've heard that before."

She turned away from him and rested her arms against the parapet, her gaze on the moonlit forest instead of him. Radu had brought her to the tower roof to view his kingdom. Now he was jealous that she seemed to prefer the vista to gazing into his eyes.

She showed no concern for the whereabouts of her companions. She'd seemed content in his company ever since they'd parted ways with the others near dawn the night before. They had shared loveplay after the excitement of the hunt. Then they had slept in each other's arms. At nightfall they'd feasted together on an outcast a wandering gypsy band had left bound outside the castle gate for him to deal with. She had laughed at such a quaint custom. The sound of her laughter had been so pleasant in his ears that he'd spent the last few hours regaling her with the history of his land, and his place in it. He treasured each word, each laugh, each smile his tales managed to conjure from her.

"I wanted the company of my own kind when I invited LaCroix here," he told her. "Now I want him to go away and leave you behind. Stay with me."

Radu watched her as she looked into the night. Minutes passed, and she showed no sign that she was aware of him, that she had heard his words. Of course she felt his craving for her, as he felt hers. Need burned between them while the silence stretched out. She

73

wanted him, but her control was strong, her desires tangled up with her loyalties.

"Stay with me," he repeated when the stillness had spun out for too long. His tone was harsh, and he received a withering look for it. He looked at her through half-closed eyes, his head tilted boyishly to one side. "I am used to commanding," he told her, "but with you, it seems I have to learn the art of persuasion."

"I'm not yours to command."

"You are LaCroix's."

She gave the slightest of nods. "But I am also my own."

The relationship between LaCroix and his children was complex. Far more than it needed to be, Radu thought. Power shifted between them, they played games with each other's emotions. It was foolish. A master should rule his creations with an iron hand. That was the way it had always been, the way it should always be. It was not the way it was with LaCroix, and perhaps that could prove to be to his advantage.

He took her by the shoulders and turned her to face him. "I would make you mine."

Anger flashed across her eyes, followed swiftly by teasing amusement. "You cannot *make* me do anything." After a tense moment, she relaxed and traced her fingers across his lips. "But you might persuade me."

"I could learn this art of persuasion for your sake, Janette." He kissed her throat, ran his fangs back and forth across the pulse points in her neck until her breath caught and her fingers tangled in his hair. "I will do what I must to keep you here. Do anything to please you."

She took a small step away, but she stroked the places where his fangs had touched her. "I enjoy being here," she told him. "For now."

"My company pleases you?"

"Yes."

He circled her waist with his hands and drew her back to him. "My touch pleases you?"

Her hands roamed boldly over him. "Your touch interests me."

"Stay with me," he urged. "Hunt with me. You've brought excitement back to the chase for me." Radu looked deep into her eyes. "I see how weary I've become being the only one of our kind to roam these lands."

"Then leave. Come with me."

He shook his head. "I hunt in my own territory."

"The world is large, Radu. There is life to take everywhere."

"Not for me. For over a thousand years this has been my place. I want no other." He touched her cheek, her lovely throat. "Stay with me and I will never be lonely."

"You could make companions for yourself. You need never be alone."

He glanced contemptuously at the creature that crouched near the tower door. "I have no interest in children. I want a companion."

"A consort?"

He did not answer Jeanette. He kissed her instead.

Only to be interrupted within moments by a hand on his shoulder.

Awareness of the intruder's identity hammered against Radu's senses even before he raised his head with a snarl. The young one answered the challenge, eyes glowing gold. The energy Nicholas threw off lit up the night. He shimmered with righteous outrage, concern, caring— every emotion a bone-deep part of him.

Radu threw back his head with a howling laugh as they circled around the tower roof. "You're so *good*," he

75

sneered. "How can LaCroix bear to put up with you?" He glanced to where Janette stood, back pressed against the wall, arms crossed beneath her bosom. "Why do you stay with this fool?" he asked her.

Her angry attention was all on the fair-haired lad. "Nicholas, stop this," she called. "This is none of your affair."

Nicholas ignored her, and pointed at the creature. "What are those monsters? Where do they come from?"

Radu laughed again. So this interruption wasn't about Nicholas's jealousy of Janette.

"Janette." Radu spoke her name like a prayer.

The mortal writhed and twisted in an attempt to escape while Radu looked up at the sky and tried to think through the hatred that roared through him. Nicholas was here. He was sure it was Nicholas.

He was going to have to find Nicholas and destroy him.

"Janette," he repeated. "Beautiful Janette." He shook the mortal and heard bones break. "Be still."

He had to have her for himself.

Why was he bothering asking this human rat questions when he had to find Janette?

First he must feed, and feed and feed until he came into his full strength once more. Only then could he hope to win her from that fool Nicholas. So Radu drained the mortal, forgot about the body even as he dropped it, and went after his next kill.

Within minutes after Radu killed him, the body stirred, stood, burned with hunger. Eyes that perceived only the heat of living blood looked out of the pale face. Sensing life nearby, it stumbled out of the alley on an insatiable search of its own.

"So happy to see that you could join us this evening." Nick was nailed by Captain Reese's sarcastic comment the moment he walked into the squad room.

He turned to face the big man. "Sorry I'm late." He didn't have to be a vampire to sense the palpable thrum of excitement in the room. It almost overpowered the fear and a faint scent of blood coming from a woman surrounded by a group of uniformed officers in one corner. "What have we got?"

Nick started to move toward the group, but Reese stopped him and pointed. "Talk to your partner." Then Reese turned to deal with the situation.

Nick shrugged and moved to stand by Tracy's desk. She was bright-eyed and a bit pale. Her fingers clicked quickly across her computer keyboard. Her lips were pressed tightly together, and her gaze was fixed on the screen. "Writing up the initial report on another headless murder victim?" Nick guessed.

She nodded, keyed in a few more words, then looked up at him. "Where have you been?"

"Checking out a lead."

"You say that a lot." Tracy's voice was shrill with anxiety. "You could have mentioned this lead earlier."

"It just came up." He shrugged. "Didn't pan out anyway."

"You could have called in."

"But I didn't."

She stood to face him. "I was warned that you were too much of a loner when I was assigned to Homicide," she complained. "But the captain said, 'Nick's the best. Work with him and he'll take care of you.'"

"He didn't say that."

"No, but that's what he meant."

"You don't want to be taken care of."

"No," she agreed. "But occasionally I'd like to show up at a crime scene at the same time as my partner instead of having to explain all the gory details at your convenience. We're supposed to work together, Nick."

He put a hand on her shoulder. She was trembling. Not with anger but with nerves. "This is another bad one, and I wasn't there for you."

She made a face. "You make me sound like a needy child. Every murder scene is bad, I know that. I'll toughen up eventually."

"Don't toughen up too much. Makes you cynical. So," he firmly got back to business, "what have we got?"

"Another headless corpse—as you already surmised. Male, in his forties, probably homeless. Found on Cobalt, near the stockyards."

"That's a long way from the first murder." *But then, the dead move fast, as Mr. Stoker pointed out*, Nick thought.

She nodded. "Twist on this one is that the body was naked."

"That's interesting." He recalled Natalie mentioning that the person she'd nearly hit with her car the night before was naked. Chances were, he wasn't anymore. He asked, "What about the ex-con? Drezerdic?"

"I'm still checking out his alibi for the first murder. As soon as Natalie gives us a time of death for the latest victim, I'll check him out for this one, too."

Nick had no doubt that Drezerdic wasn't involved. Nevertheless, he told Tracy, "Keep on him."

"I don't know if he's our murderer, but I've got a bad feeling about Drezerdic. There's something sinister about that man. I've never met anyone so focused on a goal. I almost wish I could find some reason to put him back in prison again, even if he isn't our man on this one."

"Go with your instincts, then. I better view the body."

"Natalie's doing the autopsy now."

He turned to leave the squad room. To see Natalie, he would have to go to the CFS building just behind Police Headquarters, where the city's forensic work was done. Before he reached the door, his attention was drawn to the woman in the corner as she abruptly stood up.

She shouted, "I know what I saw! I know what that thing did to me! I *am not* hysterical!"

Nick came closer as Reese said something soothing. Whatever the captain said, it didn't help.

"You're laughing at me," the frightened woman insisted. "It was trying to eat me." Nick got a good look as she thrust a blood-covered arm toward Reese's face. "Look at these bite marks."

"An emergency medical team is on the way," Reese told her. "We'll take your statement after you've been taken care of." He gave a stern look to a man with the woman. "You should have taken her straight to the hospital."

"She insisted on reporting the attack first," the man answered. "Those do look like human bite marks," he added. "If some crazy man is running around attacking people, the police need to know about it."

The woman grabbed a watching detective by his shirt, and shook. "Listen to me. A dead man attacked me tonight. I saw his face, his eyes. He tried to eat me. I was lucky to get away."

"We understand that, Mrs. Adams," the detective told her. "You need to calm down."

The woman looked around the crowd. "You people have seen *Night of the Living Dead*, haven't you?"

Nick's stomach knotted with tension at her words. Having heard more than he wanted, he backed away. He, at least, believed. Luckily no one else would. At least not about being attacked by a dead man—even though Nick knew it was the truth.

"This woman needs a sedative," Reese said.

"And a splash of holy water on those wounds wouldn't hurt, either," Nick muttered.

He had to talk to Natalie.

"Are we alone?"

Natalie glanced from the Y-shaped incision exposing the cadaver's chest cavity to the person on the other side of the autopsy table. She put down the cassette recorder she'd been using. She kept her movements precise, her tone flippant. "You're joking, right?"

Nick didn't look like he was joking. He seemed almost nervous, as though he were checking out the shadows as he glanced around the brightly lit room.

"There's just you, me, and a couple of my clients." She pointed to a covered body waiting on a gurney across the room; a victim of a vicious animal attack. "I don't think they're going to interrupt the conversation."

"This one won't, at least," Nick said as he looked down at the headless corpse.

Natalie also glanced at the body. "I'm just going through the motions here, Nick. There's a bite mark on the throat below where the head was severed." She looked up, annoyed. "We both know the cause of death, but how do I put that on a report? And how do I condone my own silence?" Her gaze dropped again as she added softly, "This is starting to get to me, Nick." Her hands clenched into fists, stretching the thin latex of her surgical gloves.

She hadn't meant to say that. Knowing that vampires existed was hard enough on her sense of reality, but she tried to keep her misgivings to herself. Because she was trying her best to cure her friend of an addiction she was certain was as much psychological as it was physical, she always downplayed the more gruesome aspects of his supernatural life. She was careful not to condemn, not to judge, though she knew unnatural death went on all around her every night in the city. She was always careful in whatever comments she made when faced with the evidence that vampires fed off the blood of mortals.

She supposed she excused it because Nick wasn't one of the ones who killed, because he did his best to keep in check the ones who did. Because once, in this room, she'd told a fascinating stranger who'd gotten up off an autopsy table and told her he was a vampire, that she could help.

Also, she kept a discreet silence about Nick's kind because she had seen enough mindless killing of mortals by mortals who didn't have to hunt to live.

With this second hideous death in two nights she wasn't feeling particularly objective anymore. She made her hands relax, but the tenseness didn't leave her voice. "Do you know who's doing this?" she demanded.

He looked sheepish, gave her a faint, apologetic smile. "Not yet."

One of the problems with Nick was that he could give her a "little boy lost" look that simply melted her insides. He could give her a lot of looks that left her totally befuddled, and that wasn't even counting his gift for hypnotism and mind control. As much as she tried not to think or talk about it, the fact was, she was in love with Nick Knight. He knew it, and sometimes he used it. She told herself he couldn't help it, didn't even notice he was doing it, but it was definitely getting to her.

All these thoughts ran through her mind as he gave her that calculatingly persuasive look. Then again, maybe he wasn't using over seven hundred years of experience to be manipulative and she was letting her suspicions otherwise get the better of her again. Most of the time she took Nick at face value, believed his side of past events he chose to share with her.

Maybe she was just feeling resentful that she was going to have to lie to cover his immortal butt one more time. "You know what's amusing?" she asked.

Nick thought that his reason for coming here was a bit more important than whatever was bothering Natalie. He also knew that he frequently, and mistakenly, thought that way. He'd had a long time in which to learn to be selfishly autocratic. It didn't help that he'd started out that way, as a nobleman used to peasants obeying his every wish, and that immortality had made a natural tendency worse. Natalie was a friend, a confidante, and a woman he deeply cared for. He had to remind himself that sometimes he had to accommodate her needs, to help her cope with the worries that were part of the mortal world.

He tried his ingratiating smile again as he answered her question. "I'll bite."

"Ha, ha." She tapped the cadaver on the shoulder. "What's amusing, Detective, is that if I put the actual cause of death on this man's death certificate, I'll be the one who gets in trouble. 'Well, Dr. Lambert's lost it,' they'd say, and there would go my reputation and my job. So the best thing for me to do is lie, and sign my name to it."

82

"I don't blame you for hating to lie, Nat. But what else can you do?"

She let out a hissing sigh. His impulse was to offer the comfort of an embrace, but the table was between them. He could sense a certain emotional distance between them as well. No, not between them, he realized. He was holding this conversation with Dr. Lambert, not his friend Nat. Here, in the autopsy room, Natalie was wearing the detachment she needed to distance herself from the gruesome details of her trade.

"I know there's nothing else I can do," she told him. "Sometimes living with, and dealing in, lies gets to me, Nick. But as long as I get vampire victims to examine, I'm going to have to lie on my reports." She glared at him.

He accepted the challenge in that look and made a promise, friend to friend more than detective to coroner. "I'll make sure you don't get vampire victims to autopsy. Then you won't have to lie."

"I'd appreciate that. But don't worry, I'll concentrate on this poor John Doe's loss of his head and play down the lack of blood when I fill out my report. I hate paperwork anyway."

Paperwork, he recalled, was something he did because it helped him think and act like a human. It reminded him of what he wanted to be, but it was still a charade, like target practice and training classes. He truly enjoyed his work as a police officer, but it was a life he chose to lead. He had been a police officer before, and would probably be one again in the future if no cure for his condition was found in the next few years. He'd also been a doctor and a history professor in the near past. He'd tried on all sorts of mortal masks in the last couple of centuries.

For Natalie, her profession wasn't a mask, it wasn't a

diversion from an existence she hated, or a way to atone for past sins. She was a real, mortal doctor doing the best job she could. This was her real life, paperwork and all. She couldn't walk away and start over as someone else.

He did ask too much of her sometimes. He did forget how much he complicated her life. And he didn't have more time to be reassuring, or to commiserate with her just now.

"I'm sorry, Nat. I really am. The problem is, if you report the real cause of death, you won't just be in trouble with the CFS's Office." When she gave him a puzzled look, he added, "There are those in our community who make sure our existence remains secret."

Natalie shuddered at the reminder. "Oh, *them*."

He'd told her all about the rules vampires lived under. She knew how dangerous it was for her to be aware of his kind's existence, how dangerous it was for him to confide in anyone. Very limited contact was allowed between mortals and vampires, everyone involved walking a very thin line where the two worlds touched. Step over that line, and vampire police called Enforcers moved in and destroyed both the mortals and vampires who'd broken the rules.

"What happens if this keeps up?" she asked. "What if some other coroner gets assigned to work on the next victim? I've already had a call asking if I'd like any assistance."

"You're the senior coroner on night rotation."

"Yes, but this could shape up to be a very media-intensive investigation. The Coroner's Office might want to bring in some more forensics experts to make it look like we're working extra hard to solve the case."

"We are. I am," he amended. "We can't let the media get too close to this."

"Captain Reese likes the media." She sighed. "I really miss Captain Cohen at times like these. She never let politics get in the way of her investigations."

She mourned the late Amanda Cohen, murdered along with Nick's partner, Don Schanke, in an airplane bombing, for many reasons, not the least because Homicide's former captain had been as hard as nails. Captain Reese was likable, good at his job, compassionate, but also politically accommodating. He brought a different agenda to his running of the Homicide squad, one that sometimes got in the way of investigations.

I'll talk to Captain Reese," he assured her. "Make sure he doesn't let CFS assign anyone else to the investigation."

Natalie wiggled her fingers in the air. "Going to use a little of the old vampire mind control magic on the Captain?"

Nick noted that Natalie smiled as she said it, unsuspecting that he'd used the old mind control magic on her a few times. Which was the point, of course. That didn't keep a stab of guilt for the uses he made of his powers from searing through his conscience. He never got used to those jabs of guilt, and prayed to the God he'd abandoned that he never did.

Nick rubbed his unshaved jaw. "I'll have a normal talk with Reese. Only"—he repeated her finger wiggling— "if I have to."

It was a promise he made to himself, a reminder to behave humanly as much as possible. Then he looked at the corpse, and recalled that human behavior wasn't going to get this case solved.

"Whoever is killing these people," he told Nat, "is doing them a favor when he takes their heads off."

Her eyes went wide with shock, then Dr. Lambert

clamped down on Natalie's emotions. The tone of her answer, "Oh? And why is that?" was quite calmly professional.

"It keeps the dead from walking."

Nick watched her carefully after this revelation.

She crossed her arms beneath her breasts. Slowly. Calmly. She schooled her expression to neutrality. Her voice as well. "What's going on, Nick?"

It would be easier not to tell her. His natural reaction was to think it was easier and safer for the vampire community to keep mortals out of it. Seeking out mortal help had always been strictly forbidden in the past. But the twentieth century was far too complicated, mortals far too aware of the world around them, for the old rules to apply. Mortals were far too curious, information traveled too fast, and there were far too many of them. That curiosity was dangerous to everyone involved, mortal and immortal alike, but Nick thought human curiosity was probably more dangerous to his kind than to Natalie's.

The night no longer belonged to his kind. They had to exist in shadows now far more than they ever had before, but the shadows were getting thinner and thinner, and mortal sight far too good. Mortals had given up the superstitions that had given his kind power. They fearlessly ventured outside after sunset, found the howl of the wolf charming rather than an ancient warning to keep out of the forest. They had forgotten to believe in monsters.

Nick feared the reaction when the monsters proved to be real. He was certain there would be a backlash of violence against anything that was *other* when mortals finally discovered that the world was as demon-haunted as their ancestors had known it was.

He wanted to stop being a vampire, but he didn't want it to be at the price of having a stake driven through his heart by a mob of enraged gang bangers, or suburbanites—or his fellow police officers.

Nick had to stop the deaths, and the worse than deaths. He wanted to do it as quickly and quietly as possible, and on his own. But in this modern, high-tech, Communications Age world, he needed mortal help to cover up the supernatural aspects of the truth. The only mortal he could trust was Natalie. Fortunately, she just happened to be the one mortal in a position to keep what looked like vicious but understandable murders from turning into an epidemic of monsters.

So, with Natalie watching him closely, he took in a deep lungful of air and began to explain.

"I don't know if I've mentioned this before, but there is more than one kind of vampire."

"You've mentioned it. Back when some lower order of vampire attacked the guide dog, and brought it across instead of killing it."

Nick nodded. "There's a lower order than the kind who attacked the dog. I don't want to even call them vampires, though they feed on blood like we do, and make more of their own kind, and must hide from the light."

Nat shrugged. "Sounds like a vampire to me."

Nick fought the impulse to draw himself up haughtily and deny any connection to the foul things he was talking about. Instead, he forced his lips to form an ironic smile. "What I'm talking about are—perhaps—very, very distant kindred to my kind." He made himself look at the headless corpse and admit, "Created by my kind. I think."

"You think?"

"I can't explain it all, not yet."

"You can, but you don't want to."

He flinched from the undercurrent of annoyance in her voice. Nick gave Natalie a pleading look, then spoke with his emotions rather than the logic he'd mentally gone through only seconds before. He found that after over two hundred years, it still unnerved him to think about those *things*. Talking about them was worse.

I'm still a medieval man in many ways, he thought. *No matter how much time changes the things mortals believe, deep in my thirteenth-century bones I believe words have power. That the priest has only to speak the right words to make the wine into blood. That I can make those creatures more real simply by speaking their name.*

It was foolish, he knew. Primitive.

Dr. Natalie Lambert, who had not the slightest belief in magic, wouldn't understand. She might even laugh at him if he tried to explain.

"The less you know, the better it is for both of us." He rushed to explain. "I think I know what's going on. I suspect I know who. I just don't know why or how, yet. I could be wrong. If I'm right, the explanation is a secret even among most of our kind."

Natalie wasn't having any of his obfuscation. With her head cocked skeptically to one side, she said, "And that secret is?"

"I'll tell you when I'm sure."

"Nick!"

"I promise." He deliberately crossed his heart. The gesture raised no more than a blister on the skin beneath his shirt. He deemed the slight stinging fair payment for annoying her and giving in to superstition. It brought an acquiescing smile to her lips.

"All right. Just tell me what I need to know. Because

the way you're fidgeting and dodging issues, there must be something you want me to do that you know I'm not going to like."

"Cut off their heads," he answered promptly, before he could talk himself out of giving the necessary information.

She blinked. "Whose heads?"

"Anyone you suspect might have been killed by one of my kind in the next few days."

Nat's voice seethed with fierce anger when she replied. "Expecting an epidemic of vampire attacks, are you?" Her eyes flashed with fury as she stepped around the autopsy table to confront him toe to toe. "I do what I do to solve crimes, Nick. I know we've already been through this tonight, but let me explain once more. The coroner's job is to find out the cause of death, not to cover it up."

He put his hands on her shoulders. She was trembling. "I swear to you, Nat, that what I'm asking you to do has nothing to do with concealing a crime. This is to protect the public. This is what we do, remember? Serve and protect. I will take the heads off of any victims I find, but you have to make sure any that come through here have their spinal cords severed."

"Why?"

"To keep them dead. To keep them from turning into something less than human but more than a corpse." He added, "I will make the murderer pay. The deaths will stop. Until they do, we have to keep him from creating more."

"Him?"

Nick didn't offer any more explanation. "I have to go." He had to hunt while the night lasted, and the ancient one roamed the streets.

7

SHE LET HIM GO. NATALIE TOLD HERSELF THAT SHE'D RATHER have Nick working the case right now than hanging around *not* answering her questions. The strange thing was, once he was gone, she didn't feel like she was alone. Natalie found herself stepping into the center of the room and turning slowly around, arms crossed tightly. Her mind chased phantoms that couldn't be there. The room was brightly lit and cool, but as her gaze ran over the familiar territory, the temperature seemed to drop even further, the air to grow thick and heavy; the bright green tiles that covered the walls threw back shadows instead of reflected light.

It was all her imagination, of course. All because Nick had insisted on being mysterious and ambiguous about just what sort of crime they were dealing with.

Something less than human but more than a corpse, Nick had said. The memory of his words, the desperation in his eyes, sent a shudder through her.

Once she felt that ridiculous physical reaction run through her, she angrily set her jaw and made herself go back to work. Not on the vampire victim's corpse; there was nothing for her to do but write up the results there. She turned her attention to the body bag on the room's other table.

While her work was gruesome by its very nature, Natalie was not prone to any creepy feelings while performing it. It was a coroner's duty to have the utmost respect for the dead. Her mission was to help find justice for those who had suffered wrongful death. She reminded herself of these things as she approached the second body. She was calm again, ready for an objective, thorough examination.

As she reached to unzip the bag, the corpse sat up.

Natalie jumped back.

The thick plastic burst open from within as though shredded by giant claws; something awful struggled to get out. Natalie scrambled to grab a long knife off an instrument table.

She'd had people rise from the dead on her before. That was how she'd met Nick Knight. One moment she'd been about to start an autopsy on a man who'd died saving others from a pipe bomb, then that dead man woke up and changed her life. She hadn't screamed that time.

This time, as a dead man turned cold, hungry eyes on her, Natalie's grip on the knife tightened, and she screamed at the top of her lungs. Not a sound of panicked terror, but a cry for help.

"Nick!"

She backed slowly toward the door, the thing stalking her. She wanted to run, but it was impossible to turn her back on the walking dead. It was covered in torn clothing and its own dried blood. It face, throat, and thorax were a mass of torn, hanging flesh. Something had shredded this man's skin and muscles, and gnawed on his bones, but he still walked.

She'd often looked into eyes like those, the pupils blown and dilated as though the victim had died from a head trauma. This man's eyes should have been empty of expression, and they were. But they weren't. No matter how hard she tried, she couldn't drag her gaze away from those empty/needy eyes.

She felt like an animal caught in a cobra's gaze, growing more confused and terrified by the moment.

"Nick!" she shouted again, as her shoulder touched the door.

Then the door hit her hard in the back, and she was flung across the room. The knife went spinning out of her hand as she sprawled across the desk. Files and a computer crashed to the floor. There was a furious roar behind her, and the heavy sounds of bodies colliding.

Natalie pushed herself to her feet, shook hair out of her eyes, and looked up to see two impossibly strong bodies struggling back and forth across the autopsy room. Since there was nothing she could do, Natalie pressed herself against the wall next to the desk, watching Nick and the animated corpse battle with each other.

"What are those monsters? Where do they come from?"

Radu's mocking laughter was even worse than the derisive look on Janette's face. Worse, but also better, because Radu's attitude fed Nicholas's anger. It helped him keep his attention on his purpose in confronting their host. Still, it was Janette's gaze he felt on his back as he grabbed Radu's pet by the throat.

Nicholas forced the creature to its feet and thrust it before him as he turned back toward Radu. "How was this thing made? What is it?"

The thing clawed at his hand and arm; the stench of rotting flesh rose up in a cloud as it fought him. Nicholas paid it no mind.

"It belongs to me," Radu answered. "Let it go."

"Did you make it?" Nicholas demanded. "Is this filth your child?"

"It is mine," Radu answered. His tone and words admitted nothing.

Nicholas shifted his gaze to Janette. Her dark eyes flashed with outrage, anger brought spots of fresh blood to flush her cheeks. "Leave this, Nicholas," she said. "Leave us."

"Not until I have answers about these monsters."

"They have nothing to do with Radu," she said. "Nothing to do with us, either. It's none of your affair."

"A stake through the heart is my affair."

She made a sharp, denying gesture. She glanced from Radu back to Nicholas. "We are in no danger here. Why would we be?"

"Because of these creatures. There's more than one of them. I saw one die like a vampire this morning. Those mortals knew what the thing was even if it was only a shadow of what we are. I think they killed the one I saw as we traveled to the castle. Now here is a second one. Sometime soon the mortals are going to come after the source."

"Are they some freak of nature?" he demanded of Radu. "Or do you make them deliberately? For sport? Or did you try to bring them across, and fail?"

Nicholas shook the struggling creature. It made no sound. It was soft and rotten to the touch, but strong, nearly as strong as he was. Fury and stubbornness helped him keep an iron grip on the thing.

"There's a plague of these monsters. It has to stop."

94

"Radu has nothing to do with this," Janette insisted.

"How do you know?"

"How do you?" she shot back. "Keep your suspicions and jealousy to yourself."

"This has nothing to do with jealousy." Though it did, by all the saints he reviled, he knew it did. Not that even his aching love for Janette mattered. He could not do as she said. This thing had to be stopped.

"I'll kill them one at a time if I have to."

Before either of them could stop him, Nicholas drove his free hand forward, fingers thrusting through rotting flesh with the force of a steel blade. He plunged his hand into the thing's chest. Old, reeking blood spurted as he closed his fist around its heart. The thing writhed, its back arched as Nicholas twisted the heart in his hand. Arteries and veins snapped and broke free. Then Nicholas brought his bloodied hand back out, tearing the gaping chest wound wider.

When he was done, he dropped the finally dead body onto the stone floor at Radu's feet.

In the silence, someone began to clap.

"Bravo, Nicholas. I so enjoy the times when you act excessively."

Nicholas looked up to confront the one who had spoken. LaCroix came out of the shadows, hands coming together in slow rhythm, taunting him even though he'd done the correct thing.

Nicholas held the still-beating heart in his hand.

Nick held the still-beating heart in his hand.

He looked from the body on the floor to Natalie. "There's something I forgot to tell you."

Her face was pale, her eyes incredibly wide and full of shocked terror. After a few moments she responded by

95

closing her eyes. Nick was afraid she was going to faint, but didn't think racing forward to grab her in his bloodied condition was the most gallant gesture he could make.

So he stayed anxiously where he was and said softly, "Nat? You okay?"

Natalie wished she could faint, but she'd lost the capacity for it years ago. Instead she kept her eyes closed until she could face the mess in the autopsy room, if not the one in her head. The trouble was, with her eyes closed she could actually hear the soft thud-tha-rump of the heart beating; it was like something out of Edgar Allan Poe.

She made herself look. Nick was splattered in blood, not in itself an unusual occurrence. Of course it was someone else's blood—also not unusual. There was a body on the floor at his feet. Dead bodies were her stock in trade; she could deal with that. The autopsy room was wrecked, blood spattered all over the place; it could be cleaned up.

Nat pushed herself away from the wall, hands slipping a little from the cold sweat on her palms. To avoid dealing with what he was holding, she looked Nick in the face. "You said there was something you forgot to tell me. Whatever could that be?"

The heart was cold, like grasping a slippery chunk of ice. Nick waited until he was sure the beat was dying before putting it into a metal dish probably designed for just such a function.

"The other way to destroy them, besides cutting off their heads," he said, as Natalie pragmatically tossed him a towel, "is to remove the heart."

It had been a typical night for Tracy Vetter. Typical in the sense that her partner hadn't reappeared after going next door to the morgue. He had called to say that he was going to help Dr. Lambert clean up a mess, then head out to check on a lead. He hadn't explained why *he* was helping Natalie, or what the lead was. In other words, Nick Knight had acted in his typically maverick fashion, and left her to do the same.

She didn't mind, not too much, though she spent a great deal of her shift at her computer attempting to run down connections between the latest headless victim, the first murder, and Constantine Drezerdic. Another street person had finally ID'd the newest victim as one Terence Donen. Terence Donen had nothing in common with the antique dealer or the one person who was even vaguely a suspect in the gruesome deaths. Tracy had suspected as much going into the database searches, but she'd also made a thorough job of looking for connections.

Once satisfied that the computer had done all it could, Tracy hit the street. She wanted to have one more talk with Drezerdic before she checked out the latest crime scene one more time. She didn't completely trust computer information, and the parolee set off too many warning bells in her head for her to let her suspicions go completely just yet.

It didn't help Drezerdic's case any when Tracy questioned several of his nosy, suspicious neighbors, and found out the man had mentioned that he was going to hunt for his daughter in the club district. The latest victim had been known to spend a lot of his time panhandling around the clubs, and slept in the alleys behind them more nights than he did near the stockyards, where the body had been found.

"Not good for my boy Drezerdic," she murmured when she returned to her car. "Not good at all."

It was late by this time. The clubs would be closing

soon, the streets in the district emptying of all but the hardiest party animals, the street people, and the hungriest hookers. Drunks, addicts, the homeless, and desperate women did not make the friendliest of witnesses. So asking after a lone, nondescript man wasn't going to get her anywhere with the locals. Knowing this full well, Tracy headed in the direction of the clubs anyway.

Drezerdic was hunting for his daughter, she reasoned as she drove through the thin late-night traffic. Maybe he was chopping off the heads of people he thought were getting in the way of his hunt. Or of people he thought were connected with her in some way.

Or maybe it was just a coincidence.

Somebody had used a sword to cut the antique dealer's head off. The sword had been the murder weapon. Drezerdic had stabbed his wife, then cut her head off with a chain saw after she was already dead. Tracy couldn't picture a weensy little dweeb like Drezerdic wielding a sword. He just didn't have the strength for it. Even enraged and pumped up on testosterone and adrenaline, she didn't think he could manage more than a knife.

Actually, the part that really bothered her was that she hadn't seen enough blood at either crime scene. The lack of blood added a possibility that wouldn't have occurred to her a few months ago. Despite having a mortal suspect, there was a possibility that there was some supernatural force was at work in the killings.

When it came down to it, the supernatural explanation was the easiest one, but it was also the hardest to deal with on many levels. Tracy decided not to deal with it for now. Maybe sometime around dawn she'd look the supernatural in the face, but she would deal with the murders as a normal police investigation while the night shift lasted. So she pulled into a parking space in the center of the club district, checked to make sure her gun was well-concealed by the light linen jacket she wore over jeans and a cotton shirt, and got out of her car.

Where she finally found her suspect did nothing for Tracy's vow to keep away from the supernatural for now. Drezerdic was standing outside the Raven. Tracy knew what sorts of—people—frequented the place.

She speeded up her steps, and put her hand on Drezerdic's arm before he could go in. "That's not a very good idea."

He tried to pull away, but she had a firm grip on him. She pulled him back a few paces. He turned an angry gaze her way. "How dare—! Ah, the policewoman." His expression went from angry to hopeful. "You've come to help me find my Tamara!"

"I've come to keep you out of big trouble," Tracy answered. "You can't go in there."

"My Tamara's in there. I'm sure of it."

Tracy checked her watch, but she didn't need it to tell her that it was near dawn. Since meeting Javier Vachon she'd come almost to feel the passage of night in her blood. "It's nearly five," she told the distraught father. "The place is closed. I know the owner," she went on. "He'd report your trespassing, and you know what that would do to your parole."

She didn't actually know who owned the Raven, but she suspected it had to be a vampire. It wasn't as if she hadn't tried to get information about the place. She'd asked Javier about the vampire hangout, of course, and he'd been, of course, evasive. Crimes never occurred at the Raven. All the licenses necessary for operating the club were impeccably up to date; the actual ownership was neatly buried in several layers of front organizations.

There had proved to be no legal way for her to investigate the Raven. With no real need other than boundless curiosity, she only occasionally attempted to find out more about the workings of the vampire center of the city.

Right now, however, she had no intention of letting her chief suspect in two grisly murders run afoul of whoever or whatever owned the Raven. She guided his lingering, reluctant steps back toward her car.

"I have to see her," he insisted. "Save her from him."

Tracy knew she shouldn't be drawn into his obsession, but she still found herself asking, "Who?"

Only because he'd singled out the Raven, she told herself, not because she thought Drezerdic's daughter might somehow be involved with a vampire. There weren't that many vampires roaming the world, were there? Not every crime of passion could be laid at their door. Wherever Mr. Drezerdic's daughter was, was no business of Tracy's. No business of Mr. Drezerdic's either, if the young woman didn't want to see him.

"From the man on the radio," Drezerdic said.

Tracy hid her relief that the man didn't claim his daughter was in danger from vampires. "What man on the radio?"

Drezerdic's features screwed up with disgust. "The one who calls himself Nightcrawler."

"The call-in talk-show host?" She always dreaded when Nick turned on his car radio on the nights she rode with him; the channel was invariably tuned to the morbid rantings of the CERK disc jockey.

Drezerdic turned fevered eyes on her. "You know about him?"

"Unfortunately."

"You've heard my Tamara talking to him, then?"

"No," she answered carefully. "I don't believe I have." They reached her car. She kept her hold on Drezerdic's arm, and subtly made sure he was positioned with his back pressed against the door. He wasn't leaving until she was done speaking to him. "You've heard her on the radio?"

He nodded emphatically. "Last night. A girl with a pretty voice. He said she was in the studio with him. A lost girl in need of her father. I can tell it's my Tamara. She calls herself Tammy, but I know. He wants her, too."

The man's eyes practically glowed with rage when he said it. She was used to the eye-changing phenomena in vampires, but the way fanaticism radiated from Drezerdic in an almost physical way disturbed Tracy. Everything about this man disturbed her.

"What," she asked, "does the Nightcrawler have to do with the Raven?"

Drezerdic gestured wildly toward the club. "He broadcasts from there."

"Really? I didn't know that." Maybe his search for his daughter had something to do with vampires after all. Or maybe he was delusional. More likely he was delusional. "You have no proof that this Tammy is your daughter."

"She's mine. I *know*!"

"Or that anyone at the Raven is involved with someone named Tammy. Leave it alone, Mr. Drezerdic. You've got more important things to worry about."

"There's nothing more important than reclaiming what is mine."

It took all of her self-control to keep Tracy from shouting at the man that he didn't own his daughter. It wouldn't do any good. Besides, it had nothing to do with the case. A *good* cop concentrated on solving the case.

"Where were you earlier tonight, Mr. Drezerdic? On Cobalt? Were you near the stockyards?"

His face wrinkled with disgust. "Why would I go there?"

"Looking for Tamara, perhaps?"

He shook his head. "I have been looking for Tamara all night. On the phone, mostly." He pointed up the street. Tracy followed the gesture, and could just barely make out a phone booth in the center of the next block. "There," he told her. "I called radio stations and night-clubs looking for the right place. I was never out of sight of people on the street. There must be hundreds of witnesses to my whereabouts, Detective."

Tracy loathed the smug sound of his voice and the triumph on his face. She did admit it was a pretty good alibi. She took a step back. "I'll check it out." She would have liked to take him into custody while checking it out, but she had absolutely no probable cause.

"Can I go now?"

She nodded. "Sure. Why not? Just stay away from the Raven," she added as Drezerdic hurried away.

"That's sound advice if I've ever heard it."

Tracy did not jump at the sound of the familiar voice at her back, though awareness of his presence sent a warm shiver through her. She turned around when Javier added, "Who was the creep?"

"Someone I wish was more of a suspect in a murder investigation."

"Gives off bad vibes—as we used to say in the sixties."

"I'm not sure I want to know what you said in the sixties. The sixties were *boring*, Javier."

There was a twinkle in his large, dark eyes. He draped

an arm around her shoulder. "You mean hearing about anything before you were born is boring, don't you?"

She frowned. "If you want to put it that way."

Vachon very nearly reached out to smooth the line between her brows. She wondered if it was more than serendipity that brought them together on the curb so near the Raven, or if he'd been lingering in the retreating shadows, waiting for her.

Vachon had stayed at the Raven until closing time. He enjoyed the place, but his presence was partly a vague attempt to keep his promise to Urs. Much to his relief, LaCroix had not put in an appearance during the rest of the night, nor had anyone who much resembled Urs's description of the girl. When Vachon left the club, he'd felt a certain tension in the air. It had kept him in the neighborhood when he should have hurried home ahead of the sun.

Maybe what he experienced was a subliminal signal, something involving a familiar scent, body temperature, heartbeat—something that drew him to Tracy Vetter. The question of why he was drawn to her was something he'd rather not explore. Not here and now, at least, in the growing light. It was time to find shelter. It would be faster if he flew back to the church.

He glanced at her car. "Give me a ride home."

"Sure."

When she would have opened the passenger door, he stopped her. "Sun'll be up in a minute." There was no one on the street but the two of them. He went to stand by the rear of the car. She nodded and obligingly opened the trunk. "You should get a bigger car," he told her as he slipped into the cramped space. "Something like your partner's Caddie. Lots of trunk space in a Caddie."

She slammed the trunk lid, closing out the growing

light. Her answering voice was muffled by the metal. "Like I'm going to invest in a gas guzzler for your sake."

"If you love me, you will," he called back, and hoped she didn't hear him. He decided to pretend he hadn't heard those surprising words himself.

If Tracy had heard him, she was as willing to ignore what had only been a joke anyway when she let him out of the car in the church's shadow. When she would have left him, he grabbed her by the wrist and quickly hustled her inside.

"I've got something for you," she told him when they reached the loft where he lived.

Screed had helped him hook up electricity in the abandoned building, but he preferred more traditional lighting sometimes. It was a mood thing, and he tended to use it when Tracy was around. He tried not to question why. So he waited until he'd lit several candles before he turned back to his guest.

"What?"

She held out his pager.

"Oh, that." He palmed it, then stuffed it into his coat pocket. He waved her to a ragged couch, then took a seat beside her. "I've been thinking about getting a nicer place," he told her. "What do you think? I like the atmosphere, here, though. It has character."

"It has rats."

"For which Screed is grateful. Shows I'm a good host, he says. Speaking of which. . . ." He bounced to his feet. "Can I get you anything?"

Tracy shook her head, then yawned. "I'm beat, Javier. Time both of us went to bed."

He sat down. "I'm more of a day person than most of us. Not that I plan to work on my tan, or anything."

She smiled. He'd been hoping to see that smile for

some time now. He wanted her relaxed, comfortable. He also had a few questions. To lead into them, he said, "You said the creep was a murder suspect. What'd he do?"

"He *might* be a suspect."

She stretched and craned her neck. Vachon slid the short distance between them and began to massage her shoulders. "Then what's he suspected of?"

"Double homicide. Two people got their heads taken off." She glanced at him over her shoulder. "You know anything about people getting beheaded with a sword?"

He shrugged. "I occasionally watch *Highlander*." When she responded to his joke with a confused look, he said, "No. I don't know anything about it."

Tracy gave a frustrated sigh. "No vampires involved, eh?"

"We aren't responsible for everything."

She chuckled. "I was thinking that earlier."

He ran his thumbs up the back of her neck. She had a very attractive throat, the skin warm and yielding beneath his hands. For safety's sake, he quickly moved his fingers back to her tight shoulder muscles. "Thank you for cutting us some slack. Mortals can be much worse than we are in the murder and mayhem line."

"I know. That feels good."

"I've had lots of practice."

Vachon wondered why she stiffened slightly at his comment. He decided it would be better to wait and ask his questions once he had her at ease again. Besides, he enjoyed just touching her. Human warmth was something he'd never given up craving.

Eventually, though, when she was all soft and pliant and his hands had inadvertently wandered away from her shoulders and down and around to places she didn't complain about his touching, though he'd had to toss her gun aside to get to some of them, he decided it was time to bring up the subject that interested him before he forgot what it was.

One of Vachon's hands drifted up to Tracy's shoulders, his other arm came around her waist. He sat back, and she leaned against him. It was a wide old couch; their bodies easily fit side by side on it. But he had promised Screed he'd check out the mysterious creature. Detective Vetter came to him for information; it was time he returned the obligation.

"I don't suppose," he said, leaning to speak into her ear, "that you've had any reports of zombies wandering the streets, have you?"

It was the sort of question that should have elicited at least a startled look from the homicide detective. When she didn't look at him, or answer, or even tense up again, he realized he'd done his work of relaxing her too well.

Tracy Vetter was sound asleep. In a vampire's arms.

Vachon was momentarily outraged, along with being amused. He'd always known he wasn't the fiercest or most frightening of his kind, but Tracy had this way of trusting his better nature that was embarrassing. Frustrating. Touching.

For a while he just lost himself in her gentle breathing and the steady strength of her young heartbeat. Time passed, drifting from dawn into early morning and beyond. He watched the candles burn down while he wondered just what he was going to do with the mortal woman he was so comfortable beside.

When it came down to it, there were only two choices in his repertoire. Screed had quite luridly laid those choices out for him when Vachon first brought her into contact with his kind's world. Since she was a Resister, totally immune to psychic influence, all that could be

106

done with Tracy Vetter and her growing database of forbidden knowledge was to bring her across or kill her.

He wasn't prepared to kill her. He wasn't prepared to kill anyone anymore. It wasn't fun to kill people anymore, even the ones who deserved it. Tracy didn't deserve it. So the easiest solution was out of the question.

That left bringing her across. He could just brush her hair aside, lean over, and just do it. Vachon's fangs ached at the notion. It would be more than pleasant to bring her into his world. If he gave in to the urge, he could make this one of the most pleasant mornings of both their lives. He could end all the ambiguity of their current situation in one long, blazing moment. But the complications that would arise from it would be a major bitch.

Nick Knight would probably stake him out in Death Valley, to begin with. Knight was just a bit protective of his young partner, even if she didn't know that Knight was one of the senior vampires on the planet. Or Knight would leave it to Tracy to find a just punishment for making her the second homicide detective in Toronto with a nasty sun allergy.

Of course, she might like it.

It had to happen eventually.

Didn't it? It depended on what Tracy wanted. Vachon forced himself to believe that unwelcome thought. It was the late twentieth century. Women had rights, and free will, and the vote, and control of their bodies and reproduction, and all that. Besides, he'd learned his lesson with Urs. He'd told himself he'd never bring anyone across who didn't want it.

Trouble was, Tracy never gave him any indication of what she wanted.

In fact, he thought, as the candles burned out and he sought sleep, he wasn't sure anymore what anybody— especially women—wanted.

8

WHAT DO MORTALS, ESPECIALLY MORTAL WOMEN, WANT? Normally the answer to such a question was an easy one. It wasn't even one he would ordinarily ask. The answer should be, Why bother with what those complicated mortal creatures wanted?

"Do what thou wilt, as dear Aleister used to say, back when he was mortal," he murmured, and took another sip of blood.

It was actually quite easy being a vampire. One had hunger. One satisfied it. Easy. Uncomplicated. All one had to do was anything one wanted between dusk and dawn, and even afterward, as long as walls kept out the sun.

He wasn't enjoying his meal. The young man slowly dying in his embrace just didn't taste right. His hard, angular body didn't feel right.

"You taste too much of testosterone," he complained to his victim.

He'd taken the young man off the street just before dawn, stopped him from beating a prostitute and turned him into breakfast instead. He decided that such chivalry was a mistake; he was more in the mood for a woman. But the whore had been pathetically grateful in the moments before she looked deep into his eyes and forgot the incident. Her attitude had touched some freshly stimulated chord of compassion in him.

"Women!" he complained.

The man groaned, as though in answer, which brought an ironic smile to LaCroix's lips. It was not an easy expression to manage around his fangs. Still smiling, he bent over the bloody throat again, his thoughts far away from what he was doing.

Women, emotions caused by women, had ways of complicating the simplicity of one's life. If one let them. Sometimes one couldn't help but let them. There was a certain helplessness the male of any species endured in the face of dealing with females of his own kind.

Even when the female was of an other kind, a child of a species the vampire had left behind but still resembled, there was room for complication.

He dropped the drained body to the concrete floor of the Raven's basement storeroom. A *carouche* would crawl up out of the sewer to collect the remains at some point, and do whatever that kind did with carrion. LaCroix paid it no more mind as he took himself off to rest in the bedroom he kept in another part of the building's commodious basement.

Some of the younger ones Janette had taken in slept down here. They jokingly called it the crypt. LaCroix passed several of their sleeping places on his way to the room that had been Janette's. They looked like sleeping children to him, their humanity still clutched to them like invisible security blankets.

LaCroix thought that his resemblance to humankind

was merely superficial, yet, after all this time, emotions remained. Either his emotions were remnants of what he'd once been, or they were simply part of all creatures. He'd rather think that emotion was something all creatures shared. Higher life-forms such as himself could exploit them, while mortal animals merely had to live with them.

Fear, he knew, was universal. Be it rabbit or raptor, fear touched them all. He could admit to experiencing fear, since it happened so rarely that it was almost pleasurable to have that scalding jolt run through him now and again. Possessiveness he'd always had in more than full measure. He took what he wanted, kept and protected what was his.

Loneliness. Yes. Loneliness was a dragging weight, a gnawing creature in the brain and gut and heart his kind knew far better than any mortal could imagine. Humans thought they knew about loneliness, but they were . . . clueless, as Tammy would say.

He slammed the door hard behind him as he thought of Tammy. He was annoyed that he thought of the child at all, even more annoyed that she could in any way influence him.

Something had to be done about the child. Perhaps he should not have sent her on her way to wherever she lived, and then talked himself out of following her home after the Raven closed. Perhaps he shouldn't have told her to stay away from him, knowing his words were an invitation for her to do anything but.

Then his gaze stabbed through the complete darkness, touching the luxurious furnishings in the quarters where his daughter no longer lived. He fell heavily onto the wide bed, at once sated and restless, aware of the familiarity of the place, and of all the changes as well.

He did not mind change, he told himself. He minded not being the one who instigated change.

Control was everything.

"You have to do something."

"Do I?"

LaCroix continued to look at the stars outside the tower window, enjoying them while Janette stood at his back, fuming. He enjoyed absorbing her mood as much as he did the unrelieved darkness that gave him such a clear view of the sky.

Behind him was a bedchamber of Turkish opulence, decorated in many shades of blue and silver. Radu had a taste for silver. The castle was full of it; its public room contained great chests of silver coinage, and even more silver cast into plates and trays and decorative casks and boxes lined shelves and walls. He had collected fortunes in silver jewelry over the centuries. Radu had once worshiped the moon, perhaps he still did. To Radu, the moon was a beautiful woman draped in disks of silver.

"You like it here," he told her, "the silence, the vastness of the forest, the isolation." He put his hand on the cool stone of the windowsill. Janette's hand was no warmer when she laid it over his. "You're happy here."

"I am," Janette admitted.

"Happier than you've ever been before?"

She replied to his viciously sarcastic tone softly. "Perhaps."

"Do you think you've found true love at last?"

She didn't answer that question.

When he turned to face her, he saw that she was wearing a great deal of silver. Candlelight gleamed off the highly polished jewelry at her throat, in her hair, at her wrists, off the metallic-shot black silk of her dress.

He touched a Scythian comb that held up her dark hair. "A beautiful woman draped in silver. Does he worship you, then?"

Her eyes would not meet his, nor did she answer his question. "You have to do something about him."

"Radu?"

She stepped back angrily. "Nicholas."

LaCroix clasped his hands behind his back. "I frequently do things about Nicholas. What do you suggest this time? Torture? Shall I send him to his room —and wall him up inside it? I haven't done that for quite some time. While that would be amusing," he continued harshly, "it isn't Nicholas's behavior I find disturbing at the moment."

She refused to question his meaning. "His behavior toward Radu—toward a host who has been nothing but gracious—is impossible. Ridiculous. Dangerous. Radu has taken great offense. It is up to you to deal with him."

He touched her cheek, then slipped a finger beneath her chin and forced her head up. When she unwillingly looked him in the eye, LaCroix said, "Nicholas has done nothing to give offense."

"He killed Radu's pet."

"So he did," LaCroix conceded.

"He might have attacked Radu if you had not taken him away."

He shrugged. "It was time to hunt. We were hungry after a long day in less than comfortable accommodations. I notice that you show no concern about my and Nicholas's whereabouts yesterday."

She pulled away from him. "How you spend your time is none of my affair."

His voice was softly menacing as he asked, "You weren't worried about us?"

113

"I feel no need to worry about you, LaCroix."

"Because you trust in my strength? Or because you don't care what happens to me?"

"I don't want to argue with you."

"You want to give me orders?"

A slight, enigmatic smile curved her lips. "No."

It occurred to him that perhaps she disregarded his authority over her enough to not worry about his displeasure. Or, perhaps, she didn't realize how annoyed he was with her attitude toward Radu. He didn't know. Did she even know what she wanted?

"You want me to punish Nicholas?"

"Of course not!"

"But you want me to do *something*."

"Yes."

"Why?"

She looked restlessly toward the door. "Because of Radu, of course. He deserves an apology from Nicholas at the very least."

"Why?"

"Because he—"

He cut her off with a gesture. "No. Why do you want to mollify our barbaric host? Are you afraid he'll send us packing? Don't you want to leave?"

"I don't want to leave."

"Not yet, you mean?"

She turned her head away. She walked to the door. "Not—yet."

"If we leave," he told her, "you come with us."

"I—" She opened the door. "Perhaps." A shrug. "Perhaps not. Radu's waiting for me," she said, and then was gone, the door firmly closed between them.

She might not know what she truly wanted, but

LaCroix was certain of one thing. "Something permanent," he said, "has to be done about Radu."

"He didn't mean it, of course."

Tammy spoke to her reflection in the mirror, her voice was too low to drown out the sound of the Nightcrawler's voice in the background. It wasn't a live broadcast. A tape of an older show played in the old boom box on the table next to the bed. A bookcase underneath the studio apartment's one window held cassettes of all the Nightcrawler's broadcasts for the last year.

She would go back to the club as soon as she'd built up the courage to defy him. She glanced at the autographed photo of the decadent-eyed, white-haired man she'd gotten from the radio station. She'd framed it and hung it over her bed. What she felt looking at him was more respect than fear, and more longing than anything else. She craved to be with him, just to *be* with him. But he'd said no. He'd said to go away and not come back.

He wasn't someone to be trifled with, not someone to be disobeyed. She didn't want to oppose his wishes, but she was going to have to.

"I've been a fan for too long to be sent away. You'll understand. You understand everything. This is a test, isn't it?" she said to the photo, then turned away and sat on the bed.

Tammy clasped her hands in her lap, closed her eyes, let the Nightcrawler's taped voice flow over her for a while. She didn't actually listen; she knew the words too well to have to listen. It was the voice she needed. Soothing in its certainty as he spoke to his children. She found the caustic inflection reassuring. He was strong, in control, sternly demanding that she listen to his wisdom.

She was more than willing to listen. To be a good girl for him.

"Though I had to be bad to get your attention. I'll have to be bad to come back. Then you'll let me be good for you. You'll take care of me. And I'll take care of you. That's what you want, isn't it?"

Tammy clapped a hand over her mouth and sighed. She was talking to herself too much. She was alone too much. She'd always hated being alone, even though she'd never gone out of her way to be with anybody. Why bother?

She had a dead-end, mindless clerical job. She had no respect for anyone she worked with. She didn't bother keeping in touch with long-lost relatives or anybody she'd known through the years in foster care and group homes. She didn't want to remember the past. Until recently the present had just been a big, empty hole. She hated being with people her own age, even though she spent a lot of her time in the dance clubs. Those places were all right for finding sex, but they did nothing for her craving for companionship.

Nothing and no one had touched her until she'd found the Nightcrawler.

He commanded her attention, her respect. He demanded that she think, and learn, and make judgments and decisions. She'd discovered the library because of him, found herself devouring books on history, philosophy, poetry. He'd given her life focus and discipline. She hadn't even known she wanted such things until the first night she turned to CERK and heard him talking.

She would go back to the Raven. She'd go tonight. And she wouldn't leave again. She'd stay with him. He could arrange that. He had that kind of power. She was sure of it.

Then she'd be his little girl forever.

Nick came out of his bedroom as he heard the door open downstairs. He tied the belt of his black silk robe, then leaned against the railing as he watched Natalie enter the living area below.

"Yo, Nick," she called. "You awake?"

He jumped over the rail to stand in front of her. "I'm awake."

Natalie's reaction to his moving faster than mortal eyes could see was an amused shake of the head. She stepped around him and headed for the kitchen area. "Please tell me you don't still keep the coffee under the sink."

"In the freezer," he answered. "Just like you ordered."

"Good boy."

"Just trying to do the mortal thing, Dr. Lambert." Nick checked the time. They would have to be at work in a couple of hours. He went upstairs to dress while Natalie made a pot of coffee. "That smells good," he said when he came back down and found her curled up on the couch, holding a fragrantly steaming mug between her hands.

She nodded. Her eyes teased him over the rim of the cup. "Try some."

His stomach lurched at the thought. "I don't do caffeine." She made a skeptical noise as he sat down beside her. "Well?" he asked.

"I checked on Mrs. Adams. Her bites and scratches were treated at Toronto General, where she was admitted for observation. So far she hasn't shown any tendency to bite anyone else."

"That's good." She didn't look as if she'd brought good news. "What?"

Natalie put down her coffee mug and looked at her hands. "I just came from a couple of hours at work."

Nick understood the implications of her words instantly. "More—animal attacks?"

She nodded. "Two."

"You took care of them."

She nodded, then raised a worried gaze to meet his. "And one more headless body. This one wasn't beheaded with a sword, though." Nick did not look surprised. Concerned, but not surprised. "You want to explain what I just told you?"

Nick thoughtfully ran a thumb along his freshly shaved jawline. "One of my kind is strong enough to take off a head without using a sword."

She could tell that he wasn't going to elucidate further at the moment. "I see." She added, "The media have gotten hold of the beheadings, Nick. Big time. They don't yet know about the newest twist—actually, it was more of a pull and twist—but they're bound to find out about the heads being ripped off soon."

Nick resisted the urge to turn on the television. He wasn't sure he wanted to know the local news broadcasters' take on the situation. It was Captain Reese's job to handle the newspaper and TV reporters. It was his job to stop the deaths. He had hunted the streets last night until dawn, and found nothing. Tonight he would have to do better.

"They're speculating about a gory serial killer or a satanic cult doing the murders," Nat said. She sighed. "That's better than the truth, I suppose, even if it's guaranteed to put people in a panic."

If people panicked, he thought, remembering a stake being driven through the Serbian creatures' heart, at least they'd be hunting for a human monster instead of a real one. "There are advantages to living in the twentieth century," he murmured.

"I'm not sure mass communication's one of them," Nat replied. Then she stood and faced him. "Where do those things come from, Nick?"

"Just what are you looking for? And *why* are you looking here?"

LaCroix's voice grated along Nicholas's nerves, but he continued to examine the crypt door rather than look around. "I did not ask for your company," he answered.

"No. You never ask for help, either."

"Not from you."

"Nor do you ask the right questions."

It was a dark night, moonless, the sky full of thick black clouds that had blown on a cold wind from the north an hour before. The graveyard beside the castle's roofless chapel was small, deserted, shaded by a stand of dying trees on one side, the high stone curtain wall on the other. No mortal had stood by these graves for a long time. Nicholas fervently wished that LaCroix hadn't searched him out as he inspected the crypt and graves.

The castle gate gaped wide a few yards away. Nicholas pointed toward it. "Why aren't you out hunting? Didn't Radu and Janette wish your company?" he couldn't help but add spitefully—though the spite was as much for himself as for LaCroix. He regretted his pettiness instantly, for he knew LaCroix would not let him get away with it.

"They don't wish your company, either, Nicholas," LaCroix answered. He jumped down from his perch on the edge of the crypt roof.

"I know," Nicholas answered as he walked slowly from grave to grave. He felt nothing—not life, certainly not death. Unfortunately, there was none of the tainted, rotting, spiritless disquiet aroused by the creatures, either. "Where do they come from?" he muttered. "Where?" He had decided to stop this strange menace before it led mortals to the discovery of true vampires. He didn't know why Radu hadn't seen to destroying them himself. "What perversity creates such creatures?"

"Who do they come from, don't you mean?" LaCroix blocked his path. "Why do you care? Do you study those revenants in order to keep your mind off a greater problem?"

Nicholas turned his back on his creator. "I don't have any more serious problems."

"Haven't you?" The voice behind him was a near whisper, but all the more vicious with its softness. "What of Janette?"

It was hard to say it, but Nicholas lifted his head and managed. "Janette goes where she wants, and with whom."

LaCroix's hand landed hard on his shoulder. "There you are wrong. She goes where I say, and with whom I approve."

"Radu is your friend," Nicholas was compelled to say. "You brought her to him."

"But *not* as a present."

"She'll come back to you, LaCroix. She always does, you know that."

"But will she come back to you, Nicholas? Does she see Radu as a better, a more fitting consort than you could ever be?"

He whirled furiously to face LaCroix. "*I* will not interfere with her wishes. It was a hard-won lesson to do it once. I won't help you drag her away unwillingly."

His maker was not perturbed by Nicholas's anger. In

fact, he smiled. "I won't have to ask for that help." He held his hands up before him. "But I think you will decide to stop Radu."

A sound in the castle courtyard drew Nicholas's attention before he could answer. He took to the air to investigate it. Unfortunately, LaCroix accompanied him. The courtyard was a wide space, paved in weed-grown cobblestones. The castle was flanked by the old chapel on one side, and the dilapidated stable where Radu's two human servants slept with the horses on the other. At first, Nicholas thought he would find nothing more than one of the cowed servants moving stealthily about his business. He told himself that he was reacting to nerves and LaCroix's taunting, that perhaps he had heard nothing.

He knew that he was frightened of facing another of the creatures.

He loathed being frightened, so he ignored it. What he found as he settled once more on the ground was just what he'd expected. It was no servant that stumbled in through the open gateway.

"Another revenant has come to visit, I see," LaCroix said as he settled to the earth. Nicholas could barely hold his ground, but LaCroix did not show that he felt any effect from by the sickening energy that surrounded the creature.

Nicholas made himself present a casual demeanor as well. "So it would seem."

He took a step toward it, and the thing's dead/hungry gaze swiveled his way. It held out a blood-crusted hand. The temptation to flee was strong, but Nicholas stayed where he was. He made himself study the thing.

It was male, young, a few days dead. Its throat had been torn open, making it look like it had a second,

121

raggedly gaping mouth along with the one that was full of fangs. Not a villager, he thought. The clothes, though filthy and torn, were well made, of a different cloth and cut than worn by the locals. Something about it was familiar. The realization chilled even his cold blood. Nicholas stepped forward to end the thing's existence.

Before he could touch it, LaCroix said, "It's one of the musketeers."

Nicholas recalled the hunt, the way Radu had torn at his victims. He'd dismembered the Austrian soldiers with sword and bare hands while Nicholas and the others simply made their kills and left the bodies for the scavengers.

"He didn't tear the life from all of them," LaCroix reminded Nicholas, catching his thoughts. "Near dawn he just drank from one last soldier." LaCroix pointed. "That one. Don't you recall how the boy begged for his life?"

Nicholas made himself study the desiccated face, stabbing through the darkness to make out detail with his kind's special vision. "Yes," he agreed, dumbfounded. "That's the one."

"Radu's child."

"Yes." He could see the truth of it, hating the knowledge that even a damned creature such as himself could have such progeny. "Do you make them deliberately?" he had asked Radu. "For sport?" Or did he try to bring them across, and fail?

LaCroix moved in front of him and grabbed the creature by the throat. "Radu did nothing to this man," he said as he slowly twisted its head off. "Radu did not bring this thing across. He killed him. He should have stayed dead. But he walks, Nicholas."

"How? Why?"

"The dead should stay that way." LaCroix dropped the body but gripped the severed head by the hair. He turned the dead face toward Nicholas. "It's a pity Radu's meals persist in following him home."

Nicholas touched the stinking corpse with the toe of his boot. "Radu doesn't make them deliberately." The revelation shook him to his core. "The very act of his killing them assures this—this hideous continuation."

"Yes."

"He must know he's responsible."

"Oh, yes."

"It's an abomination, and he doesn't seem to care."

LaCroix held the head up at face level. He looked into the decayed visage as he spoke. "Were you looking for your daddy, little boy? You walk because his blood touched yours. You are a part of him now. Or were, rather." He tossed the head away. Nicholas heard it land with a meaty thud in a distant part of the courtyard. LaCroix turned an intense gaze on him. "Radu is endangering us all with these revenants." His voice grew low, mocking as always but seductive as well. "The question is, Nicholas, what are you going to do about it?"

"Revenants?"

Nick nodded at Natalie's question. "That's what LaCroix called them."

Natalie tried to recall the definition of the word. " 'One that returns after death.' " She'd looked up a lot of terms like that in her study of the causes of vampirism.

He shrugged. She'd never seen him look more uncomfortable. "I've always just thought of them as The Creatures."

Natalie checked her watch. He'd paced the whole time he'd talked, and he'd talked for quite a while as he'd told

123

her about a vampire named Radu. "Sit down. We don't have much time, and I have a lot of questions."

Nick crossed to the refrigerator and brought out a bottle of something she knew wasn't wine. He poured himself a large glass of dark liquid before he came and sat beside her. "Breakfast," he said when she gave him an exasperated look.

"You don't need it. It's a bad habit."

"Drink your coffee."

"Point taken." She sighed and got herself another mug. Once she came back to the couch, she said, "You haven't thought through the implications of this, have you?"

Nick ran a hand through his hair. "There are monsters roaming the streets of Toronto, Nat. Monsters such as Radu created. That's implication enough for me."

"He was the vector for a blood disease!"

Nick nodded. "Yes."

She shuddered at a sudden thought. "Was? Or is? Is he still alive, Nick?"

"He wasn't alive to begin with, Nat."

"You know what I mean."

"Radu is the only vampire I ever met that actually had this—disease."

"So he's creating the revenants?"

Nick drank all the blood in his glass before he answered. "I don't know."

"You suspect?"

"But I don't know. I just know that it has to be stopped, and quickly. Remember what I told you about these things last night."

Natalie was still shaken by the information. It seemed that the revenants were flesh eating creatures. The bodies of those they killed were then turned into walking corpses. Apparently it took longer for each generation of reanimated flesh to wake up and walk, and Nick didn't think the creatures made by the creatures lasted very long. Long enough to be hungry and hunt. Long enough for some virus or bacteria in their blood to attempt to reproduce itself in another host, Natalie speculated.

"But the revenant doesn't—arise, for want of a better term—if its head is removed."

"Head or heart."

"Right. So Radu normally took off his victims' heads?"

"So I eventually found out."

"He knew he was causing this disease? And how to stop it?" Nick gave her a brusque nod. "So whoever is spreading the disease here knows that the heads have to come off, but doesn't always bother?"

Nick got to his feet. "That's what I surmise." He held out a hand to help her up. "Come on, Nat. Time we got to work."

9

THE MOON GAVE HIM STRENGTH. IT WAS THE MOTHER OF ALL HIS kind. No matter how much the world had changed, it was good to hunt beneath its sheltering, cool fire once more.

Radu turned his face to the sky. He saw only a wedge of it between the clifflike walls of the buildings on either side of where he stood. He drank in what light that came from the sky, and not the glow of the thousands of fires that lit this overgrown habitation. The moon was just past full; the taste of it on his skin was only a faint reminder of its glory, like watered wine. Like the thin blood of the aged crone he'd fed on moments before.

His day had been spent in an airless room below ground. It was some servant's room in a great house, he guessed, though the building was nothing like a proper castle. He had sensed hundreds of other mortals going about their lives during the day, but none came looking for the man Radu had killed after he'd come through the ground-level window just before dawn.

The man had been fat and full of blood, and his bed had proved comfortable. It had been a good place to hide.

Perhaps Radu would return to it if he could find his way back through the labyrinthine confusion of pathways that made up this hellish place.

Despite having found some comfort at last, he had dreamed all day of holding a female in his arms. He had always loved the taste of women above all else, though for the sake of keeping his strength he mostly feasted on warriors. Women were a delicacy, their essence prized above any other taste on his tongue.

Therefore he sought out a woman for his first kill of the night, but all he'd found after an hour was the shriveled husk at his feet. She must have been well past eighty—who knew a mortal could live so long?—and had tasted every day of it. Her flesh had been dry and papery against his grasping fingers, the veins in her throat soft and full of sluggish blood. There had barely been any dregs left of the distinct female flavor he loved. Cheated, hating her taste, he had killed her quickly, thrown her to the ground, then turned his sorrowing face up for the consolation of moonlight.

He knew he could not linger, that there were things he must do, someone he sought. Someone he had every right to hate. Someone whose heart he wanted to hold in his hands. He could not remain hidden among the refuse heaps while he had the freedom of the darkness, but where could he go? Confusion ate at him. For all his strength, for all his purpose, he knew that this place made him mad. He killed, but he was still the prey. Prey to the noise, the crowds, the strange structures, and the metal beasts with the fiery, darting eyes.

Could even the moon save him from such a place?

The moon goddess had almost saved him once. Her cool hands had compassionately touched him when he'd thought he'd been going mad. Her name had been Janette, but he had recognized his goddess just the same.

They stood side by side on the grassy bank above a deeply rutted road, waiting for a coach they could hear in the far distance. He took her hand. "There are things you want to know."

Janette wore a black cloak. Beneath it, he knew, she gleamed with silver. Covered in the heavy velvet, she blended completely with the forest night.

"You are the moon hidden by clouds," he told her when she didn't speak.

His words were received with a slight turn of her head, a faint smile. "You don't have to explain to me, Radu."

"There are things I want to tell you, then." Her calm, her stillness, the gentle encouragement of her gaze were those of an ancient priestess, one his spirit longed to confess to. "Something has happened to me. Something has changed me. There is this slow fire in my veins all the time."

"You're in pain?"

"It's hard to remember pain." He nodded. "Yes, that's what it is." Her features showed surprise but, fortunately, no pity. He was encouraged to go on. "Decades pass, and sometimes I remember nothing about them. Time confuses me, Janette."

"Because you pretend you are stronger than time itself."

"Perhaps," he agreed. "I face everything as a warrior. The sword is all I know."

"The days of the sword are passing."

"Not for me."

"Even for you, my dear." She stroked her hand up his arm. "You fight change. No warrior can win the battle with time." Her voice was reassuring. "Everything else

129

you can master, yes, but time rules everything that lives."

"Time has taken away my strength," he answered, as the heavy rumbling of the coach wheels grew louder. He sucked a deep breath into his lungs, and rushed to say what needed to be said. "Since the fire in my body started, I can no longer bring a child across. You say I am too much alone. It is because I must be. What is worse is that I am not even sterile. That I think I could accept after all these centuries, but. . . ."

"I see."

Of course she did, but he went on just the same. "What I make are—those mockeries of our kind your friend Nicholas is determined to destroy." He couldn't look into her eyes as he finished. "It is not even a deliberate thing. It happens whenever I feed, if I don't take off their heads."

"I see," she repeated.

Her calm reply annoyed him. "What is it you see?"

"That you tell me these things because you want me to stay with you."

"You deserve the truth."

"When does our kind—with the exception of poor Nicholas—tell the truth for anything but our own reasons?" She ran a cool hand down his cheek. "You want my sympathy. You think that I will stay with you and take care of you. You think I have the heart of a woman."

He smiled. "Don't you?"

"Perhaps."

In that moment the coach came up beside them. Before it passed, by Janette leaped onto the driver's box. The driver raised his whip to fend her off, but she was too fast, too strong for that. Radu ripped off the carriage door to the sound of the man's shrieking. There was a

130

noblewoman crouched against the side of the coach. Radu grabbed a fistful of her velvet cloak and hauled her forward. He gave her no time to scream, but he did bestow a hard, fierce kiss before he ripped into her throat.

Janette was beside him when he finished feeding. He turned to her and their lips met, tasting the blood of each other's kill along with the passion of the hunt. They came together there, in a space hardly bigger than a coffin, the limbs of each entangling with those of the other, and the body of the woman he'd just killed.

When they were done, it was the dead woman who moved first.

Janette reared up in shock, with a small cry of fear. Then her face turned to a mask of fury and she grabbed the woman by the hair. "You must always remember," she said sternly, when she was finished with what he should have done, "to take off the head."

Janette had the heart of a huntress as well as the heart of a woman. She should have stayed with him; why she didn't, he couldn't recall. Nicholas would know. Nicholas had something to do with it. He would find Nicholas.

But first, he remembered to remove the old woman's head. In memory of Janette's actions that night in the carriage, and because an old woman hardly deserved a sword stroke, he used his hands.

"I want to belong to you," Tammy said.

She had stood for hours at the entrance to the Raven, waiting for the doors to be unlocked at sunset, waiting to walk in and say those words to the Nightcrawler. He surprised her by coming up behind her, through the crowd that had gathered in the last hour, to join her in the wait for the club to open. She said the words, even through the frisson of shock at his sudden appearance.

"Do you?" he asked, tilting his head to one side and studying her intently as they stood close together on the busy sidewalk. Most people gave off warmth, and they moved ever so slightly even when they were standing still. LaCroix gave off no heat; he was perfectly still, except for his probing gaze. People walked around them to get into the Raven, paying them no mind. Tammy knew that was his doing. "Do you, indeed?"

She saw the faint gold glow deep in his eyes, and it didn't frighten her. "You know I do."

"Think carefully. I never release what is mine."

She balled her hands into tight, tense fists to keep from touching him. She knew without being told that he was very particular about people touching him. "I want to belong to someone. It's all I've ever wanted."

"Psychologists would say that is not a particularly healthy attitude."

She'd heard those words from shrinks and counselors and social workers ever since her mother had died. They'd all had her best interests in mind. They'd all been wrong. She didn't want anything to do with their definition of normal. "I don't care what they say."

"I can see that."

"Neither do you."

He laughed, the sound faint and chilling. "You disobeyed me."

Tammy made herself sound bold, without being defiant. "You knew I would. You didn't want me to stay away. The important thing is to give you what you want." She rushed on, "You don't always want what you say. It's up to someone who loves you to know what you want."

132

He tucked two fingers beneath her chin. "Why are you plaguing me? Do you know what you really want?"

"Yes." Her voice was low, fervent, pleading.

"I seriously doubt it." The strange glow in his eyes deepened.

He wanted her to look away, but she wouldn't. "Yes," she repeated. Or at least she thought she spoke out loud. The world spun around her for a moment, and she wasn't sure what was real and what wasn't.

This isn't what you think it is, he seemed to say in her mind.

She didn't blink when he looked away. "Yes," she answered. "It is. I want to be with you."

He took a step back and gestured for her to enter the Raven ahead of him. "I'll think about it."

Even the cool amusement of his tone couldn't dampen the joy she felt. She looked over her shoulder at him. "You'll make me—" There was a word she wouldn't say in public, even if a warning hadn't sparked in his eyes. "You'll—adopt—me," she said instead.

A blare of bass-driven music erupted from the open door of the club. The sound drew her forward, with LaCroix close on her heels.

"I'll think about it," he repeated.

When Tammy turned around to speak to him again, he was gone.

Javier Vachon scratched his head in puzzlement. "This is definitely not what I had in mind," he murmured as he looked down at the ground.

A dead woman lay at his feet, at least part of her did. Her head was nearby, wedged between a pair of garbage cans. It looked as if, in his attempt to fulfill his promise to Screed, he'd stumbled onto Tracy's headless corpse

133

case instead. He knelt beside the corpse, touching the old woman's body gently. It broke his heart to see death come in this way.

Humans could be such monsters with each other.

Vachon touched cold flesh, then drew his hand back quickly, but not quickly enough to banish the knowledge from his mind.

No mortal had done this.

He stood, stiff and tense, mind fully open. Though Vachon hated doing it, he forced all his senses to search. The psychic impressions were fading fast, but what he perceived was disturbing enough. The memory of human fear hit him, like a splash of acid in the face. Violent hunger, and the orgasmic pleasure of stealing life that only his kind could feel, seeped into Vachon's awareness.

Whoever had done this was strong, as only the old ones were strong. Also quite mad.

LaCroix?

No. He'd never felt LaCroix kill, but he was sure this wasn't LaCroix's doing. He surmised that the old one had an oedipal thing going with Nick Knight, but otherwise he wasn't crazy. Decadent, haughty, and terrifying but not crazy. Whoever had done this was insane, and something else; his spirit was tainted. There was something definitely toxic about the aura this murderer left behind. He was mad, Vachon concluded, but far from mindless. So he couldn't have any connection with Screed's creature.

Unless he'd made Screed's creature. Which wasn't possible. Was it?

No explanation jumped into his head while Vachon stood in the dark alley.

"Well, somebody must know something," he muttered,

and looked sadly at the headless form on the ground. "This shouldn't have happened."

"Police! Don't move!"

"Get your hands up!" a second voice shouted.

Vachon looked toward the figures in the mouth of the alley, momentarily blinded by the beam of a flashlight.

He'd let himself get too immersed in his other senses and lost track of the here and now. And look where it had gotten him. The cops finding him standing over a headless corpse could get him in big trouble. Those uniformed men were aiming guns at him. The tension radiating from the pair was anything but reassuring.

"I said hands up! Do it!" The shout was just a hair's breadth away from hysteria. The cop's hands were shaking.

Vachon carefully raised his hands above his head.

One of the officers hurried forward while the other one stayed back to cover him. Vachon had every intention of taking off faster than the pair could track him, but he needed them both to come closer first.

"Is it another one?" the cop at the alley entrance called to his partner.

The other cop took a quick look at the body. Every bit of color in his face faded. "We've got another one, Jeff."

"Son of a bitch!" Jeff snarled.

"Hey, I just found the body," Vachon told the angry officer.

"Shut up!"

The one approaching him took a quick look around the alley. "Not much blood, Jeff."

Officer Jeff followed his partner into the alley. *That's right*, Vachon thought. *Come just a little bit closer.*

"What did I tell you, Neil?" Jeff said to the other cop. "I don't care what the coroner says, this bastard is drinking the blood. Between the beheadings and the wild animal attacks, I'm beginning to think this town's turned into Spook Central." He turned an angry glare on Vachon. "What are you? Some kind of sick vampire?"

"I'm not sick," Vachon responded calmly, while the men's conversation set off terrified alarms in his head. "And I had nothing to do with this woman's death."

Neil took out a pair of handcuffs. "On the ground," he ordered.

"No," Vachon replied. The policeman came closer. He reached for Vachon's arm. "Look at me, Neil," Vachon said, voice low, intent, and full of power. The officer's gaze flashed up to meet Vachon's. He was caught, unable to look away. "I'm not here. I've never been here. You didn't see anyone in the alley when you found the body."

"What the hell are you doing to him?" the other cop demanded. "Get away from him, Neil!"

"Who?" Neil responded.

Vachon carefully moved away from the officer. Neil knelt to examine the body, totally oblivious to Vachon's presence. That left Jeff, his shaking hands holding a very large gun, to deal with.

Vachon had taken no more than a step forward when the man shot him. The bullet entered through his rib cage, exited through his shoulder, then ricocheted off the wall to his left. The impact of the high-caliber bullet jarred Vachon, but it didn't slow him down as he ran forward. An instant later, Vachon had the gun in one hand; the fingers of his other hand circled the terrified policeman's throat. Fangs bared, he slammed the cop against a wall.

"No one's shot me in a long time," he told the strangling cop. "I don't like it. It ruins my wardrobe, and doesn't do anything for my temper."

Which reminded him that the policeman's unprofessional use of his firearm probably didn't give Vachon just cause to kill him. Cops weren't supposed to panic, but this man was panicked. Vachon had to deal with the situation as it was, not the way it was supposed to be. And he had to get out of the alley, fast, before more cops arrived.

He dropped the gun to the ground and loosened his crushing hold on the man's throat. "Forget about this," he ordered as he forced Jeff to look into his eyes. "Forget you ever heard the word 'vampire.' Understood?" Vachon waited anxiously through the moment it took the shaken policeman to nod. When he did, Vachon said, "Good."

Satisfied that he wouldn't have to kill either of the officers to keep his presence undetected, Vachon took to the air. He hovered above the alley only long enough to make certain that neither of the policemen's gaze followed him. After he was satisfied that their only interest was in reporting one more mysteriously decapitated body, he took off.

"I've got to talk to Knight about this," he said as he flew in the direction of police headquarters.

"All right, people, quiet down."

Nick watched Captain Reese's frustrated effort to get the squad's attention as he leaned against a wall near the meeting room door. The big man looked harried and tired, his tie loose, his shirtsleeves rolled up over his meaty forearms. Too many people were talking at once, and very few in the crowd were even looking Reese's way. Nick thought the mild-mannered Captain seemed about ready to wade in and knock some heads together to get people's attention.

"I said quiet down!" This time Reese shouted, and most of the squad finally did.

"What's the matter with you people?" Reese demanded once there was silence. He stepped forward and leaned his hands, palms down, on the end of the conference table. "Is this any way to conduct a briefing? Did professionalism get left at home today? By all of you?"

Nick was at the back because there were no more seats in the crowded briefing room. Every member of the Homicide Squad was there, squeezed around the long table and bunched up two deep in places along the walls with officers called in from other divisions. Nick didn't need extra senses to feel the tension in the atmosphere. People were not only angry and nervous, there was plenty of fear in the room.

A great deal of sheepishness joined the mix of emotions at Reese's reprimanding words. He gave the squad a second to squirm, then said, "People, we have two different cases to deal with, possibly three. They're all grisly, we're not getting a lot of physical evidence at scenes, and we don't have any solid suspects. What we have to do is work harder, not start listening to the wild stories the media are making up." There was a brief, embarrassed murmuring before he went on. "There are no werewolves loose in the city of Toronto. No zombies. Not even any vampires."

Nick wished Reese hadn't spoken the words, even in derision. Mortals didn't need to hear about supernatural forces, even to be falsely reassured that there were no monsters walking among them. The last thing Nick wanted was people on the Homicide Squad thinking about vampires. Of course they wouldn't believe, not consciously. But subconsciously, they might begin to equate more than just the current batch of unexplained deaths with dark forces—or at least begin to wonder about a fellow officer with strange sun and food allergies. He couldn't hypnotize the entire police force out of their suspicions. These were intelligent, curious, well-trained people. Once they had suspicions, it wouldn't be long before they found proof.

These killings had to end, and very soon. Nick ached to be out of the meeting and hunting the streets, but he made himself stay put. He had to play the mortal police detective for a little while longer tonight. This was no time to draw attention to himself in any way.

Tracy flinched when Reese mentioned vampires. She hoped no one noticed, but she received a touch on the hand from Natalie Lambert, who was seated beside her at the table. Fortunately, the pragmatic coroner was something of a friend, one who would put her reaction down to nerves.

Tracy desperately wished that rumors of supernatural occurrences weren't flying all over the city. She didn't know why it worried her that such talk could put Javier and his kind in danger, but it did. She longed to get out, to find out what was really going on. The fact that heads were now being pulled off as well as cut off had pretty much eliminated Drezerdic from her list of suspects. Somebody from the night side of town had to be involved. Apprehending the real perp was the only way to squelch the crazy, media-driven rumors. Only she knew that the rumors weren't crazy; all the wild talk just didn't happen to apply to the vampire community.

At least this time. Or so Javier had assured her. She was sure he'd told her the truth. If he knew the truth.

She suspected that he didn't, that he needed to be warned before some rogue put his kind in danger.

Her whirling thoughts were interrupted by Reese's deep voice. "Dr. Lambert, please assure the squad that the beheadings and the animal attacks are not connected. Or in any way supernatural."

Natalie didn't dare risk a quick look at Nick as she stood. She didn't dare glance at Tracy Vetter, either. The last thing she could do was reveal that she knew that Tracy knew about vampires—which would give away to Tracy that Natalie knew about vampires. She was well aware of Tracy's involvement with Vachon, but Tracy didn't have a clue about what Nick was. Nick wanted to keep it that way. It wasn't easy to refrain from exchanging tips on personal relationships with vampires with Tracy, but Natalie had managed so far.

"Dr. Lambert? You're supposed to be reassuring us about vampires."

Natalie blushed. She wondered how long her mind had wandered on the subject she and Tracy couldn't talk about. No more than a few heartbeats, she hoped. "Sorry, Captain." Natalie pretended to look at the notes she'd brought with her, then proceeded to lie.

She looked around as she finished, but didn't see any reassurance on the faces of the anxious people watching her. This time she did glance at Nick. No one would find that strange, she told herself. Everybody on the squad knew they were friends, right? Instead of being bolstered by the sight of him, she noticed that he looked pale, and there was the faintest yellow glow about his eyes. He looked like a vampire. Only because she knew he was a vampire, she reminded herself sternly. And the glow was simply the reflection of the overhead lights bouncing off a yellow folder someone next to him was holding.

Natalie forced herself to look away from Detective

140

Knight after he gave her a brief nod. She cleared her throat. "Any questions?"

"If feral animals are responsible for the bite marks on the corpses you've examined, why aren't we getting reports of wild dog packs?" Detective Krause asked.

"What we're getting are plenty of reports of zombies," a uniformed officer added. "But nobody's calling in dog attacks."

Natalie was saved from answering by Reese's deep, scoffing laugh. "Come on, people! We're dealing with mass hysteria whipped up by the media. If people kept their televisions off, we wouldn't be hearing anything about mindless, crazed killers or bloodless corpses. What scares me is the possibility that some poor homeless drunk is going to be attacked by a mob because he's acting funny. What *really* scares me is that we've got a serial killer who's cutting off his victims' heads working our streets. We need to stop him, people!"

He slapped his hand down on the table. The noise sent a rippling jolt through the people in the room. Rather like a slap calming a hysterical person, Natalie thought. People gave each other embarrassed sideways looks; there were quite a few blushes as well.

"Stopping him tonight would not hurt my feelings," Reese added. He waved toward the door. "Go."

There was something of a mad scramble to get out of the annoyed Captain's sight. Nick waited for Natalie. Before he could speak to her, one of the dispatchers fought her way through the exiting crowd to come up to him.

"Good, Dr. Lambert, you're here, too. We've got a fresh one," she said to Nick. "Officers on the scene say he's headless but still warm." She handed Nick a message slip with the address where the body had been found.

He nodded to the dispatcher, who then disappeared back into the crowd. "Tracy," Nick called to his partner, "we're rolling."

"I've got to pick up some things at my desk," Tracy said, and quickly pushed past him.

"Meet you at my car. Nat?"

"I'll get my kit and meet you there," Natalie answered.

Nick spared an instant's glance toward Reese before he hurried out. The Captain was beaming, no doubt pleased at his squad's intense response to his inspirational words. Nick just hoped all that inspiration outweighed primitive fear long enough for him to get the killer vampire and the revenants off the street.

Reese no doubt wouldn't have been smiling if he had to face the gauntlet of television crews and print reporters waiting outside the building. Nick would almost have preferred facing a howling pack of torch-wielding peasants than people with microphones, but he steeled himself against the onslaught and walked out the door.

Vachon was glad to find both Nick Knight's and Tracy's cars in the parking lot. Knowing that sometime during the evening they would have to leave the building, he waited outside. His original plan was to linger in the darkness near Knight's ragtop green Cadillac, but the activity in front of the building drew him to the edge of the crowd.

At first he wondered why so many people with Minicams and microphones were milling around. The energy in the air was a strange mixture of excitement and fear. He understood the excitement, but he expected more of a cold, sharklike relentlessness from the ladies and gentlemen of the modern press. There was a lot of talk, and he listened. What he heard among the gathered reporters was as disturbing as his run-in with the cops, if not as hard on his wardrobe.

When a group of detectives and uniformed officers came out of the building, the reporters surrounded them. They ignored the police's media representative, and thrust their microphones into the face of the most authoritative-looking and photogenic detective in the group. Who happened to be Nick Knight. Vachon watched for a moment, a bit amused, but also more than a bit appalled. Then he retreated, with proper vampirish reticence, into the shadows.

Nick wasn't sure what he said in response to the badgering questions. He concentrated on breaking through the mob, managing it with a bit more ease than the other police officers. He wasn't pleased when one more hand landed on his shoulder after he thought he was through the gauntlet.

"Whoa!" Vachon said when he whirled to face Nick. "Oh, it's you."

"Thank you very much," Vachon responded to his annoyed tone. He looked around. "What's the matter? Didn't you feel me coming?"

Nick didn't want to let Vachon know that there had been several instances when he hadn't detected his presence. Nick didn't know if it was because he wasn't as much of a vampire as he used to be, or if there was something intrinsically neutral to Vachon's mental signature. "The media people are giving off enough negative, hungry energy to mask any of our kind's presence," he answered.

Vachon nodded, then glanced back toward the building entrance. "Quick, before Tracy spots me, what's going on here?"

"Nothing I can talk to you about now."

Vachon was not satisfied with Knight's evasiveness. "It sounds like this—whatever it is—affects our entire community. Screed's seen one of those dead things you just told the press don't exist. I've seen one of the headless bodies. Are mortals going to be coming after us with stakes soon?"

Knight gave him an arrogant look. "Not if I can help it."

"You're not the only vampire in Toronto."

"You offering to help?"

Vachon gestured wildly. "I don't know. Maybe. You've forced me to help you often enough lately."

"This is my responsibility."

"Yeah, sure. That's what you always say. Maybe taking care of mortals is your business, but—"

Nick stopped Vachon with a touch on the arm. "Tracy's coming. Get out of here. We'll talk later," he added as he looked straight ahead and walked away.

"Where?"

"I'll find you. Go."

Vachon turned quickly, and saw that Tracy was nearby. He took to the air, but not before she saw him. All Vachon could do was hope that Knight had managed to make it look like he was avoiding approaching her because of the presence of her mortal partner. He also knew, as he took off for the Raven, that he'd just ensured Tracy's as well as Knight's—paying him a visit before the night was through.

10

"WHERE'S THE BLOOD?"

Natalie sighed, but didn't immediately respond to the question from the policeman who hovered too close to where she knelt.

"Well?" the man demanded nervously.

The corpse had been found in the children's playground at a park. A bank of portable lights had been set up to illuminate the area. One end of the crime scene tape was fastened to a swing set; the other, to the ladder of a slide. The ground was damp from a recent shower.

"The blood has soaked into the sand beneath the body," she answered the man's question.

"There weren't any footprints when we got here. Why no footprints in a soil area like this?" the officer went on. He sounded as if he was blaming her.

"Not my department, officer," Natalie answered. "Could you move back before I trip over your feet?" The man moved away while she made herself stay where she was a few seconds longer. Her impulse was to stand, dust her hands together, and walk away. There was nothing to be learned from studying the corpse before her, but she forced herself to go through the motions. Not just for Nick's sake, she told herself, as she glanced up to see Detective Knight talking to a couple of teenage males on the other side of the yellow police tape.

In an effort to keep from staring at Nick, Natalie found herself looking into the dead eyes of the head that lay near the corpse's left hand. He had been young and blond; the glassy eyes were blue. They had been full of life not long ago. She imagined she could still detect the remnants of fear in those eyes. She wanted to tell the dead man that he was lucky. That she'd looked into the eyes of many bodies, but had had no fear of death until one of those bodies looked back at her. *Better to be a headless corpse than a walking one*, she thought. Not that this victim of the diseased vampire was aware that he'd been dealt the better alternative.

"This has got to stop," she murmured. She stood, and rubbed sweaty palms on her suit jacket before balling her hands into fists. Nick was the detective in charge. She had no excuse not to go up to him. She still felt furtive as she approached him.

He turned the questioning of the young men over to Tracy as Natalie came up beside him. "How long?" he asked, brisk and professional.

She decided that he was a much better actor than she was. Of course, he'd had a few hundred years more practice. "Less than an hour," she replied. Then, in a whisper, added, "I hate to nag, but—"

"It has to stop." He nodded. "I know. This is the second one tonight," he added. "We just got the call. The other one is an elderly female, found on the other side of town. He didn't use the sword on that one. Word is that a crowd gathered at the scene, and a small riot is currently in progress."

"News crews with Minicams are no doubt on the way," Nat added cynically.

"Already there," he replied.

"That's not going to influence the populace to remain calm."

"Stopping the deaths is the only thing that's going to keep the situation from exploding. Some television channel has offered a reward for videotape of the revenants. So there are people wandering the streets with video recorders."

"What happens if they find the revenants?"

"Other than get attacked?" He shook his head. "I don't know."

He looked like he did know, but didn't want to tell her. Natalie thought she could guess, then decided that if he was going to be secretive she could keep her speculations to herself. Besides, maybe there were some things about the vampire community it was better not to know.

"Did those kids you were talking to see anything?"

He shook his head. "They heard screams, and one of them *thought* he saw a big bat flying away from the body."

"Right." She considered for a moment, then asked, "Your kind can't really turn into bats, can you?"

"Right." The word sounded more disgustedly sarcastic coming from him than it had from her. "Please, Nat, not you, too."

She shrugged. "Things are getting a little more supernatural than even I'm used to. Makes me realize the old fear of monsters lurking in the darkness is closer to the surface than we think."

"That civilization is just a veneer?" he asked.

"Something like that."

"It's not," Nick said. His voice almost shook with fervent belief. "We have to believe that civilization does hold back the night. That the monsters will never be in control."

She heard the craving to return from the night in his words. She knew how he longed to be a part of her "civilized" world, to escape from the company of monsters. That the civilized world was teetering on panicked, violent resurgence of belief in his kind had to be hard on him. Nick Knight had enough problems with guilt and self-loathing. Natalie hated the thought of his having to deal with revulsion from the mortal world he so longed to return to. Especially when he spent most of his time protecting mortals from their own predatory kind.

But could the monsters be in control if they wanted to be? She wondered. It was a question she carefully kept to herself.

Without any conscious deliberation they had moved well away from the knot of people gathered around the crime scene. They were now standing amid the shadows of a cluster of old oak trees. It was much cooler here, and quiet, away from the lights and people. Natalie glanced over her shoulder, glad that no one seemed to have noticed their absence. Her crew was bagging the body. Soon she'd have one more useless autopsy to perform. Still, she didn't want to be away from the CFS building too long tonight.

"They'll be bringing in mauling victims soon."

She sighed, not quite resigned to her role of killing the dead. The only even vaguely good point in this madness was the blood and tissue samples she was taking from each victim. She had hopes that when this was all over those samples would help in her research to find a cure for vampirism. But this wasn't over yet, so it was no use speculating on any future good that could come out of this macabre situation.

Though she was wearing a light jacket, the coolness beneath the trees seemed to be seeping into her bones. Natalie rubbed her arms and shivered. It did no good to linger here, even if being near Nick gave her an odd feeling of reassurance. It wasn't as if he was actually in control of the situation, or as if she needed his protection from creatures of the night in the midst of a crowded crime scene.

"Going to be a long night," she said, and started to walk away.

"Wait."

The warning in Nick's voice stopped her more effectively than his touch on her shoulder. In the blink of an eye, things changed. The world around her took on a sudden, deeper darkness. Silence pervaded the park. Though there was plenty of noise from the people surrounding the body, it became muffled, as though blown away on a ragged wind. The people themselves seemed to recede into the distance. She felt like she was watching them through the wrong end of a telescope.

The dizzying change of perceptions made no sense to Natalie. She told herself she was experiencing some sort of exhaustion-induced hallucination. Then Nick pointed, and she saw the man-shaped apparition rise above the trees and float over the playground. The glare from the portable lights hid the figure from the people on the ground. No one seemed to hear the creature's maniacal laughter. When Natalie covered her ears to block out the horrible sound, she realized it was inside her head.

When the laughter died, she was kneeling on the

ground. Her heart raced, and her throat went dry with fear. She did manage to croak, "What? Who?"

"Old," Nick said. "Powerful. Projecting it."

He wasn't talking to her. Natalie knew Nick wasn't aware of her anymore. She didn't think he was aware of anything but the other vampire. Natalie could barely bring herself to watch as the dark form in the air spun slowly about, arms outstretched, then rose above the city skyline until he was out of sight.

"Radu," Nick said, and leaped into the air.

He'd been told that the old ones had tricks he'd never dreamed of. After nearly eight hundred years of his cursed life, Nick didn't feel particularly young. Still, he had never felt anything quite as strongly as Radu's presence in the park. One moment, nothing; the next, Radu was there, calling out to those disposed to detect their kind. It had been a deliberate broadcast of energy. An invitation.

Nick accepted, and trusted the two mortal women involved to keep the knowledge to themselves.

Nick had seen Tracy look up, he knew Natalie had seen Radu as well, but he didn't think any other mortals had responded to the other vampire's presence. He didn't think anyone had noticed him leap into the air and follow. It almost didn't matter. Radu had to be stopped. If that meant Nick had to be reckless in chasing him, so be it.

Though he would hate to lose his current identity among mortals, he'd pay that price to stop the killings if he had to. Among the numerous things that annoyed him as he sped along the psychic trail left by the other vampire was knowing that he might have to make sacrifices to save the vampire community as well.

Why had Radu shown himself like that? Who was he looking for?

What is he doing alive? Nick asked himself as he reached the edge of a darkened warehouse district.

That was the better question.

Spreading his foul plague again, was the answer. But how?

Nick settled onto a flat roof; the heat of the day still radiated from the corrugated metal beneath his feet. This echo of sunlight sent a pang of longing through Nick. Because he had no time to waste, he ignored the call of the melancholy streak in his nature. He was night's creature right now, in search of one of his own.

He turned in a slow circle, taking in a trio of boxy structures bulging up from the flat surface of the roof— vents or exhaust pipes for the building, he supposed. He could hear the whirling of giant fans in one of them. The structures all cast square black shadows where the darkness was even deeper. Nick swung his gaze back and forth as he moved cautiously toward the central projection. The world narrowed down to the rooftop, and he searched it with all his senses.

Radu remained invisible in the darkness, but within moments Nick could feel the other vampire's presence in front of him. His impulse was to rush forward, to bare his fangs and attack. So Nick took a slow step backward, thrust his hands into the pockets of his jacket, and made himself remain perfectly still. He faced the predator in the semblance of a civilized man.

His stillness served to draw the monster out, but not for several minutes.

"You act like a statue in a stone garden," Radu said as he stepped in front of Nick. The old vampire's eyes glowed a dim gold that faded as Nick watched. He snarled, and gestured angrily. "This place is nothing but stones and steel. Why did you bring me to this ugly, dead place?"

"It was not my doing." Nick got the impression the older vampire had expended a great deal of energy in sending out his call. "It is you who have brought death here."

"Good." Radu's laughter boomed, drowning the deep whirring of the giant fans behind him. "You wanted me in hell, as I recall. Wasn't that the last thing you said to me? 'Burn in hell, you cursed bastard.'"

"I don't recall swearing at you."

Radu ran his hands through his filthy hair. "Perhaps I heard you incorrectly."

You were screaming, as I recall. Nick carefully kept the thought to himself. "You were surrounded by a great many angry mortals during our last meeting," Nick reminded him. "I thought they were the ones who sent you to hell."

"Mortals are no good at killing, but they've built hell on earth in this place. There are no stars here. The moon can barely break through the city's wall of light. Hell doesn't burn it seems, though it is bright."

Radu began to pace restlessly before him, but Nick still didn't move a muscle. "This isn't hell."

"Where is it, then?"

Radu must have no idea that centuries had passed since they'd last met. Nick didn't offer him any information. Nor did he remind Radu of the part he'd played in the mortals' attack on the older vampire. He did say, "The mortals are very efficient killers. They've grown more efficient at it while you've been sleeping. You are no less dangerous to their kind in this place than you were in your own land. They will not let you continue to exist here."

With or without the aid of mortals, Nick had no intention of allowing Radu to continue existing. His impulse was to attack the monster, but he knew this almost automatic response to an enemy of his own kind was a dangerous thing. He needed cunning, a plan, the correct weapons. Unfortunately, all he had at the moment was a gun.

Radu's laughter rang out again. "Nicholas, you have the instincts of a sheepdog—and always treat me as the wolf who has invaded your herd."

"A *diseased* wolf," Nick amended, and rose swiftly in the air as Radu leaped forward.

Radu whirled around as LaCroix's pup landed on the other side of the roof. "Coward!" he called. "Always the coward." Contempt boiled in Radu's blood. "Traitor to your own kind." He shook his fist at Nicholas.

He drew the sword, only to see that Nicholas did not wear one. It was not the fashion for men to look and act like men in this place. Radu knew that Nicholas was not man enough to answer a challenge if he carried a sword. Radu had no taste for fighting with any weapon but cold iron and steel. What use was a weapon of honor in this mad world where no one would fight him? He should hack the young vampire's head off. That might give him a moment's satisfaction.

Instead, howling with frustration, he aimed the sword like a spear at his enemy's heart, and threw it with all the force he could muster. Nicholas streaked into the air and caught it, letting the steel bite deep into his palms as he grabbed it. The blood was already drying as he broke the sword across his knee. He tossed the broken pieces onto the roof.

Radu flung words next. "Janette loved me!"

Nicholas was on him instantly. "Liar!"

Radu laughed in the boy's face. Just as he'd laughed that night.

"He's not like us, Janette!"

"You're not like us, either, Nicholas."

"Do you know what he does? He carries a plague, Janette."

"And you do not?" Her laughter was cold and cruel. It warmed Radu's heart to hear it.

The boy's reply was hurt, indignant. "What do you mean?"

"Your *humanity* clings to you like a leper's dead skin. It cripples you, Nicholas. I keep hoping, century after century, that you'll be cured of this longing to be what you're not. I'm about to give up hope."

"There is nothing human left to Radu."

"I know."

He had to concentrate very carefully, and such effort took more energy than it once had, but through the thickness of two walls, Radu could hear Janette and Nicholas arguing. The young one's voice was full of fear. Radu smiled. It was good that Nicholas feared him. The boy had no courage; he was no threat. Not against a warrior like himself. Not as a rival for Janette.

Radu did find the conversation entertaining, however. He leaned his head against the wall as he concentrated on listening. As he did, his cheek rested against the cool silver blade of a dagger, one of the many trophies he proudly displayed. How he loved silver.

For a moment he lost the thread of the distant conversation as he recalled that this bauble had last been held in the trembling hand of a Khazar princess who thought to die by her own hand rather than join him against her will. She had been the last child he'd made. He'd called her Kesef, "Silver" in her language. He'd never been able to tame her independence, and she had left him. He deeply regretted her loss, but their time together had been wild. Janette would stay willingly. He listened to her scoff at Nicholas, and laughed silently. It would be better with Janette.

"He is monstrous. Disgusting."

"Far from disgusting, Nicholas."

"Is that what attracts you to him? Do you know what happens to those he kills?"

"He kills to live. What happens to the corpses is nothing to be concerned about. Why do you care? Do you think you can make me hate him by sharing this horrible knowledge of his illness?"

There was a long pause. Then Nicholas finally answered, "Yes."

Radu very nearly doubled over with laughter.

The boy's honesty was touching.

But Nicholas could never take Janette from him.

But he had.

An angry snarl sounded in Radu's ears. He faced glowing eyes and bared fangs, and feared nothing. There were hands around his throat. He tore them away. He tossed his attacker aside, then shook his fist at the sky.

He could not remember how, but Janette had been taken from him. By Nicholas. Yes, of that much he was sure. Whatever had happened, Nicholas was the cause.

"She was mine!" he shouted to the night. Then he looked down, barely aware of his fallen attacker. "She came from the land of the Franks," Radu said, as the pain of loneliness ripped at memories and sanity alike. "She would have stayed with me, shining like the moon. I would have called her Argent, after the glow of the Goddess in her own tongue."

Argent.

"Silver." The craving struck Radu suddenly, a combination of greed, desire, and religious fervor. "Janette," he whispered, staggering under the force of his need. "Janette . . . and the silver."

Silver, how he missed the silver. There had been peace within the silver. No noise, no rushing lights, no hiding from the sun. No dreams. No hunger. In the silver had been nothing but the bliss of sleep.

"You will give them to me! Bring me what is mine!"

While Radu ranted, Nick came to his senses. He was shaken with surprise that all his carefully husbanded calm had deserted him in an instant. For no other reason than Radu's having poked at an old sore, one Nick thought long healed. Janette and he had come to many accommodations before, and after, Radu. It seemed the jealousy remained.

"Janette is mine," Radu ranted as he prowled restlessly across the rooftop. The old vampire seemed to be searching for an invisible presence. Nick sensed a weak mental call and the old one's confusion.

"Janette, however," Nick said as he got to his feet, "is gone."

A bit of the madness cleared out of Radu's face. The fury remained as he focused on Nick. "What did you say?"

It gave Nick a great deal of satisfaction to answer. "She's not here."

"Dead?"

"Absent."

After a long silence, Radu said, "I cannot feel her. Where is she?"

"I don't know," Nick answered honestly.

When Radu howled in grief, Nick was almost tempted to join him. "Yelling about it doesn't do any good," he said.

Radu's ceased off abruptly. He turned his angry gaze on Nick. "And where is my—?" Radu bit off the words, his expression going furtive for a moment. He shook his head, his greasy mane swinging around his face like Medusa's snakes. "Do you lie about Janette?"

"No."

"Janette travels with you and LaCroix. If you are here—"

"She goes her own way when she wishes."

It was a privilege LaCroix was just learning to allow him. Nick had often been envious of Janette's relative freedom. He'd been hurt when she'd sold the Raven and left town without warning a few months before. In all the times he'd run away from LaCroix, he'd never failed to tell Janette good-bye. Now he was delighted to have her away from the reborn Radu's insidious influence. Glad he had no idea where she'd gone.

"I need her," Radu declared.

"I'm sure you do."

Radu took a menacing step closer, but Nick was careful to keep hold of his wits as the mad vampire approached.

"You will bring her to me, young thief," Radu declared, ever the arrogant warlord. "You will bring me all that is mine."

"I don't think so."

Nick looked around cautiously. He needed a weapon. Radu might be recently reborn, but evidence suggested he'd ingested enough blood to regain his full strength.

157

That made him far faster and stronger than Nick. Nick knew he had to destroy Radu, but it would be nearly impossible in hand-to-hand combat. The roof was empty, a wide plain of smooth metal. Perhaps if he had a larger caliber gun, a few bullets in Radu's heart and brain could at least form a distraction.

Then Nick recalled the covered exhaust fans that spun behind him. Perhaps he could. . . .

Radu's laughter interrupted Nick's speculations. "A warrior chooses the site of battle well if he wants to survive. Your treacherous thoughts are clear on your face, boy. You think you can lure me into the turning blades behind you and make an end to me." Radu laughed again, and rose a few feet in the air. Looking contemptuously down on Nick, he went on, "I chose this place for our meeting. I know not what or where it is, but I know there is only that one hazard. You won't trick me into getting near it."

Nick jumped onto the top of one of the vent housings. He was prepared to leap after Radu to keep him from flying away. He decided to attempt to be reasonable with him. "Your killing has to stop," he told the other vampire. "There are too many mortals in this place. They are too powerful. They will bring you down just as they did in Serbia if you don't abide by the rules."

"Our kind does not live by rules."

"We do in this era. We must."

"Liar."

Radu flew around him, darted forward and back, buzzing at Nick like some overgrown mosquito. Nick waited with growing impatience. "Why couldn't you have stayed dead?" he muttered, just as Radu came to a hovering halt a few feet away.

"I saw you with the mortal woman. She's beautiful,

Nicholas. You care for her. Do you plan to replace Janette with her?"

Nick refused to comment on his emotional attachments, but fear for Natalie shot through him. Fear the older vampire no doubt sensed.

A light of cold pleasure filled Radu's mad eyes. "Give her to me, Nicholas. Replace Janette for me, and I might forgive you, little thief. Thief of treasures," he added angrily. "Thief of hearts. Thief of life." He rose on a long, evil laugh. Radu was high above, and far away from, the warehouse district within moments.

Nick followed, but he could not match the other's speed.

"No. No forgiveness," Radu called back. "You cannot give me what I want. I'll take her myself, and drain all the blood from your sheep before I'm done."

An instant later, even Nick's preternatural senses could find no trace of Radu anywhere in Toronto's night sky.

11

THE OLDER THEY WERE, THE MORE ARROGANT THEY BECAME. Vachon was very well aware of the faults of his kind. It wasn't just the hunger, or the fear of sunlight, or all the other restrictions that went with the lifestyle that made vampires so annoying to deal with. It was the sheer, bloody-minded, overbearing, unthinking arrogance that came with the territory that irritated him the most. The oldest ones were the worst, of course. They were the ones who'd been brought up to think of themselves as godlike even in their mortal days.

He'd heard there used to be some sort of rule about only the best sort of people being let into the bloodsucking club. Had to be an Egyptian queen or Chinese emperor—or the bastard son of a Spanish duke, at the very least. Although the Lady who'd brought him across hadn't known about his so-called noble birth. Or maybe she'd tasted it in his blood and it had made him more worthy of the gift of eternity in her eyes. He hoped not, because it didn't mean a damn thing to him.

Vachon didn't know who Nick Knight had been before

he was brought across, but he was willing to wager he hadn't been some peasant lad LaCroix plucked out of the muck for the pleasure of his company. No, Knight had strength, power, and an ease of command that spoke of their practice from birth. Death had just given him centuries to perfect the "lord of the manor" act.

Vachon wasn't even quite sure why he was so annoyed with Knight, but by the time he entered the Raven, he was furious. It had something to do with being brushed off, being relegated to being told he'd be filled in later by the city's great vampire protector. The duke's son, the conquistador, the child of the Lady, Javier decided with vampirish arrogance of his own, didn't like being ordered around because he was a mere four hundred years old.

Of course he was a bastard, a mercenary, and hardly ever deliberately obedient to the benevolent wishes of the one who'd made him. If the whole vampire community was about to be hunted down like the parasites they were, why was it of concern to him?

Because this was his home, they were his kind, and he was a sucker for the underdog. At the moment, he was one of the underdogs. Ironic, and inconvenient.

He was, when it came down to it, a leader, though he fought off the urge to be in charge of things most of the time. He had almost gotten over the impulse to *do* something by the time he lifted his second glass of a wine-colored substance.

A week from now, he thought, setting the crystal glass down on the polished wood of the bar in front of him, the Raven might not exist anymore. Vachon forced himself out of the irritated, responsible mood and took a look around.

Might as well enjoy it while it lasts, he told himself.

The band was loud, their music heavy and hot. The

dance floor was full of writhing bodies. Vachon found himself frowning at the way young folks danced these days.

How come nobody waltzes anymore? He leaned back on the bar. He let the ambience of the place along with the effects of the two drinks, soothe his rattled nerves.

He noticed Urs, wearing a tiny leather outfit, dancing on one of the tables. She had quit her job entertaining in just this way at the Raven, claiming she was no longer interested in titillating the males of any species. She'd told him that when she danced at the Raven these days, it was for fun. Vachon hoped it was really true. She certainly looked like she was having fun now. He wiggled his fingers at her when she glanced his way. Her answering smile was as bright as remembered sunshine.

It certainly warmed him, for Urs was not much for smiling. Her cheerfulness gave Vachon hope that she'd let go of her worry about the girl who'd attached herself to LaCroix.

"Good evening."

Vachon jumped and almost crossed himself. For he'd no more than thought of the devil, and there he was. "LaCroix," he said, with a respectful nod toward the owner of the Raven.

LaCroix responded with a long, intense look. A moment of such scrutiny, and Vachon looked away.

He had the most disturbing eyes Vachon had ever encountered. They were soul-searching at best, soul eating if he chose. LaCroix's demeanor often reminded Vachon of a combination of the most fanatical aspects of Jesuit missionaries and those of the Dominican inquisitors. It was an odd comparison, Vachon knew, for whatever LaCroix had done during his time on Earth, he most certainly had never been a priest. Of anybody's religion.

LaCroix gestured, and the bartender instantly provided him with a full glass. "Wretched stuff," he said after he took a sip. He watched the dance floor for a few moments before asking, "Don't you agree?"

Vachon fidgeted beside him. LaCroix enjoyed the young one's discomfort. He sensed that several things bothered Vachon, not the least of which was his presence. How nice to know one had not lost one's touch. He took another sip, then lifted a inquiring brow. "Hmm?"

Vachon took a drink from his own glass, then swirled the dark liquid with a finger. "You get used to it."

"Do you? Really?"

Vachon replied to LaCroix's sarcasm with a shrug. He'd learned from overhearing LaCroix's exchanges with Knight, and his own infrequent encounters with the owner of the Raven, that sarcasm was one of the few tones the elder chose to employ. While he hadn't actually listened to the Nightcrawler show, Vachon had been informed by Screed that bitter irony and contempt were also on LaCroix's list of approved ways to express emotions.

Not quite sure why he'd been singled out by LaCroix, and knowing that Urs was watching him expectantly, hoping that he'd confront Lacroix about the mortal girl, Vachon ventured a question of his own. "Missing the old days?"

LaCroix downed the rest of the blood substitute. "No." He put the glass down on the bar, then turned his gaze full on Vachon. He smiled.

Vachon really wished he wouldn't do that. He also didn't obey the urge to be someplace else. He hadn't seen Tammy anywhere in the crowd, though he knew her only from Urs's description. That didn't mean that the human wasn't nearby. Vachon didn't know if he wanted her to interrupt this intimate moment he was having with LaCroix.

He wished someone would interrupt them, but the crowd had thinned out in this tiny corner of the Raven. The nearest people, mortal or otherwise, were the ones on the dance floor. Miklos, ever discreet, was busying himself at the other end of the long bar. There weren't going to be any interruptions, and Vachon had no reason to walk away from the conversation.

"Are you sure you're not being nostalgic?" Vachon made himself ask. "I get the impression that you're restless tonight."

"Perhaps a little."

He was indeed restless, LaCroix reflected. Perhaps he was even a bit jealous, though it had been his suggestion that Tammy spend some time with the young mortal male he'd had her take to Janette's room. She was so eager to please. Her emotions were completely open to him. What she did, she did for him. He could feel her now, straining to make some emotional connection with the physical act she was performing. Her mind was alive with sensation, but all of it was centered on her connection with LaCroix. He knew that every bit of her pleasure came from knowing she was pleasing him.

He had known it would happen that way. What he hadn't expected was to respond with mixed emotions. He used to revel in human debasement, when he bothered to make the effort. He should be smirking with pleasure at Tammy's compliant nature. Instead he found that he was a bit sad. Still, he found her willingness to give everything she was to him quite gratifying. His ego told him he deserved no less than total submission. Yet his conscience—for lack of a better term—informed him that he'd done nothing to deserve such total devotion. Her eyes were so much like Divia's. Not in color or shape, but in the way they constantly watched and assessed him. He had found that he could not bear that gaze throughout eternity. Then again, Divia had brought him across; the roles would be reversed if he chose to make Tammy one of his own.

"It's the twentieth century," he said. "All this constant examining of motives and reasons has become second nature. I wish I'd never heard of Oedipus or Electra outside the theater where they belong. And Greek plays were always so boring." He very nearly let himself sigh. "I should have made a quick meal of Freud when I had the chance."

"Think it would have done any good?"

"No." LaCroix gestured for another drink. Soon it would be time to don his Nightcrawler guise, dispense his own brand of psychology to the masses. "But I always have been more of a Jungian. Still, mortals in this time are a bit too self-aware. Our kind has a bad habit of allowing their values to rub off on us."

"We can't stop the world from changing," Vachon replied. "We can't keep ourselves from changing with it, even when we make an effort not to."

"Pity." *Superficial values*, LaCroix thought. He hoped. "Are their attitudes, their beliefs a part of us?" he wondered. "Or no more than a coat we wear, a part of the disguise that hides our differences from them?" He was sounding like the Nightcrawler, and he wasn't even on the air yet. He waved the question away before Vachon could answer it. "An education in philosophy and rhetoric," LaCroix went on, "is inconvenient at times." He

166

twirled the glass in his hands. "How sterile our lives become. Like this drink, artificial and superficial."

Vachon chuckled, garnering a curious look from La-Croix. "Maybe it's another way we reflect mortal behavior." He finished off the liquid in his glass before continuing. "Here we have a healthy, nutritional protein substitute for the richer food we constantly crave. This is our version of diet drinks and nonfat food. Pleasure without guilt."

"Without substance," LaCroix countered.

"Without seasoning," Vachon added, and immediately regretted his words. He remembered Tammy, and Urs's concerns about the girl, and hoped he hadn't just encouraged LaCroix to take the mortal girl's life. Not that LaCroix was the sort who needed to be encouraged to do exactly what he wanted to do. Against his better judgment, Vachon heard himself asking, "Where's your young friend?"

"And how is it you know about my young friend?" LaCroix looked from Vachon to Urs, and back again. "Of course."

LaCroix rubbed a finger slowly along his jawline. Vachon wasn't sure why he found the gesture threatening. Not toward himself, but toward Urs. It made a fierce wave of protectiveness rise in him. "Urs is concerned for the girl. She sees something of herself in Tammy."

LaCroix's smile was genuinely delighted, though no less disturbing for all that. "You children have been gossiping about me behind my back."

Vachon braved the lion further by saying, "As you're very well aware. Or we wouldn't be having this conversation. What do you want from me? Advice on dating in the nineties?"

167

LaCroix's attention was still focused on Urs. "Something like that."

It occurred to Vachon that the way Urs read the situation between LaCroix and the mortal girl was quite accurate. She'd said Tammy was trying to seduce LaCroix. It looked like it was working.

"You're not thinking of killing her, are you?"

"I haven't decided yet."

"You are thinking of bringing her across, though?" LaCroix made the slightest of movements. Vachon interpreted it as a shrug. *Does Knight know about this?* It was a question he didn't ask. What went on between LaCroix and those of his making was no one else's business. Vachon did notice that LaCroix's attention was still on Urs, and that *was* his business. "You're comparing your mortal with her? Urs certainly sees the similarities. Do you want to bring someone so unhappy into our world, LaCroix?"

"The unhappy are the best prepared," LaCroix replied.

"Depends on what they're unhappy about. Will making her one of us cure her, or just make her hate herself worse?" Vachon was very careful about what he said next. "Will it make her hate you in the end? You'll be the one who has to live with her problems." As he spoke, he realized he wasn't so much talking about Tammy, or even Urs, but his own ambiguity about Tracy. He looked around the Raven, and saw at least half a dozen vampires far younger than Urs. He pointed. "Look at them. Some no more than a few months old. Our kind seems to be having a population explosion. Maybe anyone can be a vampire these days, but it doesn't mean everyone should be a vampire."

"I've noticed," LaCroix said, "that there is a certain amount of indiscretion among our kind in this era."

"Instant family," Vachon scoffed. "Instant gratification."

"Thoughtless hedonism," LaCroix agreed.

"I'm not necessarily against hedonism," Vachon said.

"Nor I."

"I made a mistake with Urs. I've learned that a great deal of thought and consideration should go into the decision to bring someone across."

"Did you make a mistake? She seems to be adjusting quite nicely."

"Now."

"A century isn't such a long time to learn to adjust to our life."

Vachon didn't think anything he'd said had made an impression on LaCroix. Why should it? LaCroix was ancient. He had far more experience in the ways of their kind than anyone Vachon had ever met. Vachon didn't know if experience equaled wisdom. He did know that age could simply make one more willfully stubborn. LaCroix would do as he wished with Tammy. Vachon had known that would be the inevitable outcome even when he'd promised Urs he'd talk with LaCroix.

"You think I haven't listened to a word you've said, don't you?" LaCroix asked. He almost laughed at the look of surprise on the young one's face. "But I have. You see," he explained, "I've always been very cautious about whom I choose as my children, since they will be with me forever."

"Over seven hundred years, and I never tire of looking at you."

He'd come into Janette's room to find her sitting before a large silver mirror. For a long time he observed her as she brushed her hair. The hairbrush was silver as

169

well. So was the heavy embroidery on the robe she wore. She was pale and still, except for the rhythmic movement of her hand, as repetitive as a mortal heartbeat. Watching her was a soothing experience, until the silence grew too long between them.

"Some of the legends about us say we cannot see our reflections in mirrors. I don't think you'd like that."

He saw the reflection of her smile. He wondered if it was a property of the silver that made it seem so chilly and distant. "I doubt if I would have let you bring me across if I'd known that legend. Fortunately for my vanity, it isn't true."

LaCroix looked around the room while Janette began to braid her hair. When they had first arrived at Radu's castle, the accommodations their host provided had been comfortable enough but hardly luxurious. While Radu showed off his treasures with barbaric gaudiness in his great hall, the private parts of his domain were more spartan. Janette's quarters had been no different from his or Nicholas's. She had been provided with a windowless cell cut into the thick stone walls of the castle. There had been no more in it than a heavily curtained bed. The floor had been covered in rushes and rat droppings, a threadbare tapestry had ineffectually held back the damp chill from the walls. The place must have looked little different to her than the Briard stronghold where she'd first taken mortal breath. She had been as disgusted by the setting as Nicholas. LaCroix had been amused by their repugnance at traveling back in time.

He saw that Janette had nothing to be disgusted about now, and he was not amused.

The room glowed.

LaCroix had noticed Janette's quarters becoming more opulent with each passing day. Silver objects now littered

170

every possible surface, and spilled over into piles on the floor. The flames from dozens of candles threw back multiplied light from the gleaming hoard.

"This room has become a shrine," LaCroix observed.

"Yes," she agreed. "To my beauty, Radu tells me."

He sneered. "Tell me, Janette, doesn't the naïveté of his laying all his treasure at your feet bore you?"

"It isn't the treasure that interests me, but I do find Radu's devotion—sweet."

"I'm glad you've found this interlude entertaining."

Janette turned to face him. She got to her feet. Her manner was calm, cold as steel. "Interlude, LaCroix?"

He spread his hands. "We came for a visit. The visit has drawn to an end. We don't want to overstay our welcome."

She tucked her hands into the wide sleeves of her robe. "Radu would be happy to see the last of Nicholas."

"You sound as if you might share such happiness."

She lifted her head, defiance shining in her dark eyes. "I will miss you both, of course."

He moved a step closer to her. "Are you saying you don't wish to leave?"

"Radu wishes me to stay."

"I wish you to leave."

"I haven't made up my mind yet."

He moved closer, close enough to grasp her shoulders. "You seem to be under the impression that you have a choice."

Her flesh trembled beneath his touch, but only for a moment. Her gaze slid away from his, then flashed up again within a second. She looked angrily into his eyes. "You told me when you brought me across that I would never have to obey the will of a man ever again. Have you forgotten that promise?"

171

"Do I ever forget anything?"

"You weren't referring just to yourself, is that it?"

"Have I forced you to remain with me every day of our lives?"

"No," she admitted. "You've let me be free enough. With your permission."

"Permission you do not have now. I do not wish for you to stay with Radu."

"He needs me."

"As do Nicholas and I."

"I owe him nothing."

"Obligation is important among our kind."

She laughed. "It is important if you are the one in control. Sometimes, LaCroix, I enjoy pretending I am in control of my own life."

"And sometimes I enjoy letting you pretend. Not this time, Janette."

"Why not?"

"Because you are my child, and I know what is best."

"You're afraid of losing me, aren't you? That Radu will come to mean more to me than you do?" She attempted to shake off his clinging hands. "Must I always remain a child? Perhaps it is time to let me grow up."

"No."

She grew calm again. Her distant smile returned. The look in her eyes turned from fury to something like pity. "Or perhaps, LaCroix, it is time for you to make another daughter."

LaCroix hadn't agreed at the time. He'd been furious, angry enough to throw her aside and stalk away. He recalled how that night he'd been in the mood to punish a disobedient child. But now—now he wasn't so sure

172

she hadn't been right. It had just been the time that was wrong.

Time he went to work. Tammy would join him in the studio when she was finished with her young man.

He put down his glass and walked toward the back of the club. The crowd parted at his approach, though many, mortal and immortal alike, didn't notice that they made way for him. He felt the curious gazes of Vachon and his pretty little girl on his back, and found their interest somewhat amusing.

He was amused enough to be smiling when Nicholas walked in and grabbed him by the arm. LaCroix sighed. "Not now, Nichola—"

"In back. Now." Nicholas shoved him toward the studio door. "Time we had a talk."

12

Nick slammed the door, then leaned against it, arms crossed. "Would you mind telling me," he said, "just where Radu came from?"

LaCroix tapped a forefinger against his lips while he considered for a moment. "Somewhere in the Ural Mountains, I believe. Originally."

Nick stepped forward. "You are not amusing, LaCroix. You have never been amusing, LaCroix."

"Only because you have no sense of humor, Nicholas."

"You know what I'm talking about. What is he doing in Toronto? Alive and just as mad, just as sick, as ever. Why?"

LaCroix responded with mock outrage. "Are you blaming *me*? Knowing how appalled I was at Radu's sickness?"

"You weren't appalled."

"Wasn't I?"

"You didn't care what happened to the mortals he infected."

"But you did. It was your concern that concerned me, Nicholas."

There was a certain seductive quality to LaCroix's voice, and the usual infuriatingly flattering appeal to his twisted logic. Nick shook his head. "You're about to say that you only wanted what was best for me—and Janette."

"Isn't that all I ever want?"

"LaCroix wants what LaCroix wants. Ultimate selfishness—that is the hallmark of our kind. As you have so often told me."

"And Nicholas always wants what he wants. You are always at such great pains to hide your selfishness from yourself. You do as you choose, and pretend it's for the good of everyone. Nicholas is forever playing at being mortal—doctor, teacher, policeman. He excuses his games by proclaiming himself protector of the weak and downtrodden. Nicholas doesn't want to take responsibility for what he is, so he decides he wants to be mortal. Nicholas wants to save the world, because it makes him feel good about himself. Nicholas, Nicholas, Nicholas," LaCroix scoffed, "do you know how *annoying* you are?"

Nick stood toe to toe with LaCroix as they glared into each other's eyes. "Yes," he answered. "I *enjoy* annoying you. I'm also not letting you change the subject. This is about Radu, not me. What happened?"

"How should I know?"

"I'm sure this has everything to do with you."

"Why must I always be the villain?"

"Because you're so very good at it."

LaCroix gave a scoffing laugh. "You wanted Radu out of our lives as much as I did. You simply needed the right excuse to do it. You," LaCroix snarled, "are the one who killed him."

"He's a danger to us all."

Nicholas sat on the stone bench in the dark courtyard while LaCroix prowled back and forth in front of him. It was normally LaCroix who remained still and silent, and Nicholas who was filled with restless energy. Tonight, their activities seemed to be reversed, though they appeared to be in a rare state of agreement.

They had Radu's castle to themselves once more. Their host and Janette had said they wished to hunt down the villagers who had staked the revenant at the cross-roads. They claimed they wanted to teach the peasants that their kind was not so easy to be rid of. Nicholas worried about their bravado.

"Janette is not normally so reckless," he murmured.

"Radu is a very bad influence on her."

Nicholas leaned forward, halting LaCroix's pacing with a touch on his sleeve. He looked up into LaCroix's angry face. "Are you concerned about the revenants? Or is it Janette's fascination with him that worries you?"

LaCroix's brows drew down harshly over his fanati-cally glowing eyes. "Radu poses a threat. I think we both realize that."

"But to whom, LaCroix?"

"Mortals and immortals alike. Isn't that the answer you wish to hear?"

Nicholas stood. "What I wish to hear isn't important." He knew LaCroix thought it was. LaCroix's manipula-tion was too transparent this time. "You want me to rid the world of Radu—for the world's sake, of course."

A smile. One that was more a flash of fang than any show of earnestness. "Of course."

Bitterness twisted through Nicholas. "And then Janette will blame me for the destruction of her lover. Your hands will be clean, and she will turn to you for comfort."

"You're not normally so cynical, Nicholas."

"I can't always be your unheeding tool, LaCroix. But," he added, "something does have to be done about Radu."

He didn't ask LaCroix for help, but he did have a plan. He told himself that he wasn't doing it to keep Janette with them. That he wasn't doing it because LaCroix wanted it done. He *knew* that the threat of the revenants had to end. Radu was diseased, a danger to his own kind as well as to mortals. The contagion could not be allowed to spread.

That was why he armed himself, and forced himself to follow Radu and Janette to the village. The place reeked of garlic; it was like breathing poisoned air. It hung from every window and door. The noxious stuff was a strong deterrent, but not absolute protection from his kind. The fumes burned like quicklime in his eyes and throat, but Nicholas ignored the pain as he ran from house to house.

He banged on doors, shouting, "Vampires! Save yourselves! The monsters are in the village!"

Windows banged open. Men shouted gruff-voiced questions at him as he ran down the narrow streets. Women screamed. Light grew as candles and fires were kindled. Half-dressed peasants tumbled out of their doors behind him. He looked back as he ran, glimpsing hands holding torches, knives, stout pieces of wood carved to sharp points. He was careful not to look too closely in case he caught sight of a brandished cross. He was certain he couldn't face garlic and holy symbols both. Despite the danger, Nicholas was gratified to see that these people were prepared for a supernatural invasion.

Once he had the townsfolk stirred up, he went in search of Radu. Nicholas found him on the far side of the village square, standing on the steps of the church. The headless body of a black-robed priest lay at Radu's feet. He had no time to find out how Radu had lured the priest from the protection of the house of God.

Janette stood on the stone rim of the well in the square's center, her fierce smile bright in the darkness. She turned an annoyed gaze on Nicholas as he approached. "What are you doing here, Nicholas?"

"Saving you," he answered. He pointed behind him. "Can't you hear them coming?"

She looked around in alarm. "The villagers? They're hunting?"

"Yes. Coming for you."

Radu ignored Nicholas. "Why do you look afraid, Janette? Has LaCroix failed to protect you in the past?"

"I would rather not face a mob," she answered.

"I would." He laughed loudly, just as the first group of villagers reached the edge of the square.

"Go!" Nicholas urged Janette. "This madman's doomed. You don't have to be! Please, Janette, escape!"

Radu jumped down off the steps, and pushed Nicholas aside. Nicholas was quite happy to be standing behind Radu, and not because he sought protection. "Go, Janette!" he shouted once more. She gave an anguished cry, then rose into the air, hidden by the darkness above the light thrown by the flaming torches.

"Monster!" several of the men in the crowd shouted. "Fiend!"

"Look! He's killed Father Stefan!"

"We won't let him kill again!"

"Numbers make you brave!" Radu shouted back.

"Knowing that you can outrun them makes you brave," Nicholas said. "But this time you won't escape justice."

Radu gave him a disdainful look. "So you led them here. Against all our customs, you led mortals to me?"

"Yes. Customs change."

Radu was so angry he seemed oblivious to the mob heading their way. He put his hand on the hilt of his sword. "You're not worth killing with my bare hands. I'm going to cut you down like a dog. Skewer your heart and give it to Janette." Radu began to draw his sword.

Nicholas smiled as he drew the pistols he'd unpacked from their case in his luggage. He thrust them into the older vampire's face and fired before Radu could get his weapon out.

Radu howled in pain as he went down.

Nicholas sprang into the air as the mob converged on the vampire writhing at the foot of the church steps.

"A pair of bullets in the brain will slow you down long enough for the mortals to finish the job," Nicholas said as the first stake was raised.

He'd made the balls for the pistols from a melted silver plate snatched from among Radu's hoarded treasure. It had seemed fitting. He'd known when he decided to kill Radu that the barbarian would not expect the use of a modern weapon. No, Radu belonged in the time of swords and challenges to single combat. Nicholas, on the other hand, had moved with the times. His experience with Radu had taught him that stagnation was the sure death of his kind.

He lingered long enough to see Radu's body set on fire.

The next night he, LaCroix, and Janette left Radu's castle. Nicholas returned to the salons of Paris. LaCroix preferred to spend his time in less serious pursuits. Janette was coldly angry with them both for a long time.

Nicholas told himself that it didn't matter, that as long as Radu was dead, he'd done the right thing.

"But he didn't stay dead." Nick pointed accusingly at LaCroix. "That is your doing. Why?"

"What? Do you I think I disrupted the universe just to annoy you?"

"You've done it before."

"True," LaCroix admitted. He stepped back, moved to put the desk between himself and Nick. "But not this time."

Did LaCroix actually look embarrassed? Yes, Nick believed he did. He let himself have a moment to enjoy his usually supremely confident maker's chagrin, but no more. He didn't have time to gloat. He needed information. He needed to rid the world of Radu one more time before sunrise. "What happened?" he asked. "We left his ashes in Serbia. How was he revived?"

"How?" LaCroix shook his head. "No, that I cannot tell you." He gave Nick an angry glare. "There are secrets we old ones must keep, to protect all our kind."

"I'm not exactly young anymore," Nick reminded LaCroix.

"You are an eternal adolescent."

Nick fought the urge to bicker, to remind his maker of who had kept him that way. "How was Radu reborn?"

LaCroix shook his head again. "It was long ago decided," he said with vicious pleasure, "that there are some secrets you will never know. Nicholas de Brabant will never be a respected elder among our kind."

"For which I am eternally grateful."

"Besides," LaCroix went on, "how he was revived has nothing to do with reducing him to ashes once more."

"Ashes," Nick repeated, and knowledge slowly dawned

on him. "You kept his ashes, didn't you? You brought them away in one of his collection of coffers."

This time LaCroix nodded. "It seemed appropriate, given his love for silver."

"The silver box that was stolen. But how did—"

LaCroix cut him off with a gesture. "This much I will tell you. It is an old custom, a pledge sometimes made among friends. Radu and I were once friends. I had no intention of ever reviving Radu, but I allowed for the possibility. Keeping his ashes was a way of keeping the potential for his return."

"It was a way of gloating and keeping him a prisoner."

"You know me so well. Actually," LaCroix said, "I'd almost forgotten Radu was in the thing. Its only relevance had come to be as a bit of decor, kept on a shelf with other mementos. How was I to know a burglar would break into my home?"

"It was stolen?"

"I already told you it was. It was chance that somehow brought Radu back to life. Nothing more."

"Somehow?" Nick almost laughed. "Just a whim of fate?"

He didn't quite believe in chance. He'd seen the workings of fate whirling around his kind for too long. Accepting immortality had released his kind from the most obvious plot of destiny, but Nemesis wasn't done with them yet. They'd escaped death, but that only gave fate more chances to play games with them. He knew very well that LaCroix didn't believe in blind coincidence, either.

"If you saved his ashes," he told LaCroix, "you're responsible for putting him back where he came from."

"I am not responsible for anything," LaCroix declared.

"You've set a beast loose in the city."

"Not I. That was done by some mortal's hand." LaCroix's tone was cold and haughty. "Let the mortals pay for it."

"Do you know how many have died already?"

"Do I care?"

Nick wanted to strangle LaCroix out of sheer frustration. This squabbling was getting them nowhere. "Will you help hunt him down?" Nick demanded of his maker.

"No."

"He's endangering all our kind."

"Let the Enforcers deal with him. I have my own plans for the evening," LaCroix added with a smirk. "Besides, it might not be such a bad thing if mortals came to fear the dark again. We had so much more control over our own lives when we weren't worried about their believing in us."

Nick didn't recall the past that way. He remembered centuries of running from the hunters. "Your memory is selective."

"And your conscience is overactive. I suppose you're going to attempt to kill Radu again?"

Nick couldn't stop the short, bitter laugh. He didn't even bother answering the question. Why had he even come here, just to confirm what he already knew? Had he really thought he could get LaCroix to help him when LaCroix had nothing to gain from the exercise?

He very nearly tore the heavily soundproofed door off its hinges when he threw it open. Nick barely noticed the gamin-featured girl standing next to the door as he walked out. He barely saw anything at all as he rushed out of the club to resume his hunt for Radu.

"I'm telling you, there's nothing else on television right now. The local channels have gone 'All Monster All the Time.' They're out to get us."

"You've been saying that for a hundred years, Sasha," Vachon reminded the blond Russian who'd come up to him just as he'd started to leave.

"And I haven't been wrong, have I?"

"Okay, paranoia has its place," Vachon agreed.

"We have to do something."

"We? What do you mean, *we*? All right," he conceded at Sasha's grim look. "Knight said he'd. . . ." Vachon's voice died as something sped toward him from the other side of the wide room. A red-shifting image, black and gold in its center, tore across his vision. A tornado force pushed him aside. Raging energy whip-cracked through his senses and was gone, leaving a buzzing wake in his brain.

"Speak of the devil," Vachon muttered, and shook his head to clear it.

Vachon hadn't seen Knight enter the Raven, but his angry exit was hard to miss. At least for any vampire who wasn't blind or deaf—which was about zero percent of the population. Chances were, even some mortals noticed the brief black and gold blur as Knight passed by, and hopefully put it down to whatever recreational substances they were currently abusing.

The vampires in the club gave each other curious, worried looks after Knight was gone. Vachon could see that Knight's behavior did nothing to ease the increasing sense of anxiety among their kind. His own growing mood of anxiety wasn't helped when the others looked expectantly toward him. To him, Javier Vachon, not to the smiling LaCroix who came from the back of the club with his new human girlfriend trailing close behind. Vachon also wondered why Knight had left in such an incautious hurry. He didn't think it had anything to do with the girl. His guess was that there was some connection with the monster sightings that had the city in such an uproar. He suspected the others were going to come to him with their questions rather than approach LaCroix, who was the one who could probably answer them.

I'm not a leader, he said to himself as Urs made her way over to him. *Really, I'm not.*

Vachon watched as Sasha ran his fingers nervously across his teeth. "My fangs ache, Javier. You know my fangs always ache when there's trouble."

Urs put her hand on his arm. "Camille told me she thought she saw one of Screed's mindless creatures on her way here."

"She thought?"

"Excuse me, young man."

Vachon glanced sideways at the man who'd spoken. There was something familiar about the older mortal who squeezed through where they stood, pushing Urs aside before she could answer. The mortal's presence reminded Vachon that they weren't exactly alone. Not even the Raven was completely safe for their kind. Vachon said, "I think we ought to take this conversation elsewhere." Then he noticed something else about the man who was barreling across the crowded dance floor.

Vachon pointed. "That's Tracy's creep."

"Who?" Urs asked.

"Somebody who's sort of a suspect in a murder case."

"Oh, that makes a lot of sense, Javier."

"What's he doing here?"

"Looks like he's heading toward LaCroix," Sasha said.

The three younger vampires exchanged glances. Without any discussion, and with infinite curiosity, they moved to follow the mortal intruder.

LaCroix had just turned to reply to his sound technician's request to start broadcasting when he heard a man say, "Tamara, I found you."

LaCroix was instantly struck by the combination of adoration and covetousness in the stranger's voice. He sounded as though he truly understood love. When he looked at the man's face, the expression he saw there was utterly familiar, if too openly and hungrily exposed.

Tammy, on the other hand, look horrified. "Go away." She looked to LaCroix. "Make him go away."

"You are Tamara Drezerdic. I know you are." The man moved closer to Tammy. "You are mine." He grabbed her wrist. "You will come with me. Now."

"Maybe she doesn't want to go."

It was Javier Vachon who spoke. LaCroix hung back as the young one stepped forward. Two of his crew were with him, that big Russian bear, Sasha, and pretty little Urs. The man—Drezerdic—turned to face them. He didn't drop his grip on Tammy's hand. The man seemed oblivious to the menace they exuded, not even aware that in the darkness of the club, these three had faintly glowing yellow eyes.

"Devotion, indeed, Mr. Drezerdic," LaCroix murmured to himself as Tammy continued to look to him. "To brave the vampire's den for his child."

"Is he your father?" he asked the girl.

"I don't want him," she answered.

"You're coming with me," Drezerdic stated, and started to pull her forward. "For your own good."

"She isn't going anywhere she doesn't want to go," Urs said, blocking the man's path.

Vachon wasn't sure why they were getting involved, other than it seemed like the right thing to do. He glanced toward LaCroix, and saw that the old one was looking thoroughly pleased with this diversion. It occurred to

Vachon that letting the mortal girl's father take her away might be the best thing for her. He tried to communicate this to Urs with a look.

"Do you want to go with him?" Urs asked Tammy.

"No." Tammy had started to cry.

"I'm your father."

Drezerdic didn't strike Vachon as devoted father material. Or maybe he was too devoted. He was certainly fervent about finding his daughter. Hadn't Tracy mentioned that he was an ex-convict? Convicted of what?

"You've been in prison—for murder, right?" Vachon demanded of the mortal.

"He killed my mother," Tammy said.

"Only because it was the moral thing to do," Drezerdic told his daughter. "It was justice. You were too young to understand. I'll explain after I take you from this horrible place. I'll take care of you from now on. See that you become a good woman."

Tammy succeeded in breaking the man's grip on her arm. She jumped behind Urs, who pushed the man away when he tried to reach the girl. The man stumbled backward, only to thud into LaCroix. LaCroix put his hands on Drezerdic's shoulders.

"I don't want anything to do with him! Please, LaCroix! Help me!"

LaCroix gave the girl a reassuring look. Then he spun Drezerdic to face him. "Look at me."

The man's dark gaze was caught by LaCroix's. Those eyes were full of complete hatred, but they were trapped just the same.

LaCroix spoke slowly, carefully, and very, very firmly. "I think you are going to go away. You are going to leave your daughter to me. You will never see her again. You want very much to be elsewhere. If you are not elsewhere immediately," he added in a whisper, "your daughter will drink your blood for dinner."

The man went pale as LaCroix spoke, his face slack. He would have fallen to his knees when LaCroix released him, if Vachon hadn't caught him. Vachon passed him to Sasha.

"Get him out of here," Vachon told the Russian, who nodded and escorted Drezerdic out the door.

LaCroix looked around, and saw that everyone in the club was staring at him. The band had forgotten that they were being paid to play. LaCroix waved his arms expansively and shouted, "Music! Dancing! Drinks on the house!"

The noise level soon returned to normal.

From the safety of Urs's embrace, Tammy looked at him imploringly. His technician reappeared after Drezerdic's departure. He pointed to his watch. LaCroix considered the competing entreaties. As far as CERK went, he owned the station. If he wanted to play three hours of dead air, or the Grateful Dead, rather than the Nightcrawler, that was his option. But it wouldn't do any good to let the girl think she had any power over him, even though his appetite was deeply stirred by the wildly throbbing pulse in her throat. Her heartbeat was a delicious thrum in his ears. Soon it would exactly match the slow, stately pace of his own—and of Nicholas's and Janette's.

"I want you to go home," he said to Tammy as her gaze hungrily searched his. He saw her devastated disappointment, and added, "Gather together whatever you wish to keep. I'll come for you."

"But how will you know where to find me?"

He touched her cheek. "Do you think I have trouble finding anyone I want?" He turned to Urs, who stood next to Tammy. "She's upset. See that she gets home safely."

Urs nodded, and put her arm around Tammy's shoulders. LaCroix followed the technician back to the broadcast booth.

Vachon stepped forward as Urs and Tammy started toward the door. "Meet us at the church after you're done with the girl. If you want to. Please, Ursula," he added politely when she tossed her head angrily and shot him a dirty look.

"I'll be there," Urs said, and hurried to escort the young woman out.

13

"YOU GOT HER HOME OKAY?" VACHON ASKED AS HE STEPPED out of the shadows by the church entrance.

He'd waited to escort Urs inside because she still had a problem with some of the old taboos; she'd been a good Catholic girl in her mortal life. Sasha was a godless Commie, Screed had never been a believer. Camille and Larry were more into *Star Trek* than Mother Church. Vachon himself had never been more than nominally Christian; his mother had been a forced convert who'd taught him to be wary of priests but not to fear God. Besides, having known nothing about vampires before he was brought across and having no contacts with other European vampires until he'd learned how to use his powers, very few of their restrictions had meaning for him. He had the garlic allergy, and sunlight meant death, but being repulsed by so-called holy images was not one of his problems. Over the centuries he'd convinced a few others of his kind that it wasn't their problem, either.

He even had major proof that the fear of crosses was all in the older vampires' minds. Nick Knight, the most

191

hidebound European traditionalist Vachon had ever met, made the assumption that the church had been deconsecrated just because Vachon chose to live there. Knight sauntered in and out of the place without any adverse effects just because he didn't know Vachon's dwelling was still, technically, holy ground.

Urs nodded as he took her arm. "And I warned her about LaCroix. Something you should have done," she added accusingly as they walked up stairs to the loft where he lived.

"When did I get the chance to talk to her?"

She sighed. "You're right."

"LaCroix really wasn't interested in what I had to say."

"I had hopes when I saw you talking to him."

"I know."

"It's out of our hands."

Urs took a seat on the beat-up old couch between Sasha and delicate, red-haired Camille. Larry lounged against a pile of pillows on the floor; nearby candlelight glinted off the gold hoops in his nose and in the multiple holes in his ears. Screed perched on a box in the shadows across the room from the others, with them but not completely part of the group.

Vachon was all too aware of their gazes on him as he leaned against a pillar next to the staircase. There hadn't been much discussion as, one by one, they arrived. Now that the old crew was assembled, he stepped forward and took over the role he'd tried so hard to abandon recently.

He rubbed his hands together. "So," he said, "what do we have?"

"Monsters," Camille said.

"Pot calling the kettle black on this one," Screed muttered. "Pot's a touch cleaner, though, I reckon."

Camille shot Screed an annoyed look. "I've seen this thing, rat catcher."

"Seen one m'self, darlin'." He leaned forward into a patch of candlelight, skull-ugly face transformed by glowing eyes and extended fangs. "Looked worse'n me, dinnit?"

"Never thought I'd agree with you on anything, Screed," Camille answered. "But it's definitely uglier than you. It's no *carouche*," she told the others.

"And there's more than one of them," Vachon said. "If the media are to be believed."

Camille said, "The one I saw used to be an Asian female. How about yours, rat catcher?"

"White. Goin' green," Screed said with a twisted smile. "And male."

"So we definitely have at least two of these things," Vachon concluded. "Whatever they are."

"The question is," Larry said, "what are they?"

"And what do we do about them, Javier?" Sasha asked.

Vachon shrugged. "Get them off the street, I suppose."

"But what do we do with them?" Urs questioned. "If they're our kind, we can't just destroy them."

"Why not?" Screed asked.

"You have to ask?" she questioned back.

"Me and mine's not nothin' but walking rotting meat, Blondie. Those ghoulies are." He looked disgustedly from Urs to Vachon. "Girl's too damn kind, mate. I say we kill 'em."

"Excuse me," Larry interjected, "but if they are nothing more than walking corpses, how do you suggest we—do them in?"

Screed scratched his bald head. "Oh, yeah. Right." He brightened. "Douse 'em in petrol? Wooshing up in a fireball ought do 'em."

"We ought to find out where they come from," Sasha said. "Stop the contagion at the source."

"Contagion?" Vachon asked. The word set off alarm bells in his psyche. He might not fear crosses, but vicious little bugs he couldn't see were another story. He wished he'd never let Sasha talk him into reading those books on emerging diseases. He wished the microscope had never been invented, since it was hard to be paranoid about something you didn't know about. Chances were that whatever caused vampirism also rendered their kind immune from disease—but you never knew when some virus was going to mutate, and feed on them the way their kind fed on humans.

"You think it's an illness?" he asked the Russian.

Sasha nodded. "Latest theory is that what we are is caused by some kind of blood aberration. That vampirism itself is a disease."

"Who says that?" Larry asked indignantly.

"Sasha, and some others, have been studying biochemistry and stuff like that," Vachon told the others.

The Russian nodded. "It is better to look to a scientific explanation of our condition than to be held in thrall to the superstitions of—"

"The capitalist running dog lackeys of the West," Larry ended for him.

"Comrades," Sasha added, with an amused grin.

"I thought communism turned out to be a myth," Camille said.

"No, vampires are myths," Sasha answered.

"Yeth, I am," Camille responded, and provocatively tossed her glorious red hair. They all laughed, but not for long. "Do you think these things are a mutation?" Camille asked. A shudder of fear went through the room when she added, "Do you think we can catch it from them?"

Sasha shrugged. They all looked at Vachon.

He was tempted to shrug as well. Instead, he found himself confiding, "Ever since AIDS came along, I've been worrying if I should wear a condom when I bite someone." He got sympathetic nods in response from the rest of the group.

"Maybe it's senility," Urs suggested after an uncomfortable silence. "Sort of vampire Alzheimer's."

Camille shuddered. "Now there's a horrible idea."

"Maybe they have nothing to do with us," Larry said.

"It followed me," Camille said. "I could feel it wanting to be with me."

"Me, too," Screed said. "They're vamps all right."

"You don't have to sound so gleeful about it, rat catcher," Sasha said. "Though I suppose it might be gratifying to discover a lower life-form than yourself."

Larry spoke up before Screed could reply. "You *carouches* could be useful in controlling these things."

Screed laughed. "Gonna 'ave us round 'em up, then baby-sit 'em for you? Oh, no, mate, I ain't sharing my sewer with any of that lot."

When Nick entered the church with the intention of giving Vachon the explanation he'd asked for, he was surprised to feel the presence of several of their kind on the second floor. He was even more surprised when he heard some of the younger ones conversation as he came up the steps to the loft. Their easy camaraderie was another surprise, though it shouldn't have been. It was just that he spent so much time trying to divorce himself from his former life that he forgot, especially without Janette there to remind him, that there was a community among his kind. Friendships, rivalries, careers, and conversations went on all the time among vampires.

To him it was a mockery of the true life they'd left

195

behind, a pretense at acting human. Then he gave a faint smile at the hypocritical irony of this thought, since he played at being mortal more than any of them. Perhaps the difference, the saving grace (if there was one), was that he desperately wanted to be a mortal among mortals.

Glancing at the group gathered in Vachon's loft as he reached the top of the stairs, Nick was reminded of those American situation comedies that were the current rage. Here were four young people, and a *carouche*, sitting around an apartment, sipping their favorite warm, dark liquid and discussing the problem of the week: in this case, revenants rather than romance, which was where the analogy got weird, and ended.

Everyone's attention was on Vachon when he said, "I asked Knight what these things are. He said he'd explain— later."

Nick knew he was sometimes considered stodgy and standoffish—"thick as a brick" was how Janette had put it—by the younger members of the community. But even he knew a cue that shouldn't be passed up when he heard it. He stepped up behind Vachon and tapped him on the shoulder.

"How about now?"

Vachon jumped—literally—about two feet in the air. He came down facing Nick, his big eyes even wider than usual. And bright yellow with defensive rage. They calmed quickly to their normal brown color as he recognized Nick.

Vachon blinked. "I should have expected that."

Nick moved to stand in the middle of the room. "I need your help," he told the group. "The revenants have to be hunted down and killed."

Vachon came to stand beside him. "We were just discussing that."

Nick watched the others silently regarding him. They were suspicious of his appearance among them, if not outwardly hostile. He got their grudging respect because abilities grew with age among their kind, and he was the second oldest vampire in the city. He barely knew any of them, except Vachon. He had contact with the Spaniard only because of their mutual connection to Tracy Vetter. Actually, Nick supposed he rather liked Vachon, and had developed a vague, sympathetic fondness for Urs in his few encounters with her. He was still a stranger and enigma to most of the city's younger vampires, and happy to keep it that way. The disadvantage to this attitude was that Vachon's crew eyed him warily as he faced them. They had no reason to trust him.

It was Sasha who spoke first. "By us, you mean."

"Why should we?" Camille asked. "Where did those things come from?"

"Can we kill them?" Larry asked.

"What's in it for us?" Screed wanted to know.

"What about the Enforcers?" Vachon questioned.

A psychic shudder went though the room at the word. Urs got to her feet. "What can we do to help, Nick?"

Nick reacted to the girl's generosity with a warm smile. Then, feeling time ticking relentlessly by, he answered their questions. "Yes, the revenants are created by a disease. They're mindless and easily destroyed." He quickly explained how, then added, "I'm responsible for destroying the one who causes the infection. Kill him, and there will be no more revenants, no more headless corpses for the police to investigate."

"Revenants? Headless corpses? Does this madman know how much he puts us at risk?" Vachon demanded angrily. "Do the Enforcers know about this guy? Are they going to blame us for letting him run loose in the city?"

"There were no Enforcers the last time this vampire walked among us," Nick answered. He shrugged. "As for the Enforcers blaming us, I can't say." He looked at Screed. "If we take care of the problem before the mortals find out about us, the Enforcers will probably overlook the whole incident. I would say that our kind's survival is what is in it for us."

"Guess we better hit the streets," Larry said. The boy with all the rings in his ears grinned broadly. "It sounds like fun."

Nick looked to Vachon. "Organize the hunt," he ordered.

Then he jumped out the nearest open window and took off for police headquarters. With the revenant problem taken in hand, he had another solution to set in motion, and not much time to do it in.

Radu, he vowed, was going to be dead again by dawn.

"She meant well," Tammy said to the picture over her bed. She spoke above the sound of the Nightcrawler's taped voice in the background. The live broadcast was over for the evening. She was replaying it while she waited for LaCroix. "But meaning well doesn't mean a thing in this world," she added.

She'd learned that long ago from social workers and foster parents and therapists. People kept feeling sorry for her. They kept telling her to want something different than what she knew she needed.

I wonder if meaning well means something in the next life, she mused, and smiled, just a little, as anticipation buzzed through her veins. She'd dried her tears and put the incident at the Raven behind her. Now she was ready to move on. In a way, the incident with her so-called biological father had made everything fall into place. Tammy's choice was made.

"Be sure of what you want," Urs had said before Tammy asked her to leave. The vampire woman had stood at the door, looking all sincere and worried, and added, "Don't let any male talk you into something *he* wants. You'll have a long time to regret your mistakes."

Urs had chosen her words very carefully. Tammy was amused at the other woman's deliberate ambiguity. She smiled at it as she selected what few things she wanted from her closet. Other women simply couldn't be trusted, even when they tried to be well-meaning.

"She was just being selfish," Tammy told the Night-crawler.

He was there only in spirit, of course, but she felt his presence all around her. Not just his voice, played so low it was almost subliminal, or his face in the signed photo on the wall. *He* was part of her. Soon she would be part of him.

"She's not happy with what she is, and thinks no one else should be, either. That's because you don't love *her*. She doesn't understand that you need me to need you." She gently stroked the picture frame, smiled at the unblinking black and white image. "You can't be whole unless you have someone to take care of. I won't be whole unless someone takes care of me." She smiled lovingly at the photo on the wall. "We're a perfect fit."

She looked at her watch. He would be here soon. There would be no need to worship an image, or a disembodied voice, ever again.

When someone knocked on her door, Tammy didn't assume it was LaCroix. He wouldn't bother knocking. She did think it was Urs. Tammy supposed Urs was intent on taking one more shot at talking her out of her destiny.

"This is *so* frustrating."

She almost didn't open the door. Then, when the knocking became quick and urgent, it occurred to Tammy that LaCroix might have sent Urs. Perhaps he was using Urs's warnings to test her determination to belong to him.

After searching for him for so long, Tammy wasn't about to fail any test he set for her now.

She hurried forward. "Coming."

The man who pushed his way into the apartment when she opened the door was the last person she expected to see.

"He told you to leave me alone!" Tammy shouted at her father as he shoved her backward.

He laughed at her outrage. He slammed the door and made sure it was locked. A quick look around assured him that the windows in the one room apartment were too small for his Tamara to crawl out of. There was only one way out, and she'd be leaving with him. "You're packing," he said as he took in the clothes on the bed. "Good. Hurry."

Instead of doing as she was told, like a good girl, she stood in the center of the room and glared at him defiantly. "He doesn't want you here." Then she smiled. "He'll kill you if he finds you here. He. . . ."

Drezerdic grabbed his daughter by the shoulders. "He, he, he. *He* isn't your father."

"He will be."

He slapped her. He hated having to hurt her, but his girl need discipline. "You've been alone for too many years. I couldn't help that, though I was in pain every day I was separated from you. I'll take care of you now. We'll

200

be together. No one but you and I. You belong to me. I won't let you become a whore like your mother."

"I belong to him!" Tammy's heart was racing. She didn't mind the throbbing pain across her cheek, but she hated the fear that had her trembling. It curdled in her stomach, and sent shock waves through her brain and limbs. She couldn't keep it at bay, but she knew it was wrong to be experiencing it. This man, this stranger, would pay for making her feel. Her emotions belonged to LaCroix!

Because she was so young, and it was hard for the young to understand things, Drezerdic said, slowly and carefully, "He's a bad influence. I've heard how he talks on the radio. Seductive, corrupting. He is evil, Tamara. Evil."

"Yes." Her adoring smile shocked him. Her eyes were full of love when she spoke. "The Nightcrawler is evil incarnate. I've searched my whole life to find him. You won't take me away from him. You're not evil enough," she added with a cruel laugh.

"I'm not an evil man."

He slapped her again. He felt how her skin was cold, how she shook with fear. It was right that she should fear her father, but he couldn't bear that she still spoke lovingly of the one he'd come to rescue her from. Anguish forced him to strike his child again. Her lip was cut, her nose bleeding, when he was done. Then he pushed her backward, forced her to sit on the bed. He stood over her, grabbed her chin, and forced her to look up to him.

"I am not evil. I am your father. I told you when they took me away that I would find you. Having you is all I've worked for all these years. I played every game, made myself be meek and cooperative, just to get to you.

The policewoman told me not to go into the Raven because she knew you were there. She hid you from me, but it didn't do any good. I came for you."

Tammy jerked her head out of his grasp. "I chose LaCroix. He ordered you to forget about me. You can't defy him!"

He stroked her hair, worshiping the feel of it as the silky dark strands slid through his fingers. "You are so beautiful. My doing. You look like me. You'll have to let your hair grow," Drezerdic went on. "And I don't like the way you dress. You won't go to those clubs again."

"He likes the way I dress. The Raven is his. I'll stay there with him."

"No."

Her adamant tone infuriated him. "He doesn't have the strength to keep you with him," Drezerdic said firmly. "You won't go there again. I know how to keep you with me. He can't keep me from being with you. I knew what he was doing when he stared into my eyes." He laughed. "I almost laughed at his silly mental game."

"He's playing a game now. You'll see."

Drezerdic ignored her childish words. "But I was too smart for him. I only pretended to obey. It was too public there. They wouldn't let us be alone. So I waited. I followed. I never thought the whore he sent with you would go away. Now we can be alone together. We'll always be together."

"No. Never. I hate you."

"You don't mean that, Tamara."

"Hate you," she said fiercely. So fiercely he almost believed her.

"You make me sad when you talk like that, Tamara."

"Tammy. I don't want your name. I'm Tammy. Or whatever the Nightcrawler wants to call me. I don't want any part of you," she added rebelliously. "I belong to him!"

She glanced past the hated intruder, toward the door. Soon he would come. Locks wouldn't matter to him, nor would the window glass. Perhaps time and space didn't matter, either. She sensed he was nearby. His dark spirit was rushing toward her, just on the edge of her awareness, relentless as the incoming tide. She was a vessel sensing the wine that would soon fill it. She took delight in being empty and waiting, knowing that she waited for him.

"This is another test," she told Drezerdic, confident, though her voice shook. "You're not strong enough to defy him."

Drezerdic couldn't help but laugh at his child's foolish words. There was so much he had to teach her. "I will not obey anyone who tells me to stay away from what is mine. No power is stronger than a father's love. Not even that monster will come between us." She tried to stand. He pushed her back down. "Don't make me have to punish you the way I did your mother. Please, don't force it to come to that."

"I'm going to be with LaCroix. Forever."

She was like her mother. That was a pity, but it could be dealt with. He would save her. What he had to do wasn't punishment, it was protection. It broke his heart, but it had to be done. "I'll keep you safe," he promised his daughter. He stroked her shoulders and throat. His hands on her soft skin were gentle, loving, as he murmured, "Don't be afraid."

She tried not to let him make her feel afraid. She tried to be happy about whatever game the Nightcrawler was playing. She stayed still, concentrated on the taped voice whispering reassuringly in the background, and tried to be good. Soon she'd be rid of this monster forever. *He* was near. It was going to be all right.

"The last thing you see will be LaCroix," she told the man who'd sired her, as his hands circled her neck.

"Javier?" Tracy's voice called from the bottom of the loft steps. "Can I come up?"

"Sure," Vachon called back, then turned to Sasha. "'Bye."

The big Russian was grinning broadly. "Didn't know the girlfriend was coming over, eh?"

"She's not my. . . ." As Tracy's footsteps pounded up the stairs, Vachon pointed at the open window. "Go," he told the last remaining member of his crew. Tracy knew about Urs and Screed and the others, but there was no reason for her to get to know every vampire in the city.

Sasha nodded. The last thing Vachon saw of him was his teeth gleaming in an amused grin just before he leaped out the window. He put the Russian out of his mind, and turned to face Tracy.

"Hey, Button," he said as she hurried toward him.

She came to a halt and grimaced. "Why did I ever tell you about my nickname?" Then she remembered her mission. "I need your help."

"I don't have time right now, Tracy." At her annoyed look he put his hands on her shoulders. "Really," he told her, "I honestly don't have time."

"You're going to have to make time. There's a vampire loose in the city. Yes, I know, there's probably dozens," she hurried on before he could make a comment. "But not like this one. I saw him. Worse, Nick Knight saw him. I'm certain he did. Because he left the crime scene right after this vampire flew overhead. There has to be a connection. Javier, we've got to find Nick. You've got to hypnotize him again—to keep him from finding out about your kind. If you don't want the world to know you exist, convincing Nick otherwise is your problem. My problem is to stop whoever is chopping off people's heads. It would help if I didn't have a constantly disappearing partner who's probably putting himself in danger by trying to chase down a vampire suspect. Of course he wouldn't ask Commissioner Vetter's little girl to help in something as dangerous as that."

She stopped speaking long enough to breathe.

While Tracy was replenishing her oxygen supply, Vachon said, "I see your point. Points? What you're getting at." He steered her toward the couch. "Sit down."

She moved with him reluctantly and resisted taking a seat. "I don't have time. I have to get back to work. There are people getting killed. I don't know if it has anything to do with the vampire that showed up near the crime scene or if that was some sort of freak coincidence, but. . . ."

"Do you really believe that was a coincidence?"

Tracy sat, then looked at him anxiously. "No," she admitted. "No, I don't."

"That's really what you want my help with, isn't it? Finding that vampire?"

He could feel her skin heat with a blush as she looked at the floor, then pleadingly up at him. "I could use your help with that, too," she conceded. "Is that why you came to Headquarters? To tell me about this vampire?"

"Uh—yeah. But I didn't get the chance to get near you."

"I've seen him myself now. He felt wrong."

Felt? Vachon filed Tracy's observation away, but he carefully didn't ask for an explanation. He knew what she meant, even though he didn't think she should be able to sense anything about vampires. It looked like she was not only a Resister, but a sensitive one as well. Somebody born to be bit, Screed would say.

No, he wasn't going to think about anything but the vampire/revenant problem right now. *Narrow your focus*, he told himself. *Concentrate on the revenants.* He might be annoyed that Knight had given him orders, but he had to agree with them. Those things had to be gotten rid of. First, though, he had to deal with Tracy.

He considered calming her down, lying to her, and sending her away. Then again, this was her case, she was involved. She hated the way people always tried to protect her. It seemed to Vachon that telling her what was going on, and giving her the choice of how she wanted to handle the knowledge, was the best way to deal with the situation.

Besides, she was the one who kept the vampire killing kit stored in a gym bag on the backseat of her car. He knew that since finding out vampires existed, she'd made a stake and the other traditional paraphernalia as much a part of her field equipment as her gun and cell phone. If there was one thing Tracy Vetter was better prepared for than anyone else on the police force, it was dealing with vampire perps.

What she did with the rest of the night was going to have to be up to her.

He ran a hand along his jawline as he mumbled, "Maybe after four hundred years I'm starting to get the hang of this maturity thing."

Tracy's glance was both puzzled and annoyed. "What?"

"Never mind." He put his arm around her shoulders. The gesture seemed affectionately casual but ensured she wouldn't move until he was finished. "Don't worry about Knight." She had no idea how much he enjoyed saying,

"I'll make sure your partner doesn't get hurt, or remember anything. I'll take care of him. Now," he added, "about the case—there's quite a lot I have to tell you."

While Nicholas's visit had been both annoying and amusing, it had also reminded LaCroix that there was something he wanted back.

"I do not let anything that belongs to me go easily. Should anyone? Shouldn't the direst retribution be reserved for those who attempt to take what is yours?" the Nightcrawler had asked this evening's audience. *"Property rights are the only rights that matter. There are Ten Commandments, I've been told, in a currently popular upstart religion. In order of appearance, 'Thou shalt not steal' ought to top the list. It should be the only commandment. What is murder but the theft of life? Adultery is theft of love. Coveting your neighbor's belongings is a depraved anticipation of theft. These are the commandments of the Lord—a grasping and avaricious godling, but one who recognized that getting and keeping is what the human animal is really all about. Not greed, but the need to have, hold, possess, is what drives us all."*

He'd spoken on the subject for quite some time. He refused to take any calls. It hadn't been a long broadcast. Long enough to give Tammy time for delicious anticipation of his arrival.

He enjoyed the building anticipation himself.

Flying across the city, on his way to claim his new possession, LaCroix's thoughts were still mostly centered on the thing that had been taken from him when his home was burglarized. Not the silver box—Nicholas was welcome to the old thing now that its spilled contents were out roaming the panic-stricken streets. It

207

would bring Nicholas trouble, for Radu would no doubt come looking for it.

Radu, he mused as he made his swift passage through the night sky, *has always understood the nature of ownership.* A small, victorious smile curved LaCroix's lips as he added, *He should have kept it in mind when he tried to take Janette from me.*

Tammy was no replacement for Janette. She was a foolish child, pathetic. Her hopeless worship was entertaining, but might threaten to become swiftly boring—if he didn't sense a potential for evil in the depths of her obvious madness. Developing that potential might prove an interesting challenge.

He chortled. "Nicholas is going to be so annoyed at having a bad little sister."

The first task he was going to give her after bringing her across, he decided, was to find his *numina.* The statue of his family's guardian god that had been stolen along with Radu's remains was probably stored in some police evidence room. Tammy could fetch it for him, and he'd make sure Nicholas was aware she was the one who'd broken into the police station. That would make for a fun introduction of the new brother and sister.

Her building was easy for him to find, even though she lived in a low-rent apartment complex with a dozen identical three-story structures. The call of mind to mind was one of the simplest of his kind's powers. All he had to do was concentrate, and Tammy's hunger for destruction drew him toward her. That she longed for it at his hand made the bond of hunter to prey even stronger.

The warm, pulsing energy of mortal blood mixed with mortal emotion was all around him in the city, but only one filament of mortality was linked to his own slow heartbeat. Nicholas would have said that her soul called to his. Nicholas would have shrunk in disgust from such connection. LaCroix rather liked the notion.

As he drew closer, he became aware of many twisting threads of emotions tangled around the girl. LaCroix felt her fighting to control those emotions. He sensed her trying to concentrate on nothing and no one but him, despite wild flashes of fear, anger, and uncertainty.

It was a concentration that was fading. All her emotions were fading into some sort of trancelike state. Yet he could still feel her thinking, *LaCroix, LaCroix, LaCroix.*

This was all very interesting. So interesting that he lingered in the air just over the roof of her apartment building to savor the lovely dark mix for a while.

First night jitters, my dear? he wondered as he floated on the breeze. *A spark of virginal terror of the unknown?*

It was too late for second thoughts. For either of them, LaCroix decided as he came to earth on the dark steps before the building's security door. The light was out over the entrance. The door, which should have been locked, opened at no more than a touch.

She was in the basement apartment, the one on the left at the very end of the hall. He was already tasting her blood on his tongue as he walked down the steps. Her door also was unlocked. He paused, his hand on the knob. Inside he heard a man's voice, speaking intently but very low. He listened for an intruder. After a moment he recognized the voice as his own, a tape of a Night-crawler broadcast. LaCroix wondered if he would find votive candles and flowers surrounding her tape player as he stepped into the room.

There were candles set on the dresser where the tape player sat, but no flowers. There was a picture of him over the bed. There were a pile of clothes and an open suitcase on the floor. Every light in the small apartment was on, but even with the added light from a half-dozen candles, the place was dim, washed in a gray aura. The air was moved by an unnatural breeze, and the room was very cold.

Pleading eyes stared at LaCroix out of the shadows. Someone sobbed, just on the edge of hearing. Invisible hands reached out to him.

He had always found such supernatural phenomena annoying wastes of time and energy. He refused to be disturbed by them or distracted. He gestured, as though he could flick the ghost away with an imperious wave of his hand. He concentrated his attention on the evidence of mortal violence.

Tammy's body was carefully arranged on the narrow bed, a pair of pillows tucked under her head. Bruise marks stood out vividly on the pale skin of her throat. He stepped forward and brushed a hand across her cheek. He bent forward to look into her sightless eyes. He touched the spot over her heart.

Nothing. Gone. Dead just when he would have given her eternal life.

Her spirit was in the room still. The ghost of Tammy waited for him, called, begged, beckoned, a thin shadow holding on to existence by fanatical will. He knew it was useless to pay it any mind. It would dissipate soon, or linger to haunt the spot where she'd died. Not even he could call it back. Her body was already growing cold. He could not share the blood of the dead, could not bring across flesh separated from essence.

She had been stolen from him.

Theft was the only sin.

Retribution would come for this theft tonight.

He stroked Tammy's hair one last time. "It looks as if

our plans for the evening have been changed." The already low temperature in the room dropped to freezing at LaCroix's cold words.

Then true anger took hold of him. His eyes took on the pale yellow tint of the arctic sun. The smile that stretched his lips was guaranteed to freeze mortal blood.

The last thing she'd heard was his voice. It was the last thing her killer would hear as well. LaCroix brought a fist down on the boom box, shattering it into a thousand pieces.

Then he left the crying ghost to its eternal, lonely fate.

14

"FIRST YOU WERE MISSING, NOW VETTER'S MISSING," CAPTAIN Reese complained as Nick made his way toward his desk. The big man blocked Nick's path as he demanded, "Couldn't you two be missing together once in a while?"

"Sorry, Captain."

"We've got another headless corpse for you to look at," Reese reported. "Found just outside a coffee shop near the Hockey Hall of Fame."

As he tried to ease by, Nick said, "You make it sound like that's desecrating holy ground, Captain."

"I don't have time for humor right now, Nick."

And Nick didn't have time to investigate a fresh murder. Pretending to investigate wouldn't help when he already knew the cause. What he had to do was eradicate the cause. He gave Reese a stern look. "I'm not here," he told him.

The big man blinked, then walked away. Nick continued across the squad room.

Once at his desk, he sat down and did something he rarely needed to do; he turned on the computer and did

213

some actual investigative work. His vampire's enhanced speed proved useful in reading and correlating data Tracy and the rest of the Homicide Squad had begun to put together. It wasn't long before he sat back and gave himself a moment to consider options. The night was running away from him, so Nick didn't have too much time for thought. With a nascent plan in mind he went to talk to Natalie.

"But Dr. Lambert, we already know the cause of death on this one," said the eager assistant the Coroner's Office had insisted she needed.

As he spoke, Natalie saw Nick enter the autopsy room. She had managed to steer the rest of her night staff to other lab duties, but this gung-ho rookie pathologist was following her around like a puppy. She gave Nick a look that was intended to keep him lingering near the door while she dealt with the situation.

Natalie pointed at the covered bodies of two bite victims on the other autopsy tables. "I've got a pretty good idea of what killed them as well, Dr. Payton." And she had to cut their hearts out before either of them sat up and gave young Dr. Payton the surprise of his life. She pointed toward the headless cadaver she'd asked Payton to start the protocol on. "These beheadings have a higher priority than the animal attacks," she reminded the younger doctor. "I know you're eager to get all the experience you can, but you're here to help with the bigger case." She touched the headless body's shoulder while Payton continued to look eagerly at the bodies on the tables behind her. "You start on this one, while I make the initial incisions on the others." Those hearts had to come out, and now.

Payton looked at her in puzzlement. Was that a hint of

suspicion she saw in his eyes? Or was working with a vampire turning her paranoid? Natalie wondered if she looked menacing as she picked up a bone cutter.

"Why on both of them?" he asked.

Nick received the expected annoyed look from Nat when he got tired of waiting and stepped forward. Perhaps it would be better, more like mortal behavior, to let her deal with this, but they didn't have the time for such niceties. The city didn't have the time. So he stepped forward, and for the second time in the last hour, Nick prepared to use his mind-control abilities.

"Dr. Payton." When the young man turned his way, Nick made eye contact. "Go get a cup of coffee."

"Good thing he isn't a Resister," Nat said when the door closed behind Payton. "Help me," she added as she turned to the revenant victims. "No, don't," she decided as Nick uncovered one of the naked bodies. "Your way is too messy, and I've already got enough explaining to do."

Nick stepped away from the table, impatient but knowing that what Natalie was doing was necessary. Removing the two hearts would take precious time, but it wasn't wasted time. He watched her work with bone cutter and scalpel. She was deft, quick, and competent. As she performed hasty surgery on the corpses, her expression became more and more annoyed. Her eyes flashed when she turned to him after placing the dead men's slowly beating hearts in a metal dish.

"What?"

Natalie stripped off her surgical gloves and threw them in the trash. "You *really* shouldn't have sent Payton away like that."

He stepped close and put his hands on her shoulders.

"I knew you could handle it, Nat. I wasn't usurping your authority as a coroner."

"You were being thoughtless with your powers. It's dangerous for you to be thoughtless."

"I was trying to be helpful."

"Do you want to be mortal, Nick? Really? Do you *ever* listen to anything I tell you? You have to act mortal *all* of the time. Not just when it's convenient."

He hated not just the anger but the look of disappointment in her eyes. "Tonight," he told her, "it's more convenient to be a vampire. I hate what I am. I want to be mortal. But tonight I have to fight a very powerful one of my own kind, and I need your help."

Natalie's anger faded under Nick's fierce response. She wondered if he knew the iron-hard strength of his intense grip on her shoulders. She sighed. "It's risky for you to do things like hypnotize people, Nick. But you aren't here to discuss your treatment. What kind of help do you need?"

Nick stepped back reluctantly, for Natalie's mortal warmth was a comfort in this cold room full of dead men. He took the silver box from his pocket, weighed it on his palm for a moment, then handed it to her.

"It's beautiful. And heavy." Natalie ran her thumbs along the embossed design on the lid and sides. "And familiar." She looked back at Nick. "Isn't this evidence from the antique shop?"

Nick took the box back. He held it up so that the overhead lights gleamed off its rich surface. "This," he told her, "is how we trap Radu." He tucked it back in the deep pocket of his black coat. "But not without your help." He held out his hand to her. "Come with me. Right now."

Natalie looked around the autopsy room. "I'm needed

here, Nick. What if more revenant victims are brought in?"

"They won't be," he promised. At her skeptical look, he explained, "Our community is taking care of that part of the situation."

"Vampires are hunting down the revenants?"

He held a finger up to his lips. "Not so loud, Nat." He nodded, and whispered, "You won't have to cut out any more hearts tonight." He had something far more dangerous in mind.

At Nick's words, a tenseness of mind and body, of which Natalie had been only subliminally aware, dissipated all of a sudden. She found herself almost limp with relief. She had been afraid, she realized. Afraid of having to face anymore awakened revenants. She didn't want to admit to fear—not of the supernatural, the unknown, because that raised the possibility of fearing Nick. That could not be. For the sake of their relationship, she could never allow herself *that* sort of fear.

She took a deep breath and made herself say, calmly and confidently, "You said something about wanting me to come with you. Where? What do you want me to do?"

Nick supposed he had better fill Natalie in before asking for a very big favor. "Radu is looking for the silver box. The antique store has been broken into twice since its owner was killed. The place was torn apart both times."

"Radu's doing?"

Nick nodded. "He was always obsessed with anything made of silver." He patted his coat pocket. "This box is especially important to him."

Probably because Radu's somewhat sentient remains had rested in it for hundreds of years. That some sort of awareness lingered with the old ones even after their bodies were completely destroyed was a guess on Nick's part, but he was certain enough of the truth of it that he was reluctant to share the knowledge even with a trusted mortal. It would be dangerous for them both if he were to reveal too much about his kind. He had broken faith with his kind many times since meeting Natalie. For the sake of their friendship, and his growing hope of regaining his mortality, he had already revealed far more about vampires to her than was safe for any mortal to know. This time he kept silent.

Before she could ask him why the box was so important to Radu, he said, "Just trust me when I say that Radu wants the thing back very badly. I want to use it—and you—as a lure."

Natalie went pale, but that was the only outward sign of the terror he felt rush through her at his words. She stuffed her hands in the pockets of her lab coat—in an effort to keep from showing that they were shaking, he guessed.

"I see." Her voice was the calm, detached one he was used to hearing from Dr. Lambert as she performed an autopsy.

She didn't see, but Nick was grateful for the way Natalie coped with the unknown. "Radu isn't used to the modern world," he explained hurriedly. "He wasn't used to the modern world in the eighteenth century. He's never going to be able handle the twentieth."

"He may not be good at coping, but he's very good at killing. Not to mention having a second career as a disease vector. He's tearing the city apart, Nick."

"All he can do is kill," Nick insisted. "He can't adjust. He can't learn to rein in his hunger. He has great power, but he's sloppy and insane. Doomed—but I'd rather see him destroyed sooner than later, and without tipping off the world to my kind's existence."

She nodded. "Agreed. But why do you need me?"

Nick hated to spend any more time on persuasion. Then he reminded himself that Natalie had to make the decision to put herself in jeopardy. "I need a mortal's help to pull this off. And Radu's always been very attracted to beautiful women."

"I see." Natalie turned her back to him.

He watched her in silence. She seemed small and fragile at this moment. He normally didn't think of her that way. He was very afraid of losing her, but he had no other choice. This was their best shot at ridding the world of a monster—one more time.

It was only seconds, but it seemed ages before she said, "You want to use me as bait in a trap."

Nick thought of a dozen different ways to phrase his answer, but settled on "Yes."

Natalie turned toward him. Her eyes were bright with what might be the glitter of unshed tears. It made him want to take her in his arms and comfort her, but he did no such thing. *It's nerves*, he told himself. *She's having a reasonable reaction to a frightening situation.*

Natalie managed to keep her voice steady. "All right. I'll change out of my lab clothes and meet you at your car." She added to herself, *And I want to get something from my locker.*

They liked vampires.

That was what Screed and Camille had said. Not in so many words, Vachon corrected himself as he strolled casually along the packed clay walking trail. The revenants didn't *like* anything. The poor creatures were well beyond anything resembling emotions. They had *needs*. Apparently the creatures were drawn to vampires.

Like moths to flames, or some such analogy. Groupies to rock stars? He smiled into the darkness, and paused to look at the bright stars overhead. It was a lovely night; as a connoisseur of darkness, he should know. Neither heat nor cold affected him on a physical level, but he still enjoyed the slight coolness of the late night air. He enjoyed the way the tree leaves brushed against the indigo sky. He liked the thick, black, still darkness of this wooded park deep in the heart of the city. Life around him was muted. He almost felt alone. It was very hard for his kind, with their enhanced senses, ever to feel alone. Lonely, yes, but that was another story, and Vachon wasn't feeling lonely tonight.

It was hard to feel lonely when you were being stalked. He'd come to this park because Tracy had said the police were getting quite a few reports of what were officially called animal attacks here. The park had been cordoned off, sensibly abandoned to the night by mortals. Tracy had made a call that had sent the officers assigned to patrol a different part of the wooded area. Their absence had left Vachon free to go for a walk in the woods. He'd been walking up and down the path for the last forty minutes. He could feel the seconds of the night sifting away. He could almost, but not quite, feel something else out there in the darkness.

He wanted to hunt, but he let himself be hunted. It was Tracy's idea to use a vampire as bait to catch a worse monster. "I saw *Jurassic Park*, you know," he said out loud. "I know what happened to the goat." No answer came from the deeper darkness under the trees. He sighed. "Revenants aren't big on conversation, I suppose." Of course the goat hadn't been put out as bait. It had always been intended as an entree.

Were revenants drawn to vampires out of sheer, mindless hunger? Did the creatures long to feast at the source? Did the blood of a vampire do anything to improve a revenant's I.Q. or chances for survival?

Are we brain food for those guys? he wondered. Knight hadn't been at all clear on any facts about the creatures. "I have a few questions that I don't want answered the hard way," Vachon said as he reached the shore of the pond at one end of the path. He looked out at the small stretch of smooth water, and listened to the world behind him with all of his senses for a few moments.

He had on his hunter's smile when he turned back and headed for the other end of the path.

With each step he fought the urge to fly forward. He kept his feet on the ground and stuck with the game plan, but it wasn't easy. He felt it drawing closer to him at last. He felt its hunger, felt its aura of putrefying evil. Mostly he felt its emptiness, its wrongness. Creatures like the revenants didn't belong in the world. A dead thing walking, Screed had called it. What was worse, it was a dead thing that projected its condition along with its sour, rotting stench. The closer he got, the more affected he was by it. The aura it gave off was enough to make a four-hundred-year-old vampire who thought he'd seen everything, want to scream and run away.

Instead, Vachon said, "Let's get this over with." He quickened his pace toward the revenant.

Fifteen feet further on, around a gentle curve in the path, he came face to face with the thing. It wore a leather vest and jeans; its pale, tattooed arms and chest were bare. Recently it had been a long-haired young man. The revenant's clothing and skin were crusted with dirt and dried blood. Bone showed through several wide gashes in the thing's skull. A flap of skin hung down like a patch over one eye. The revenant's other eye locked onto Vachon like a homing beacon.

Vachon stared back, hopelessly searching for some life in the blasted depths. He found no light, no awareness, no soul. He did see craving, hunger, addiction without understanding. This thing didn't know what it needed. It was need, elemental and awful.

The revenant's hunger washed over Vachon. It left him stunned, almost stupefied. He stood still as it came closer.

It reached for him.

Vachon held out his hands as the monster drew closer. He heard footsteps rushing forward from under the trees. The revenant began to turn his head in the direction of the noise.

"Now!" Vachon shouted. He grabbed the revenant by the wrists.

Tracy wielded the three-foot sharpened ash branch like a spear. She ran forward with it held at shoulder level, firmly grasped in both hands. She kept her thoughts focused on what she had to do rather than letting herself think or feel. She knew the thing she ran toward was horrible and hideous, a monster that clawed and chewed and ripped its victims apart to get at their blood. She couldn't let herself look or think about it as anything other than her target. Because if she did, the urge to run away screaming would take hold.

She'd always been a strong runner. The speed she built on the short sprint out of the cover of the woods added to the force of the blow as the pointed stake penetrated the revenant's back.

Syrupy, stinking blood splattered her as the force of the blow drove the revenant forward. Its body collided hard with Vachon's. They both went down, the screaming revenant sprawled on top of the vampire.

"Javier!" she called anxiously.

She could do no more than hope for an answer. Instead of trying to pull her friend from underneath the monster she had to hold onto the stake. Javier had been very clear that the wood had to remain in the monster's heart until it stopped moving. She was tossed around, and had to keep her grasp on the stake. Tracy concentrated all her energy on keeping the creature impaled until it was truly dead.

Vachon fought to keep his hold on the revenant. The thing on top of him was heavy, and it wasn't taking a stake in the heart quietly. It fought fiercely for its non-life. The stake had speared the creature's heart and come out the other side. Vachon could feel the sharp tip of the deadly wood scrape against his own chest as the revenant's body thrashed and twitched on top of him.

It took long, endless seconds before the revenant finally stopped moving. It seemed like forever before the dead body became truly lifeless. It was a heavy piece of rotting meat that Vachon finally pushed away.

Vachon gave Tracy a wary look as he got to his feet. He touched a spot on his now filthy shirt that had been torn by the point of the stake. "Good work. You're very skillful with a stake."

She was breathing very hard. Her clothes and hair were mussed. She rubbed sore, sweaty palms on her jeans. "Thanks."

Vachon touched the flesh over his heart. "I'm not sure if it should be a compliment, coming from one of my kind. You been taking lessons from Buffy?"

"What?"

Tracy thought she was going to be sick. She had just driven a stake through the heart of a creature of the night. It smelled terrible. It looked like a monster straight out of hell. Now another creature of the night had just made what was probably a joke, and she didn't get it. She didn't care.

The creature of the night gently put an arm around her shoulders. Javier turned her away from the corpse and led her a few feet upwind of it. "Never mind," he said. "It was a good plan. I'm glad it worked."

Tracy couldn't bring herself to look back at the thing on the ground. "What do we do now? We can't let that body be taken to the morgue."

Before Javier could answer, Tracy jerked her head around as her eyes tried to follow a sudden flash of movement. Before she could even blink, Screed was standing in front of them.

"This is where my lot comes in, luv," he said. To Vachon he added, "Decided to put a word in the ear 'ere and there. Got my kind doing garbage pickup. Like always."

"Thanks, Screed," Vachon answered. "I appreciate it."

"You're the only one who does, mate." Screed went over and picked up the revenant's remains. "Not to worry," he said, then took off again.

"What about . . ." Vachon began to call after him, but Sasha landed beside him before he could finish.

"You were about to ask how the rest of us are doing?"

"Yes."

"Hello," Sasha greeted Tracy. His smile was warm but showed just a bit of fang. "I admire your beauty and prowess. But please remember we're on the same side tonight."

"Hey, I'm *not* Buffy the Vampire Slayer," Tracy answered, having finally gotten the meaning of Javier's earlier joke.

Vachon frowned meaningfully at the Russian, who nodded respectfully in reply. "The hunt goes well," Sasha reported. "I have taken out one revenant. Urs and Camille have made another kill."

"Good."

"This is fun," Sasha said. "I'm going to hunt with Larry now." He gave them a wild grin, then took off once more.

When they were alone, Tracy said, "There can't be too many more, can there?"

"Let's hope not. Do you want to go looking for another one?"

Tracy shook hair out of her face, then gave him a grin that mirrored Sasha's. "Yeah."

He would have liked to take some part of her with him, but he knew it would be useless. She was lost to him, but her soul was safe. There had been no way to save her mother. At least he'd been able to do one good thing with his life. He was sorry it had to be this way, desperately sorry. They wouldn't understand, of course. The authorities would see it as murder again. They didn't understand about justice, or a man's duty to protect what was his. He'd learned not to try to explain.

He didn't return to his apartment. He didn't stay with Tamara in hers, either. How could he remain in a place *his* child had made into a shrine to another? It wasn't her fault, of course. They had taken her father from her when she was young and in need of his guidance.

"Too late," he murmured sadly. He sighed.

He sat on a bench beneath a streetlight. With his hands

resting on his knees, he watched the traffic go by. Buses stopped at the corner every few minutes, the intervals between their arrivals growing longer as the night wore on. He watched the buses pass, but never got on when they stopped and the doors opened. He heard the mechanical huffs and squeaks and sighs nearby, but kept looking straight ahead. He never moved. He had found Tamara; now he had nowhere else to go. There was nothing more he needed to do.

Someone in authority would come for him soon. Or perhaps he would go to a police station. It didn't matter. All he wanted to do was wait here, alone, thinking about the family he should have had, until morning. He spent the time mourning all his losses, regretting what he'd been forced to do.

Every now and then someone would take a seat on the other end of the bench. They never stayed long. He paid them no mind. He treasured his time alone too much to share it with strangers.

It was very annoying when a man sat down beside him and gave every appearance of staying. The stranger sat too close, for one thing. There was room enough on the bench for two. There was no reason for anyone to be so close beside him. Drezerdic tried to pay the newcomer no mind. He was very good at ignoring people. He focused his thoughts on his child, his wife.

The man was big. Even without looking at him, Drezerdic was aware of the intruder's menacing size. His presence seemed to devour the very air around them. Drezerdic had learned all about intimidation in prison, how size was far more than a physical thing. This man was large, but that wasn't what made him imposing.

Drezerdic wanted nothing to do with this stranger, but he couldn't make himself get up and walk away. Gradually, though he fought the process, his attention was drawn away from thoughts of his Tamara. Eventually, the intruder beside him filled Drezerdic's very small world.

He looked at the stranger's feet first. He wore expensive shoes, the dark leather brightly polished. They looked new, as though they'd never been walked in. The stranger's long legs were crossed, with one elegant, pale hand rested on his knee. There was something very odd about the man's hand. At first Drezerdic thought it shone so white because of the streetlight, or in contrast to the black material of the man's trousers. But he soon realized that the whiteness of the man's hand was very real, and unnatural.

It was as though the stranger were—dead.

In the fraction of an instant after this realization, the Nightcrawler flexed his pale fingers, and said, "All the better to strangle you with. Not that you'll be that fortunate, of course."

Drezerdic couldn't keep from looking at the monster's face now. He should have looked at him sooner. Should have recognized the man seated so uncomfortably near as the fiend who had polluted his daughter. As the pale demon smiled at him now, Drezerdic knew he should have looked up the instant the creature appeared. He should have looked up, and run. He should run now.

But he couldn't run. The Nightcrawler looked into his eyes, and he couldn't even move. He'd been able to resist him before, but now, but now. . . .

"But now," the monster said — it was a deeply amused drawl. "Now, you have nothing to live for. Pity." A hint of anger, a hint of the fires of hell, came into his inescapable eyes. "Because I would very much like to take something more than your worthless life from you before the sun comes up."

The Nightcrawler wasn't whispering. There were some street people with nowhere else to go loitering nearby. A bus pulled up, then huffed off. There were some cars in the street. Drezerdic was aware of everything going on around them, that there were people all around him as his life was being threatened. He knew he and the Nightcrawler were utterly alone.

It would do him no good to call for help. When it came down to it, he didn't really want to.

"I have the only thing that matters," he told the creature who was going to kill him. It took all his strength, but he was able to smile. "She won't be with you. She's safe."

LaCroix was not surprised by the look of triumph on the mortal's face. He wasn't surprised by his words. They were galling, just the same. He put a hand on Drezerdic's wrist, and squeezed until the only expression on the man's face was one of agony. The man looked much better with his mousy features twisted in pain. LaCroix didn't keep it up for long. People who were in too much pain couldn't pay attention.

"It would be futile and petty to argue over whom she belonged with. I know how you feel about property rights. Believe me, I understand," LaCroix said with all the conviction of his over eighteen hundred years. He was almost sympathetic when he went on. "I understand how a father feels about a child who wants to leave his protection. You have to be strong, you must discipline them for their own sake. You must make them behave. Children cannot be allowed to do everything they want."

LaCroix paused while Drezerdic gave him an agreeing nod. Pathetic, poisonous creature.

It wasn't even worth the effort to torture the fool. Drezerdic would never regret for an instant what he had done. LaCroix had given a great deal of thought about how the man would die as he hunted him down. Imagining detailed scenarios of Drezerdic's deserved end had been a balm to his own pain, a way of keeping his mind off the image of the dead girl lying on the bed. The reality was that this mortal's death was really no more than an afterthought, the inevitable end to a very unpleasant evening.

"It's quite pathetic, actually."

LaCroix gave a quick look at the nearby street people, who immediately moved away. He checked the sky. Dawn was very near. The last bus had come and gone. Cars were few and far between on the street. He wasn't worried about witnesses, but he saw no reason to upset Nicholas unduly over his evening's activities. He turned his attention to Tamara's biological father for the last time.

"You're going to die now," he told Drezerdic. "Not because you took her from me." LaCroix's anger had cooled, but the stab of grief for the mortal girl surprised him. He stood up and moved behind the bench. Drezerdic didn't have time to move away, but he didn't even try to make the effort. LaCroix put his hands around Drezerdic's throat. "No one who kills his own child deserves to live."

How Divia would have laughed to hear him say that.

He broke Drezerdic's neck as he spoke, a gesture that took no more effort than swatting a bug. He let the body slump forward and walked away. The sun was coming up. It was time to go home—to spend the long, melancholy day alone.

15

"How much time have we got?" Natalie asked as she followed Nick into the elevator.

"Not much."

She pressed a floor number, and the copperplated doors silently slid closed. This late, or this early, depending on how you looked at it, they didn't have to worry about sharing the elevator car with anyone else. She had seen no one but two or three members of the hotel staff scattered across the gigantic lobby as they crossed it after a quick stop at the front desk. She and Nick had received a few looks, but no real interest, from the people they passed.

The hotel was enormous, one of those big, modern glass and steel structures that stood in the heart of the city. It was functional, near everything, housing conventions and trade shows that were good for the economy. Natalie wasn't sure if she thought the building was beautiful, but it was certainly impressive. It was also just the sort of place Nick said they needed.

When the elevator stopped, Nick put his hand on

Natalie's elbow and hurried her down a hallway. Heavy carpeting deadened the sound of their footsteps. All the doors they passed were closed. Nick ignored all sensory glimpses of the life going on inside those closed-off rooms. He didn't ignore the sensory impressions he received from his physical contact with Natalie, but he was careful not to comment on them. He didn't have to be a vampire to know that she was frightened but determined not to show it. He also knew that the silence spooked her. She felt like they were the only living beings in the enormous building. Nick might have tried to make a joke by pointing out that she was the one who was living, but he thought better of it. Better not to let her know that his kind had a certain amount of telepathy. Besides, it was never wise to dispute his physical condition with the doctor who worked so hard to cure him.

They went left at one crossing of corridors, right at another. He'd memorized the layout of the building during an assignment the year before. "Stairway's this way." They reached a doorway, which Nick opened with one sharp tug, then hurried up three flights of darkened stairs. He forced open another door. They moved cautiously into another broad hallway. Nick knew that the cameras monitored by the hotel security staff were turned off unless the function rooms on this part of the floor were in use, as were the fire alarm and sprinkler systems. Despite having been fined by safety inspectors several times, this policy saved the hotel money, and was perfect for what he had planned. He pointed the way to the ballroom to Natalie. An art gallery that also served as a reception area was located on another part of the floor. Nick went to make sure any security guards who might be assigned to patrol the area took a nice long nap.

He came back to find Natalie standing in the middle of the empty ballroom. She'd found a switch and turned on a wall sconce near the door, but floor-to-ceiling velvet curtains kept the room swathed in soft, enveloping darkness. Nat seemed tiny and lost beneath the one small light. The floor was marble, and he made sure she heard his footsteps as he approached.

"Do they house aircraft in this place when they aren't having parties?" she asked as he came up to her. Her voice was soft, but still produced a faint echo in the vast, velvet-lined darkness. "This place must have its own climate."

"It's big," he agreed. "And the view is awesome. I remember how Schanke couldn't get over it that night we were assigned to play bodyguards here. He kept saying he felt like he was flying over the city." With aching regret, Nick recalled how his last partner had died: in an airplane that had exploded just as he was flying over the city. Nick touched Nat's shoulder. The gesture was meant to be reassuring, but he drew assurance from the sympathetic look she gave him. Maybe he wasn't the only one who could read minds. "I better go."

"You better," she agreed. "Before I chicken out and change my mind."

He kissed her temple. "You're the bravest woman I've ever known. You won't do that."

Nick barely heard her call after him, "I bet you say that to all the girls," as he hurried away.

Silver drew him, as it always had. Radu stood before the mound of gold and silver and jewels, and wondered once again at the purpose of such displays. The building before him did not look like a palace. It was small, made of painted brick like so many others on the long, long, straight roadway. There were no guards at the door. Only a thin metal grate and a wall of the substance that felt like

233

glass to the touch, but was far too thin and clear to really be glass, separated Radu from the treasure inside.

This world made no sense. All Radu could suppose was that the treasures were put out for the world to see as a statement of some proud merchant's wealth. Or perhaps the ruler of this land imposed such harsh penalties that no one dared to commit any sort of theft. Radu had known of such a prince once. In Wallachia in the days of Prince Vlad, it had been said that the air was full of the stench of corpses rotting on impaling stakes, but there had been very little crime.

A few minutes before, he had fed on a beggar sleeping in the shelter of the treasure house doorway. He'd not bothered to take more than a few sips from the mortal's torn throat, so a great deal of blood had spilled onto the smooth stone walkway when he pulled the corpse's head off. Radu stepped into a sticky puddle of the stuff as he grasped the metal grate and ripped it aside. Bells sounded as he smashed through the clear barrier. He didn't think the loud, irritating clamor sounded to announce the dawn, though he knew it was near. He left bloody footprints as he swept up a handful of silver and ran away.

With cool silver tucked greedily in his fist, Radu took to the air in search of shelter. Today he would sleep with treasure, like a dragon on its hoard. Silver would bring peace, and guard his dreams once more.

As Nick searched the brightening sky for signs of Radu he was more worried about being seen by a mortal on the ground below than he was about the impending appearance of the sun. At least for the moment. Flying across the city was safe enough under the cover of darkness, but right now he felt vulnerable.

It was good to know that the one he hunted was just as vulnerable as he was to the light. Age was no protection from the sun or fire. It was just the opposite. He knew that Radu would be seeking a haven from the daylight right now. The trick was to cut him off before he went to ground. Nick could sense that Radu was nearby, but that still left many blocks of territory for him to cover.

It was the sound of the burglar alarm, closely followed by police sirens, that gave Nick the break he needed. He paused, hovered in the air, and listened until he pinpointed the source of the sound. He flew north and spotted Radu flying away from the scene in moments. A stray glimmer of humor almost caused Nick to take out his cellular phone and announce that Detective Knight was in aerial pursuit of the burglary suspect.

He flew as fast as he could, very nearly at the speed of sound, in an effort to keep Radu from sensing his approach. When he caught up, Nick called out, "Looking for this?"

At the sound of the hated voice behind him, Radu slowed his flight and spun to face Nicholas. The boy floated arrogantly before him, baring his fangs in a cold smile. He held a small silver box cupped in his hands.

Radu felt his eyes go wide at the sight. A shiver ran through his being. The silver. The silver was right there before him. He would not be taunted with the most precious thing in the world by LaCroix's disobedient pup!

Radu lunged forward. "Thief!"

Nick barely managed to dodge out of the enraged vampire's way. Radu hurtled past him and downward. The old vampire nearly touched the ground before he halted his plunge and sprang back toward Nick. Nick quickly stuffed the box back into his pocket before Radu got to him.

"Peace," he called before Radu attacked again.

"Thief!" Radu accused again. "I'll take your heart out."

"I'm no thief," Nick said quickly. "I came to return

235

your property." He held up his hands. "I came to make amends."

The two vampires flew slowly around one another in a circle. They stayed out of reach for the moment while Radu seemed to consider what Nick had said. Nick heard a car horn blast beneath them, but didn't look down to see if the noise was caused by some hapless mortal having seen them. He couldn't worry about being spotted now, not when he needed to keep all his attention focused on a very dangerous enemy.

"Amends?" Radu finally sneered at him. "For what? What do you want from me, pup?"

"LaCroix is responsible for your being here, Radu," Nick told him. "Neither you nor I have any reason to be friends with LaCroix."

Radu laughed. It was a loud, hysterical sound that Nick was sure could be heard throughout the city. "You want me to help you fight your maker? Is that it?" Radu didn't sound convinced. He held out a blood-crusted hand. A thick silver chain spilled out of it and tumbled to the earth. "Give me back what is mine."

Nick forced himself to smirk, to exude sincerity. Each second that ticked away brought a bit more warmth pressing against his exposed skin. His eyes began to ache, even though the morning light was still very weak. "I want to help you," he told Radu. "In return for your aid, I'll give you back what is yours." He waved an arm toward the east, where the rim of the sun was beginning to glint on the horizon beyond the CN Tower. "Not here. There's no time. Follow me!" he shouted, and raced across the pink-tinted sky. It was going to be a clear day, and a hot one. The way the light already scorched him, Nick was afraid he'd waited too long to flee.

He didn't bother entering the hotel by the lobby entrance when he returned, with Radu in swift pursuit.

Nick landed on the roof, then wrenched off a maintenance access door in his hurry to get inside ahead of the dawn. He streaked down the service stairs, careful to note the floor number on each landing, all too aware of the furious madman racing at his heels.

Nick slowed after he reached the floor he wanted, but kept ahead of Radu until they entered the vast, dark ballroom. Once inside, Nick moved to keep himself between Radu and the door. It was the only way in, and Radu wasn't going out again.

"It's safe here," he told the old vampire. "Dark as any tomb."

Radu looked around the hall where Nicholas had brought him. His guess was that they had ventured deep into the heart of a palace. "What prince owns this place?" he questioned.

"You could," Nicholas answered, voice soft and seductive. "If you wish."

The hall was half-moon shaped. One long, straight wall was covered in white marble that shone even in the near darkness. The long wall that curved at Radu's back was completely concealed by a vast hanging of the richest cloth Radu had ever seen. He marveled at the hundreds of yards of black velvet, and the arrogance of the lord so secure in his strength that he hadn't bothered with any decoration. Instead of heraldic banners or painted armor to declare his lineage and conquests on the tapestry of his great hall, the owner of this palace allowed an emperor's ransom of black velvet to speak of his wealth and power.

There was a mortal woman standing, still and silent, in the corner where white marble met the night-dark velvet. Radu felt her presence but ignored her for the moment.

He concentrated on Nicholas, who once more held Radu's most precious possession cradled in his palms.

Radu wanted more than anything to snatch it away from the young troublemaker. He forced himself to wait, to be patient. He would hear what Nicholas had to say before deciding whether to rip the life from him.

"You want this," Nicholas said. He tossed the box from hand to hand as though it meant nothing, stopping only at Radu's warning growl. "You need my help to survive in this hostile place. LaCroix brought you here, not I."

Radu folded his arms across his chest while he gave Nicholas a speculative look. "You want me to kill LaCroix?"

Nick smiled as sincerely as he could in the face of such an unpredictable opponent. He wasn't actually lying when he said, "Killing LaCroix would be doing me a favor. What's important to me," he went on over the sound of Radu's booming laughter, "is for the public killings to stop."

Radu's laughter abruptly died. His gaze went cold. "I feed where I choose. On whom I choose."

"You can't," Nicholas told him.

His words were not arrogant, Radu finally understood, but earnest. The boy had always been earnest. "And why not?"

"Our kind cannot kill indiscriminately and survive here. There are too many mortals. They are too organized. Their city guards are far too vigilant. They are too quick to notice unexplained deaths. They hunt criminals without mercy."

Radu nodded his understanding. He was reminded of the laws of Vlad of Wallachia once more. Their kind had had trouble hunting in that land, too.

"Surely you have noticed by now," Nicholas went on, "that things are very different here from the world you remember."

Radu nodded again. "This place is mad."

"Then you should fit right in," Nick muttered under his breath. "You *need* my help," he said aloud, and waited for Radu to protest.

"You keep saying *need*."

"We all have needs."

Nick put the box on the floor. He slid it across the smooth marble surface toward Radu with his foot. Even he barely saw the old vampire move to snatch up his beloved piece of silver.

Radu clutched the box lovingly to his chest. "The silver!" The words were spoken with the fervency of a prayer.

"Your home for the last two hundred years."

Radu's shocked gaze flashed to meet Nick's eyes. "So long?"

"LaCroix kept you a prisoner. Now you are free."

Radu's fingers stroked the patterned sides of the box. Nick watched carefully while he counted off the passing seconds. A little longer. He had to draw this out a little longer.

"Free," Radu said. "Now I am free." He slipped the box into the front of his tattered, filthy shirt. "Now I have all I need. Or perhaps not quite all."

Nick's gut twisted with worry when Radu glanced briefly toward where Nat waited in the darkness by the curtains. Seven hundred and eighty-six years had given him plenty of time to lose many mortal friends. None of them had meant more to him than Natalie Lambert. Now he had deliberately brought her into danger. She had volunteered, but he had given her little choice. If anything happened to her, it would be his fault. His only consolation would be that this time he would not be there to mourn another lost love's passing.

Nick wanted to put himself between Radu and Nat. He

forced himself to stay where he was. He gestured toward her. "You expressed an interest in the woman. I brought her here as a peace offering. Her blood is yours with my blessing. Or I could bring her across to be a companion to you."

Natalie felt her knees go weak at Nick's callous words. Her reaction was so strong that she had to grab a thick fistful of the velvet drape for support. Fortunately, the knowledge that there were a few things about this encounter that Nick hadn't bothered to tell her annoyed her enough to counteract the fear. Her throat was tight with nerves. She touched it, and unfastened the top button of her blouse.

"He *wants* me?" she asked Nick, her voice barely above a scared croak. "Why didn't you tell me?" Nick didn't answer.

Radu turned slowly to face her. There was so little light in the room that she could barely make out his features, though she thought she could smell him from a kilometer away. She had seen death in every imaginable form, worked on cadavers in every possible state of decomposition. Radu's physical form held no terror for her. His size frightened her. The wild arrogance she'd heard in his voice frightened her. She told herself that she could handle the fear. Not even the yellow eyes that glowed out of the darkness, or the threat of the gleaming fangs that he meant to use to suck out her life, was enough to send the panic a sensible person should be feeling about now through her. Though she shook inside, Natalie stood her ground, one hand behind the edge of the curtain.

"Thank you, Nicholas." Radu was laughing as he started to walk toward her.

The sound was bone-chilling. It made her want to

cover her ears. As he came close, Natalie grabbed the cross around her throat instead.

It was a small gold pendant on a thin chain, a gift from a doting aunt that she had never worn before today. Natalie had never tried to explain to herself her reasons for keeping it in her locker. As Radu made his swift, deadly approach, she was just glad she'd remembered the gold cross was there and slipped it on under her blouse before meeting Nick at his car.

Once she was sure Radu was close enough to see it, she held the small cross up before her face. It was gratifying to hear his hiss of pain. He didn't think it was a psychosomatic reaction, and that was good enough for her right now.

Faith, more than the sacred shape clutched in the mortal girl's hand, slowed his steps. Belief created a radiant energy, a magic, that transformed sacred symbols into tiny, pulsing suns. The magic affected Radu, but not for long.

"My goddess is strong," he told the mortal as he took a struggling step forward. He had no choice but to move slowly, for the magic from the cross repulsed him, tried to push him back. He denied its reality and drew closer to the woman. "The moon is my lady," he told her. "Your young god is only a little challenge to her ancient power."

Natalie faced Radu, and fought the nearly overwhelming urge to run. The mad vampire was enormous! He was far too close. She couldn't wait any longer!

"Nick!"

Natalie's heart slammed wildly against her chest. She could feel the blood racing in her veins as Radu caught and held her gaze. She was no Resister. She couldn't—

Natalie barely heard Nick shout, "Now!"

Her hand moved on its own. She pressed three buttons

241

on a recessed control panel. Then she lunged to the side as Radu made a grab for her. He hit the marble wall. She fell to the floor. He followed her as she scrambled away. Radu had his back to the window as the curtain began to draw aside.

Nick watched the process from his post by the door. The heavy velvet made only the softest of sounds as the silent mechanism drew the floor-to-ceiling hangings back to reveal a spectacular daylight view of the eastern side of Toronto. The curved glass wall of the ballroom was the reason Nick had lured Radu up here. It was the reason he needed Nat as well. Though he'd hurriedly covered as much of his skin as he could when Radu turned to face Nat, he doubted he was protected enough. He knew he couldn't deal with Radu and all that sunlight on his own. He suspected that even with Nat's help, he was going to burn to death this morning.

The drapes hadn't opened more than a few inches when the first shaft of sunlight stabbed Radu squarely in the back. Natalie was on her hands and knees on the slick marble, crawling backward in the effort to escape him, when Radu began to scream. She sprang to her feet and ran toward the solid marble wall on the other side of the room. The curtains continued to open, and the room was filled with light. Beautiful, glorious, golden light, magnified by the glass, reflected by the marble. Light, light, light! Natalie was suddenly very much in love with the light.

And Radu began to burn.

Natalie had always hated and feared the sight of burned flesh. This time she didn't mind at all. She actually shouted joyously, "Burn, you bastard!" as his pain-twisted features blackened and crumpled before her eyes.

Radu twisted and writhed, lurched back and forth with his arms waving wildly as he desperately hunted for shelter. The curtains were fully open now, hidden from view, drawn back into a wall niche. The room was completely flooded with sunlight.

Nick wore driving gloves, sunglasses, a ski mask, and a wide-brimmed floppy hat. He always kept these accessories in the Caddie's glove compartment. The cloth coverings afforded some protection as the sun came in, but he knew they wouldn't help for long. Nick could barely see as Radu stumbled toward where he stood, between the window and the door. Nick's eyes were frying on the inside. The vulnerable skin on his hands and cheeks felt licked by the flames of hell. As his body heated, smoke began to rise from his clothing. It was only going to get worse.

But Radu was on fire.

The burning creature crashed into Nick as he tried to escape through the door. Nick pushed Radu back toward the window. His gloves caught fire from the contact. He bit back a scream as he pounded his hands against his coat. Radu came forward again. Nick shoved him back again. This time the momentum took Nick halfway across the wide room.

The last thing Nick saw before the sun enveloped him in white-hot blindness was Radu. The old vampire's body was a flaming torch pinned against the thick, curved glass wall.

Nick was so hot to the touch that Natalie had to strip off her jacket and wrap her hands in it before she could grab hold of his arm. He cried out in pain, and mindlessly tried to throw her off. He was terribly strong, but she held on for dear life.

"It's me, Nat!" she shouted.

243

She doubted he could hear, and didn't wait to find out. She spun him around, and hauled him out the door. Once they were in the hall outside the ballroom, she let Nick fall to the floor. Natalie slammed the door closed against the light. The thickness of the gilded wood barely muffled Radu's dying screams.

Natalie stood with her back pressed against the door for a long time. Nick lay on the floor, a faint cloud of smoke rising from his clothes for a while but soon dissipating. He'd warned her of what might happen, and told her to leave him alone. So Dr. Lambert watched helplessly as he curled around himself next to the wall and waited for some signs of recovery. She couldn't think of a thing to say. Despite compassionate urges and all her medical training, she knew there was nothing she could do to ease the burn pains suffered by a vampire. She did remember to tuck the cross she wore back under her blouse and carefully button it. She didn't want Nick flinching in more pain if he should catch sight of it.

While she waited, all she could do was marvel at Nick's bravery at putting himself through such living hell for the sake of destroying a monster. She was filled with wonder, and with delayed reaction at having almost lost him to the ravages of the sun. When she recalled that she'd been attacked by a vampire a few minutes before, her teeth began to chatter as adrenaline washed out of her system.

"What a way to start the day," she murmured.

"Amen," Nick groaned from the floor.

She was exhausted, drained, but after silence settled over the ballroom for a long time, she turned to open the door. Natalie was careful to open it just a crack, and to shield Nick with her body from even that tiny amount of natural light.

She was surprised to hear him move behind her. "What do you see?" he asked.

Natalie carefully scanned the room. "Nothing."

"Nothing?"

"Nothing but dust. The window and a bit of the floor look like they've been coated in gray dust. Radu?"

"Ash," Nick said.

She heard him gulp. She imagined that he was thinking *There, but for the grace of Nat's remembering our plan at the last second, go I.*

He asked, "Anything else?"

"A lump of something dark. Looks like melted metal."

"Silver." Nick gave a weak laugh. "Radu's beloved silver box. It went with him this time."

Natalie carefully closed the door. She was rattled that the fire that had immolated the vampire had burned hot enough to melt silver. She was glad there had been nothing else in the glass and marble room that could catch fire. She had noticed that the heat of the conflagration had burst some of the bulbs in a chandelier high overhead, blending thin shards of glass with Radu's ashy remains.

"What happens now? To Radu?"

Nick laughed again and climbed shakily to his feet. He leaned against the wall for support. She watched as he stuffed his hat and sunglasses in his coat pocket, then ever so carefully pulled the black knit mask over his head. Skin peeled away with the mask, leaving his normally pale face raw and red. He smelled scorched, and looked thin and terrible, as though the heat had wasted him from the inside.

He tried to smile as he saw her worriedly watching him. "I'm in better condition than what's in there." He pointed toward the ballroom. "What happens to Radu?

Some surprised housekeeper will mop or vacuum up the remains."

Natalie considered this comment. She thought it was more likely that hotel security would find the mess, call the police about an unexpected bit of vandalism. Then Radu's ashes would end up in the forensics lab. If that happened she could still make sure they ended up in the trash.

"That's it, then," she said, and put her arm carefully through Nick's. She helped him move away from the wall. "Let's get you out of here."

"I came over to feed him chicken soup and watch the Jays game on his wide-screen television after I have him tucked in for the night." Natalie laughed at a comment from Tracy, then listened with the cordless phone tucked against her shoulder.

It was warm in Nick's loft, so she shrugged out of her suit jacket while carefully keeping the phone in place. She'd worked the day shift today in order to spend time with her patient during the evening hours.

"Yes. I see. Hmm." She continued to make the occasional encouraging sound as Tracy spoke, while Nick sat on the other end of the couch and watched her. "This is a very bad flu bug, Tracy," she said when she could get a word in. "Nick really isn't up to visitors. He says he thinks he came down with it back in the park two nights ago. That's right, at the crime scene. He's had a very high fever. Doesn't even remember how he got home that night, or anything else about the evening. Yeah, I'll tell him." She glanced at Nick, who handed her a glass of white wine he'd just poured from a bottle on the coffee table. He was drinking red. She nodded her thanks. He still looked even paler than usual; the skin on his face and hands looked as fragile as rice paper. "Maybe he'll be well enough to be in tomorrow. Yeah. That *is* good news. I'll see you tomorrow night. 'Bye."

Natalie set the phone on the table, slipped off her shoes, and curled up on her end of the couch. She began to drink her wine.

Nick waited, but when she didn't seem in any hurry to convey Tracy Vetter's news to him, he finally cocked an eyebrow and said, "Well?"

Nat smiled at him over the rim of her wineglass. "All is well in Metro Homicide. Captain Reese isn't happy about your calling in sick for three days, but he's living with it. Especially since things are a bit quiet at the moment. Did I tell you that your only suspect, Drezerdic, was found at a bus stop with his neck broken? There haven't been any decapitations since his death. His murder is being blamed on vigilantism," she added. She sighed, then took a sip of wine. "I almost feel sorry for the man, being blamed for something he didn't do. Then again, I did the autopsy on his daughter, and physical evidence says he did it. So I suppose he did pay for a crime he committed."

Nick carefully took a sip of his own drink, though he would rather have taken a long gulp. He'd drunk an entire bottle before Natalie's arrival, just so he'd be able to fight the blood craving that had consumed him since being exposed to too much light. He needed to feed, but he didn't want Nat to know just how much, or how hungry he was for the healing tonic of human blood. He tried to tell himself that she looked beautiful tonight, not delicious.

Though he had his suspicions about how Drezerdic had really met his end, he kept them to himself. "What else did Tracy have to say?"

"That the animal attacks have stopped as well."

Nick nodded. "Sounds like Vachon and his cleanup crew have done a good job on the revenants."

"Something Tracy knows about, I bet." She chuckled. "She sounded relieved when I told her you didn't remember seeing a vampire flying over the crime scene. I made sure to let her know that while we were there, I hadn't seen anything either."

"I'm sure she thinks Vachon dropped by to tell me to forget the whole affair, and that I don't really have the flu at all."

Personally, Natalie thought it was time she, Nick, and Javier Vachon stopped playing games with Tracy Vetter. Then again, the explosion of indignation from Tracy when she did figure out that Nick was also a vampire might be fun to watch. But she didn't want anything exploding around Nick right away, she decided as she carefully watched him finish his drink. She didn't comment when he immediately went to pour himself another glass. He moved slowly, tiredly, but not as feebly as he had the night before. He looked terrible, but he was rapidly regaining his strength. When they'd left the hotel after sunset two days ago, she'd been afraid she'd have to call an ambulance, but he'd been able to make it to his Cadillac in the hotel's parking garage by leaning on her and moving slowly.

They'd spent the day after destroying Radu in the room they'd rented when they'd entered the hotel a few hours before. Nick had been prepared for being injured during the fight. He'd been right. There would have been no way for him to go out into daylight again after being exposed to the full blast of the morning sun. He was burned and debilitated and barely able to make it as far as the elevator, let alone across town. So he'd stayed in the darkened hotel room, and she'd returned to his loft for fresh clothes and bottled blood for him. She'd spent the whole day worrying about him, and expecting to be caught for the vandalism in the ballroom. She'd been more than happy to leave when night came and Nick said he felt well enough to go home.

He was certainly better now, but there was a melancholy look on his face when he sat down next to her on the couch.

"I take it you're not really interested in watching baseball?" she asked after he had just sat for a while, twirling the stem of his wineglass between his palms. Nick's head was down, his shoulders slumped.

He didn't look at her. "So many dead. All of it my fault."

It took a great deal of restraint for Natalie not to sigh in frustration. She leaned forward and put a reassuring hand on Nick's shoulder. "Radu's fault," she reminded him. "Not yours."

He finally looked at her. "I had the chance to totally destroy him once before, but it didn't work. I should have been more thorough. Instead, something of him survived, and I let a monster loose on the city."

"Did you?" She couldn't keep a trace of sarcasm out of her voice. "Did you indeed?" When he nodded sadly, she asked, "Are you responsible for every monster that walks the streets of this world every hour of every day? Are you responsible for a monster like Drezerdic?"

"He was a mortal man who. . . ."

"Who murdered his wife, and then came back years later to murder his daughter. He was no less a monster than Radu, and the prison system is responsible for letting that genie out of the bottle." She gave his shoulder a slight shake. "We deal with monsters every day, Nick.

Not just revenants and diseased, insane members of your community. Your kind of monster is far more rare than our mortal ones. We face them. We deal with them. We go on, and hope the world's a little better with each monster we destroy. And *you* are the one who stopped Radu. You should be congratulating yourself."

"I did what I had to."

She smiled encouragingly. "Which was what?" When he didn't respond to her coaxing tone, she said, "You saved a lot of people's lives."

"This time."

She punched his shoulder. "Sometimes I think you're hopeless, Knight."

"Yeah. Me, too." Nick slumped back on the couch. He drained one more glass of liquid. He was far too tired to argue. Guilt and weariness weighed him down. "Sorry, Nat," he said to his best mortal friend, "but I've got to get some more rest."

"Do you promise to be more cheerful tomorrow?"

He gave her a weak smile. "Promise."

"Then I guess I'll be going. And I was just getting comfortable."

She tousled his hair and planted a quick kiss on his cheek. The contact felt so good that he almost called her back, but managed not to when she got to her feet. He watched out of half-closed eyes as she slipped on her shoes and gathered up her things.

"Good night," she said as she went to the door. "Sleep well."

He'd told her he'd wanted to rest, not sleep. The healing power of sleep was for mortals. It wasn't a privilege the damned such as himself could call on. For him, sleep was often the place where he relived the crimes of his endless past. After Natalie was gone, he got another full bottle of cow's blood out of the refrigerator, and turned on the radio.

Though he didn't know how listening to the Night-crawler was going to help him rest.

"Have you ever had your favorite toy broken? Deliberately taken away from you and smashed into a hundred pieces?"

Nick barely listened at first, using the far too familiar voice as background noise. But as he sprawled on the couch, with the bottle in one hand and an arm thrown over his eyes, LaCroix's morose mood began to penetrate Nick's consciousness.

"It is the specter of lost possibilities that is the most galling. There is anger, regret, disappointment. They sting and they disappear, but lost possibilities linger on. 'Might have been' is a notion that can grow to fill your whole world. Pretending can become a way of life if we let it. We convince ourselves that everything would be different, everything would be all right—if only we had our toy back. Well, some of us do survive our losses. Some of us prefer to get even and go on, though we're never quite the same. Loss can be a growth experience. But lives change, lives are twisted, and all over a broken toy."

Nick was sitting up straight on the couch by this time, both hands clenched around the thick base of the bottle. He bent his head forward and listened carefully to every one of LaCroix's venomous word.

"Or is the pain that sears through you at your loss over a broken life, perhaps? Do you mourn an end that came too soon? A love that might have been? We are haunted by potentiality long after the broken pieces of our pretty, untouched toys are swept away. 'What I could have done with it,' we think. 'How malleable it was! How

bright and new and different.' It was all so illusory. *Illusion remains. Illusion is such an empty cup."*

"Illusion of what?" Nick asked the voice that filled his loft, his mind, far too much of his past. He recalled the events of the last few days, and the pretty girl who had lingered tenaciously in LaCroix's shadow. "What were you planning?" he asked his absent creator. The answer was easy enough to guess. Nick shook his head. "Oh, LaCroix, no."

But the girl was dead, and her murder had been avenged. Nick had wondered why LaCroix would go to the trouble of dispatching Drezerdic, but now his reasons were quite clear.

"Drezerdic took away your bright new toy." Nick shook his head sadly. "And now you're pouting about it." He regretted any mortal death. He picked up the remote. "But better to be dead than a slave to you, LaCroix."

"Is it?" the voice from the radio asked. Nick jumped, but LaCroix continued, *"Is it better to hold on to the illusion? To grasp the cup and drink down the invisible nectar? To dwell on our illusions, when we know that reality rarely matches expectations, might be the only way out. Hemlock and ambrosia might, in the end, taste just the same. Tell me, gentle listeners, what do you think?"*

What Nick thought, was that turning on the radio had been a very bad idea. He turned it off, and tossed down the remote. He found himself staring at the dark liquid in the bottle he held. Hemlock or ambrosia? Illusion or reality?

"It's cow's blood," he said. An adequate substitute for what he truly craved.

Illusion and reality could both go to hell. Right now he needed another drink.